*The Widow's To Do List*

STEPHANIE ZIA

blackbird
blackbird-books.com

ISBN 9781492143680
First published by Blackbird Digital Books, London 2012
This revised, retitled edition published in October 2019
Copyright Stephanie Zia 2012
The moral right of the author has been asserted
Cover Image: Sabine K/Pixaline/Pixabay
http://blackbird-books.com/

# CHAPTER ONE

When Dominic Lightfoot's coffin came through the church doors, muffled gasps of astonishment swept through the pews. All eyes were on his pearl blue Von Zipper Sizzle goggles, balanced precariously on top of his skis, making it look for all the world like he had a bug-eyed, grandstand view of the ceremony he'd so carefully planned. Cat Stevens' *Morning Has Broken* tempered the shock down to knowing inward nods as everybody slowly shuffled round to face the altar. Trust Dom, the awkward strokings of the backs of the necks and little shakes of the head now said. There's a man who knew a thing or two about making an entrance.

Petite, neat and understated in top to toe black, Dom's widow followed at a steady pace behind, her jaw set firm, determined to get through the ceremony with grace and dignity even as every particle of her insides was drowning without her.

Inside the church now, getting there. (One two, breathe and walk, one two breathe and walk.) So many people – comforting, yes. We're sharing the same secret. Maybe the refrain repeats inside their heads as well? No. Not Dom? But he was so alive. It can't be true? No? No!

(One two, breathe and walk.) A blur of stained glass up ahead.

Pillars of light slanting dust swirls down from the high windows. Cathedral windows. Who'd have thought it? Hiding away on a tiny Strawberry Hill side street. Dom must have known. He'd only chosen it for its sound system. She must ask him, she thought, keeping her gaze fixed on the back of the coffin. But she couldn't now. How strange was that? Impossible. (One foot, now the other.) She'd get through this.

Nick and Ami had refused to make up the final family foursome. They hadn't quite believed that she'd go through with it. Everybody knew how much Sally hated ritual. Being the centre of attention even more. That's why they'd married in Vegas. That's why she'd always been the backing singer and never the diva. But Dom had thought this through. For her. For all of the build-up she'd kept out of sight, and now all eyes were still pinned, bug-wide in astonishment, upon the coffin.

Sally hadn't been sure about the yellow theme. Dom's favourite colour had been reserved for his car, iPods, screensavers and the bits that weren't black on the Australian rugby strips. Not clothes. Not in church. She'd worn black to give the traditionalists confidence. Yellow wasn't her colour.

(One, two, breathe and walk.) Sensing a movement ahead, she looked up. Who were all these people? There were hundreds of them.

Oh ffff... (NO, Sally, no. Don't even think-swear in here.) She had to turn soon. Right? Or left?

The kindly young vicar looked as cool and comfortable in his robes as he had in his baggy jeans sitting in her kitchen. He gazed in rigid serenity into the middle distance somewhere above her head. Is that a smile flickering over his holy lips? (No, stop it Sally. This is a good man, good God man. Yes.)

Were there relatives' and friends' sides, or did you sit anywhere? She'd better not be left hovering or crash into the vicar. The makings of a nervous giggle hovered at the bottom of her throat threatening to surface. She'd better not laugh. Or stop in front of him. Not a wedding, no.

She'd be with Rocky in a moment, and Ami, and Nick'd be there – sort of. They were the most important thing now, she had to keep strong. She mustn't become a burden, or embarrass them. (Keep walking, that's all you've got to do.)

Cat Stevens DJ-mixed into Ella Fitzgerald. Sally felt a

firm grip on her arm, pulling her to the right.

Smart Rocky. She glanced gratefully into his troubled eyes. He steadied her. A long, inward sigh of relief turned her knees to mush. His presence was reassuring. Almost as if Dom was on the end of a phone somewhere, barking instructions down to his old roadie mate.

Ami threw her a well-done nod across Nick, sitting erect and stiff between them, his left foot tapping noisily. Which cocktail of drugs and alcohol had he put himself on to get through this? Though he'd probably survive better than any of them, in that shambolic, chaotically successful way of his.

Everybody stood up to sing.

Ami would be more of a problem. She'd always believed that if she put in enough preparation and hard work her life would continue forever more in its A star upwards trajectory. Too many corporate brainwashing courses, Dom always said, but Sally blamed herself.

'Let Us Pray.'

Sally sat down. Rocky dropped to his knees. Surprised but impressed at the old rocker, Sally got down next to him. (Is anybody else kneeling? Don't look round, you can't look round. This isn't a kneeling contest.)

After the prayers came speeches. The vicar talked about unconditional love. They hadn't loved each other, she and Dom, they were each other. Conditions didn't apply. Rocky picked nervously at a fingernail. Nick's foot tapped. Sally put her hand on his knee, lightly, so it fell into the beat, absorbing, she could only hope, a fragment of the tension.

The Meltdown Maniacs assembled awkwardly at the

front looking like holiday reps in their matching yellow suits. They sang a three-part harmony version of Blackbird. Frank Warner would sing next and she still hadn't decided. Everyone said she didn't have to sing. Widows didn't. It wasn't normal.

Fear pierced her numbness. Dom had built in the choice. He knew how she'd feel, watching others pay their respects in the way they knew best. He didn't expect her to sing but would leave it up to how she felt on the day. With the last Maniac note still ringing in the air, Frank was already moving down the aisle in his mustard tux, arms stiff at his side, his grey head bent low.

At the first note of the opening bar, Sally leapt up and rushed to stand beside him, a half pace behind. All fear gone, the song was in her chest now, a living thing, ready to rise out. She let her voice take it. Her eyes filled – Dom and his bloody Christmas carols. Her tone complemented Frank's, becoming the notes as the song became her. She gave it all her guts, power and strength, her voice enhancing without ever taking over. Sally was the perfect harmoniser. Dom would have been proud. Blissfully, she escaped her own thoughts until the last refrain of *sleep in heavenly peace* stilled. Scattered sniffs and muffled chokes brought her back to the present. She returned to her pew in a humming silence but for the beats of her footsteps, strangely magnified.

The municipal graveyard was a slow, formal car ride away. Sally, Nick, Ami and Rocky settled into the limo's dark, unreal hush. Sally wanted to run over every tiny detail of what had happened. (Relief?) Like that feeling she used to get clambering into the transit after a gig that had gone well. (She shouldn't be feeling this.) After the cold, empty, surreal days she'd been through, to share the horror and disbelief – yes, she could. So many people. Sad, like her. Shocked, like her. Had anybody ever been so loved? Would be so missed?

Rocky patted her arm.

Thank God for Rocky.

'Are you getting enough help?' was almost the first thing the vicar had said when he'd come to the house.

'My daughter's here, and my son, I mean they're both out at the moment, but they're doing everything. Keeping his Aussie mum as far away as possible mainly. Too much.'

'It's often the way. So much confusion, it's understandable. Perhaps somebody a little less close. A friend of Dom's perhaps? When people ask if there's anything they can do at a time like this, they usually mean it.'

'What? Like a best man, you mean?'

Rocky's team of nubile PRs had snapped into business, organising everything from the slippery-eyed bouncers and the car parking to the chaperoning of the Aussie visitors to the running order of the service. Now a high-profile festival organiser, he was probably the only person in the world who could have mediated a friendly billing arrangement between the Maniacs and Frank Warner, whose ego had spiralled out of control since his unexpected return to the charts. Sally's main job had been toning it down, vetoing the laminated passes, the roped-off VIP area and the numbering of seats, but she couldn't have done it without him.

The vicar had been surprisingly compliant. When

she'd confirmed she was a believer, he'd assured her that a sense of humour was one of God's greatest and most mysterious gifts, and that if that's how Dom wanted to be remembered, well he'd do his very best to oblige. This immediately sent Sally into her private default guilt mode. Her faith in some mysterious other was real enough, but so were her beliefs in feng shui, the I Ching and the evil power of witches.

'May I ask, did your husband, um, it's slightly unusual for the details to be so precise. It being an accident – in somebody so – young.'

Sally explained how, years earlier, Nick had done his work experience at a TV production company researching a possible new show called *Design Your Death*, offering up Dominic's name without asking. When it had been picked up by Channel 4, Dom had obliged with his usual generosity and enthusiasm.

'So – Dominic was famous?'

'It was only a pilot. A trial show that was never shown. It got good feedback but they couldn't get the sponsorship in the end.'

'Death not sexy enough for them, eh?' The vicar looked thoughtful. 'Even someone so um, famous? as….'

'Like I said, he wasn't famous.'

'Oh.'

'By association I suppose,' she added, sensing his disappointment. 'He produced the Meltdown Maniacs.'

Silence.

'Frank Warner?'

Quizzical frown.

'The UK answer to Andy Williams? Christmas

number two last year?'

'Oh? Hold on a moment, yes. Yes!'

'I'm sorry this is all so – unusual.'

'Designer funerals are nothing new to us my dear. Trickling in now, trickling in. John Peel's Undertones started it. Ely Cathedral on the 6 o'clock news, years ago now, time does fly for us all doesn't it, in the end. We have new guidelines now. Mostly it's the graves. Um, yes. All in all, a good thing I'd say. Our bishop says, in – confidence – you understand, it's only a matter of time before tombstones start appearing racked up next to the toasters in Tesco. Profit and prophets getting dangerously close these days.'

'Dom would have loved you,' Sally blurted, wanting to hug him, marry him even, for being exactly the kind of understanding jokey vicar he would have wished for. She beamed widely, choked on her smile and burst into tears.

'I know, I know,' the vicar said softly.

'You don't.' Sally felt in her bag for a tissue. 'You're not old enough to have been with someone for 25 years for them to go pftt, and disappear off the face of the earth all of a sudden.'

'Terrible. A terrible time for you.'

'When we'd got everything so nearly sorted as well. I knew it was too good to... sorry,' Sally dabbed at her eyes. 'I've actually been laughing more than crying lately, believe it or not. I can feel all the tears piling up inside me, like a heap of stones stuck in my chest. They pour out of me whenever they feel like it, all by themselves. There's no warning or anything like that.'

'You're still in shock.'

'Shock. Yes, yes, I think so.'

The car stopped at traffic lights. Crowds surged in front of them. A girl with giant hoop earrings adjusted her toddler's hat. He pulled it off and threw it to the ground. A bald man in a donkey jacket bit into a sausage roll. The shop windows were covered in red January sale signs. A pub board advertised salsa and Frank Sinatra nights.

Normality seemed very far away.

Sally felt the strange once removed, underneath the pier, feeling she used to get when she had a hard time on tour. Like being on a holiday beach at the height of summer, looking out at a sparkling blue sea. Whether they were dozing, swimming, reading or chatting, everyone appeared content. She was on the beach too, but underneath the pier, stuck in the shadows where the sand was brown, wet and cold and splatters of rusty rain and pigeon shit dripped from the girders above.

She looked across at her children. A paler than ever Ami, a stiff and staring Nick. They were all in it, poor things. All of them there but not there at all. Ami had her intimidating frown on, not directed at anyone but turned inwards. Probably, like herself, repeating why, WHY? Nick's shirt, she noticed for the first time, was dotted with yellow faces. Happy or grimacing? She wasn't going to put her glasses on to find out.

The procession turned into a long avenue lined with yew trees. It was a relief to be away from the world again. They purred past tombs, mausoleums and tranquil, towering angels green with lichen. The ivy, the moss and the tangles of hawthorn soon gave way to the manicured, disturbed, multi-coloured new.

Reaching the grave was a jolt. Rocky jumped out importantly and held out his hand for Sally. She leant back to let Nick and Ami go first. The sun was bright but had no warmth in it. She pulled her coat close. It felt tight around the shoulders and had no give in it, a piece of TK Maxx tat she'd bin tomorrow. They passed a cluster of girls huddled together with a hysterical fairground vibe about them.

'Always a fuckin few,' Rocky growled under his breath. 'Don't worry, Sal. It's all taken care of.' He gave a nod to his bouncers, hovering attentively a short distance away. Coiled and ready to pounce, they appeared far scarier to Sally than the kids, but she thanked Rocky all the same. He was only trying to help.

She squeezed Ami's arm. 'Harmless,' she whispered.

'Pa – thetic,' Ami muttered breathily.

Men, no more than boys, in off-the-peg black were moving the flowers from the car to the grave. Sally's throat tightened, and direct tears threatened. She looked quickly to the ground then up, ready to nod to anybody who caught her eye, but nobody did. They milled, stamped their feet and studied the ground. Some greeted each other quietly, shaking hands respectfully, nodding. (The sacred cocoon is disintegrating here. Where's Father Simon?)

'Be here any second,' said Rocky. 'Gone on the Meltdown detour. Didn't want too many fans about did we.'

Her eyes rested on the graves. She elbowed Rocky, 'Do you think we could request an upgrave?'

Rocky rolled the tip of his tongue across his top lip and glanced to the left and to the right.

'Rocky, it was a joke.' She huddled into his bony shoulder.

Together, they looked down at a grave covered with teddies and brightly coloured chrysanthemums, squashed upright into ugly vases way too small, like battery chicken flowers.

'*Gone are the days we used to share, but in our hearts you're always there*,' he read. 'Who writes these fuckers? Gary Barlow?'

'Bling graves,' Sally agreed. 'Who'd have ever thought it.'

'I blame Princess Diana myself. That's when all this started.'

'Give it another 100 years or so and it'll all be as Farrow and Ball as that lot.' Sally looked longingly across at the angels reaching earnestly for the skies out of the distant weeds.

'Come on, what's the Man's inscription going to be?'

'Inscription? He'd wanted a solar powered video.'

'A what?'

'It's a little schmaltzy film with music built into the stone.'

With a wry grin, Rocky shook his head. 'Gadget man to the last, eh?'

'He'd seen one in the States.'

'Had to be ahead of the pack.'

'He'd have done it ironic,' Sally said defensively.

'Ironic,' said Rocky dryly.

'Right off the municipal graveyards' radar. We've settled on his memorial web address and No Chrysanthemums.'

'Never knew he had it in for flowers?'

'No Effing Forecourt Flowers would never had cleared, it has to go to the diocese as it is. You know, the church elders, or is it the council, or both, I can't remember.'

'How did this lot get away with it? If Dom'd seen this he'd have had a quick rewrite, wouldn't he?'

'He'd have died!' Sally's hand flew to her mouth. 'Shit, I didn't mean, I didn't realise…'

'Behave, woman,' Rocky said and they laughed. She imagined Dom laughing with them and listened for his Muttley giggle. Imagined his elbow nudging her. But there wasn't a murmur. Just the howling, cold continuum.

All she'd read about the closeness of the newly dead around their loved ones hadn't happened. If she'd half-believed in life after death before, she didn't now. He was Gone. Not here anymore. Wouldn't be again. Ever.

'What about "Can't choose your fuckin neighbours anywhere these days"?'

'A bit long, Rock'.

'Keep the noise down!' Rocky chuckled, his eyes suddenly narrowing into a cold, lizard-like stare. Sally followed his gaze, fixed on the music business contingent gathered across the pathway. A girl Sally didn't know glowered at them.

'What's that minxy little ligger's game? She can fuck off and all. Who the FUCK is she, what does she…'

'Leave it,' Sally gripped Rocky's arm. 'She's too young to know. I never realised that you laughed almost as hard as you cried at times like this.'

She felt him relax and let go, he kept his arm behind her and rubbed her back, 'If that's how you want it Sal, what's the difference.'

'Nothing means what it means anymore.' Sally grabbed his hand and led him over to join Ami and Nick. They all stood silently staring down at a grave crammed with football flags, helium balloons, fairy lights, cans of Fosters, cigarette packets, ashtrays, wind chimes and vigil candles.

'Chavs,' said Ami. 'I bet they put Christmas lights all over their houses.'

'Snob,' said Nick, the first thing he'd said all day.

Excited, muffled squeals came from the gates. The Maniacs were back from their decoy run, led by a worried-looking vicar. A handful of fans followed at a distance, clutching their phone cameras like a game of What's the Time Mr Wolf.

Ami tutted. Rocky tensed and made to move.

'Leave them,' Sally said gently. 'They'll settle down.'

'Tell her that,' said Rocky, eyeing Ami warily.

Frank Warner sidled up to Sally. 'Thank you darling,' he whispered in her ear, 'you were magnificent.'

'So were you.'

Frank tightened his lips into a brave smile, lifted his chin into the air and stepped back.

Poor Frank. His fans weren't as persistent, and he needed the reassurance. As for that lot, Sally looked across to the music business crowd. They were history. Her husband had gone, her life had gone, her job with it. There'd be no more Strawberry Hill Studios to run, no more music. But one, perhaps the only consolation, no more music business. No more of those kooky girls with their big handbags and clingy little retro dresses; no more of that scary promo witch over there with the white hair and red lipstick; and no more of those up-themselves execs with their squared off glasses and shadowy metrosexual chins, fingering their BlackBerrys more lovingly than their balls through their deep, tight pockets.

Her eyes rested on a jumpy little guy in a gruesome probably Prada mustard knitted jacket. He was talking to a greying exec type in a bulky, black cashmere overcoat. Her eyesight may be shot, but Sally's hearing was 100/100.

'I know, I know, listen mate, whilst I've got you…'

'Leave it to me… Talk later, mate, afternoon tea. Brown's! Excellent, I'll get Amber to fix it.'

Looking more than pleased with himself, Prada prat did a little bow and turned away as if for a pee.

'Mate!' he said to his hand.

'Listen. Guess who I've run into…'

Sally felt a rush of air sweep past her.

'Man, man, take it easy,' Rocky darted forward and reached out but Nick slipped his grip and was there, snatching the phone out of Prada prat's hand and throwing it hard away. In a cartoon split of a second, everybody watched it pause in the air before landing in the grass several grave rows back.

'Missed. Fail fail FAIL,' he said loudly, striding back to his mother's side.

'Strike a light,' Rocky breathed. 'Do you know who that is?'

'I don't give a flying, tossing fuck who that is,' Nick shouted.

Trying very hard not to be there, Prada prat looked up at the sky, repeatedly stroking his bald patch. His over-urgent assistant retrieved the phone and rushed to his side.

Sally pulled a shaking, shivering Nick proudly close to her side.

'There's nothing they can say to that, is there,' Sally whispered to him. They slowly and casually turned their backs.

'Uh oh, Wallace and Gromit alert,' said Nick.

Sally caught the watery, helpless-to-help eyes of her next-door neighbour Valerie Wallace, leaning into her hunched-up husband.

'Keep turning, keep turning,' Sally mumbled, the image of a pair of Emperor penguins who'd lost their egg leaping unstoppably into her mind.

# CHAPTER TWO

*One Year Later*

'They only had one blueberry left so we've got lemon and cinnamon today.' Val thumped her Bag for Life on Sally's kitchen table. 'I could have taken the one but I didn't want muffin decisions this early in the day and I didn't think you would either.'

'Nothing like a change,' Sally said warmly. 'Lemon and cinnamon too, my favourites.'

Val looked at Sally carefully. 'No, Blueberry are your favourites. That's why we've been having blueberry every day now. For nearly a year.'

'And they've been great.'

'But you just said lemon and cinna…!'

'I like them as *much* as blueberry, Val.'

'But don't you see, that changes everything.'

'Why's that then?' Sally turned on the gas. It whooped as the flame caught it. She lowered the heat and took two plates and two mugs down from the dresser. Steady, she told herself, taking two teabags from the tea caddy. Go along with it and keep steady, this is the good part of the of day, remember, the best that it gets.

'We could have a variety,' said Val getting the milk from the fridge. 'Blueberry on a Monday, lemon and cinnamon on Tuesdays, raspberry on Wednesdays, something like that, and chocolate on Fridays as a treat maybe?' A naughty little rounder-offer for the end of the week.' She stood behind Sally to pour in the milk.

'Sorry,' Sally stepped away from the warmth of Val's breath on her neck. 'I need some water.'

'Remind me to write it down later will you?' said Val, taking the teas through to the conservatory.

Sally pressed her glass heavily against the ice dispenser. It growled as the cubes fell into the glass with a satisfying clatter. Unable to keep up the good mood vibe any longer, she let the thought surface. If Val and Tony hadn't been their neighbours, if Tony hadn't organised that trip, Dom would be here now and Val would be with her husband, where she belonged, wittering away about muffin rotas and polishing her ornaments. Their only contact would be at neighbourhood parties and the farmers' market, where it belonged.

Don't do anything rash. That's what everyone said. She hadn't. All the crazy, silly urges to up and go and live in a Jamaican beach shack or ride a white horse across Spain had been sensibly suppressed.

Hating herself for thinking badly of her well-meaning neighbour, Sally took her glass of water through to the conservatory. Val's bossy Boden-blue aura of contentment could be a trial, but in the year since Dom's death her daily visits had become a welcome weft to the warped fabric of Sally's life. If nothing else they forced her to get up in the mornings, put herself under the shower and cover herself with clothing as if a new day was something to be welcomed rather than endured. With an inward sigh Sally sat at the long pine table that ran down the centre of the room, her Val-default position.

Val had, as always, perched herself on the edge of Dom's battered old tapestry chair next to the radiator, last night's Evening Standard folded sharply into four on the Sudoku page.

Sally ran the palm of her hand across the thick old pine. The table was always polished now and clear of clutter, but its random rings of dark and pale water marks and little hillocks of white and crimson candlewax were a comfort. The black cigarette burns and the scribbled signatures, trophies of all the bands who recorded there, literal signs of a life once lived. The kitchen end was more wholesome, sparkling mutedly in the winter morning light with Ami's silver and gold childhood glitter that'd worked itself deep into the grain. If there was one reason why she didn't want to sell the house, this table was it.

Time. That's what everybody said. Till when? She was still trapped in anger. Anger at the stupidity of the accident. Anger at Val and Tony. Anger at Dom for vanishing off the face of the earth so thoughtlessly, abandoning her to all of this – life – stuff. Anger at all the time she had, floundering about in all the hours, minutes and seconds she'd been dealt and Dom hadn't. What the hell was she supposed to do with it all?

Outside, the sky was so low it almost touched the trees. Rain drifted in a light mist across the long, white studio building that took up half the garden. Permanently locked and bolted now, but the emptiness of it – the rows of off-white plugs and the coils of wire snaking across the brown, coffee-stained carpet –

seeped out of every brick. Whatever the weather she could sense a tangible stillness out there. Not the unearthly, misty stillness of lakes and mountains. The other kind, hollow and full of echoes. Like the one that followed her around at parties. The one people were scared to death of.

'The offer stands,' Val said without looking up. 'Tony can sort out some friendly Poles and have the studio knocked down in no time. Be gone in a day and you'll have a lovely lawn there in no time. Such hard workers as you know, though they know their rights, comes from living under communism for so long, Tony says. You have to have the correct paperwork.'

'I don't think so.'

'You need to get a bit of air moving through there. I know I've said it before, but renting would solve all your problems. It doesn't have to be a music studio. You could still do your catering – have you thought any more about cooking for the homeless?'

'In Strawberry Hill?'

'What about a yoga studio. Or pilates!'

'Oh great. Having a load of strangers wandering about, seeing what a slob I've become.'

'It's the perfect size.'

'And I'm not. The last thing I need is a stream of healthy, bendy people trafficking through my hall with their mini Evian bottles. Just as I'd be tucking into my cheesy Doritos and guacamole Deal or No Deal slob outs no doubt.'

'Box Fifteen had the quarter of a million in it again yesterday did you see?'

'I saw.'

'She shouldn't have dealt.'

'Dealt way too early,' Sally agreed. She'd long ago let down the veil of irony she used to hide behind when she read self-help books or watched crap TV.

They both looked out into the garden. 'I'll work out what to do eventually. It'll come.'

But when? How the hell could she do anything with his studio when half of her genuinely expected him to casually stroll through the door one day, fling his beige Muji laptop bag down, say 'Hi honey,' pour them each a large G&T and flop down in his chair. Or Val's chair, as it had now become.

'You've been doing some more clearing I see.'

'If I waited for Nick and Ami to turn up and decide what they want to keep it'd never get done.'

A glint of fear shone through Val's filmy grey look of concern. 'I hope you haven't been getting any more daft *Place in the Sun* ideas.'

'No no, it's come from that *How to Win As A Widow* book I told you about.'

'And?'

'It's the music.'

Val frowned. 'As you know, music isn't my...'

'I mean Tony. Do you think he'd download some tracks onto Dom's iPod for me?'

'Indeed, he'd be glad to,' Val said generously on her husband's behalf.

'I fancy hearing some metal.'

'Good for you!' Val studied the wall.

'Not metal radiators, Val. You know, AC/DC, a bit of Sabbath maybe. Black Sabbath? I've only got a few tracks from an old compilation, but it feels like they're reaching the parts my usual music isn't. Something about all those crashing guitars and wailing vocals,' her voice faded away.

Val's eyes were waving vaguely in different directions. No, Val didn't know did she. This was a woman who thought a fender belonged in a fire grate and a high hat was something worn in Jane Austen novels. Was heavy metal before or after Val's time, Sally wondered. Had Val ever *had* a time.

'Are you talking about that dreadful swearing man? Married to that lady with those horrid little dogs that poo?'

'Ozzy Osbourne. Yes, Val, you got it!' Val's knowledge of the 21st century surprised her sometimes. 'Maybe a bit of Metallica too. Raw energy.'

'But Sally you know how that all works, I mean even I, not knowing one end of a computer from another that I am...'

'Oh, and I want Dom's tracks wiped.'

'Ah.'

'I don't want to find myself on his skiing mix by mistake one day. It'd set me back years.'

'I can't remember these names you'll have to write it down.'

Sally dug out a pen and a Post It from the dresser drawer, took a sip of water and made a list. They both knew she was more iPod savvy than Tony, but she'd got away with it. However many times removed from homicide Tony was, they were almost in as dark a place as she. Needing her to need them was all tied in with their own recovery plan.

The last time she'd seen Dom had played over in her

head so many times the memory had worn as thin as an old video. Boys' weekends away had never been Dom's thing but Tony's skiing weekend with the lads would do him so much good. Sally had pushed him into it. After weeks of living in the dark finishing that difficult *Hard Drive* second album, she thought the mountain air would kick-start him into the new year. If only she could hit rewind. Haul him back inside by the scruff of his neck. Hide his suitcase. Confiscate the car keys.

'New year's resolution?' said Val.

'Eight glasses a day.'

'Ice water's no good, it's meant to be lukewarm. Goes into the system quicker that way. With a squirt of lemon. Fresh, preferably. Do you have any in?

'No.'

'I'll bring you one tomorrow, you can never have enough lemons in the house. The eight has got to include food you know. Too much water can be most bad for you. Flushes all your vitamins away. Is this that widow book again?'

'Yes.'

'Thought so.'

'It's quite good actually. Changing small habits leads to changing big habits, so it says. I mustn't directly confront my worries. It's supposed to happen unconsciously at first, then consciously, without trying.'

'By listening to rock music and drinking eight glasses of water? But that's marvellous, Sally, wonderful!'

Sally didn't really believe it either, but it was worth a shot.

# CHAPTER THREE

The morning pensioner rush-hour was long over but the H22 bus was packed. Sally folded her umbrella, climbed the steps and blipped her Oyster pass card like it was a badge of honour.

Spotting a free stretch of pole to hold onto near the folds of the exit door, she squashed her way through the damp, Pacamac pensioners and stared out at the rain.

When had these people accepted themselves? When had they given up on the mirror twirling and given in to the sight of their wispy grey helmets and corrugated skin without mourning the loss of their older, younger selves?

They hit traffic. She automatically scanned the distant faces of a group of students hanging around outside the college. Crowds were an addiction. Any gathering got her Dom-antenna up. Parties, the high street, traffic jams, TV, even old black and white movies, every back of head of every broad-shouldered blonde man in a white T-shirt still churned her up. He *had* to be somewhere, said the logic in her brain. His clothes were in the wardrobe, his car parked in the drive, the little yellow rectangular Juicy Fruit chewing gum pack on the dash. Still in first gear, in the annoying the way he always left it, making her leap forwards into the garage every time she used it. Except she hadn't since.

Her mobile trilled. The phone was as bad. Whenever it rang a little part of her still said, 'there, you see!' to herself. (*Hi, it's me. What? Were you worried?* and then he'd put on his silly fake French accent, *I'm soreeee, I'm zo zorreeeeee.*).

'Hi, mum it's me, I'm at work so I can't talk long. Why did you text?'

'I heard from Nick yesterday.'

'He phoned?'

'Tweeted, four direct messages in a row so I called him.'

'What's up?'

'He's out of the squat.'

'Great!'

'Only because it was raided. Don't worry it was the bailiffs not the police. So he's not in custody or anything like that,' Sally looked up at a marble-eyed woman staring straight down at her. 'Ami can I call you back? I'm on the bus.'

'I'm in my loo break minutes mum.'

'Oh…'

'Not a problem, so you know I haven't got...'

'Hang on here's a stop,' Sally rang the bell. 'I'm getting off right now. 'Nick wouldn't say where he's living but that wasn't why I texted. Good news as it happens. He heard from Rocky. I put a note on his Christmas card asking if he could do anything to help Nick get out of his spiral. Well he did say if there was anything he could do. Anyway, I'll be quick – I'm on my way to an appointment too as it happens – it turns out he got straight onto Nick and has only offered him a job.'

'Nick?'

'As a DJ.'

'Is it true?'

'He may go off the rails big time, Aim, but he doesn't fantasise. He sounded really excited.'

'Was he high?'

'I expect so.'

'How's he going to get himself together enough?'

'Maybe it'll be the trigger he needs.'

'It's not like it's an attachment to Nat West is it mum. I mean, working in a nightclub will only throw him in deeper.'

'It's not a club it's radio.'

'Really?'

'A DJ mate of Rocky's was looking for a street music savvy kid. A late show for some local station... If he can hold it together it may be the key, we'll have to see and hope he doesn't fall in with the wrong crowd.'

'Nick is the wrong crowd, mum. But yeah, if it's true, that could be good news.'

'I'm so glad I put that message on Rocky's card. It was only an afterthought. I mean, we're all so busy these days.'

'Sometimes asking for what you want gets results, mum. Talking of busy.'

'Oh, sorry.'

'It's – I'm really pushed here.'

'So am I, got to dash, got an appointment too.'

'Where?'

'Oh, nowhere exciting.'

The doctor's receptionist stared at her screen like she'd never seen it before. Sally studied her expression.

The familiar feeling of being more isolated out than home alone surfaced. Had she got the right day? Was she still registered? Convinced that sour-mouth would crack into a cheery, 'sorry, you don't seem to be *here*,' Sally prepared herself for disappointment.

But no, life was, after all, full of surprises. She was given a pink plastic paddle with a large number 6 written on it in black marker. There, see? She existed. She was a pink number 6.

Crossing the brightly-lit, windowless waiting room, the hem of her skirt swished around her knees. Sally hated wearing skirts. This one pulled a bit worryingly on the bias when she sat down. She hadn't worn it for over a year. Not since the Brit Awards. This event held less appeal than getting wasted on champagne, watching her husband up on the podium grinning inanely at James Corden and waving a statuette, but so far she'd managed to block out the nasty reality part of it.

Considering she was moments away from unnatural intimacy-invasion, Sally felt surprisingly chirpy. Having a smear test made a nice change from schlepping about at home in her soggy-knee'd trackies waiting for Val's daily suicide-watch call.

She sat down opposite two old ladies who looked like they'd been there forever and picked out a *Country Life* magazine.

The property ads weren't what they used to be. A wizened fourth-time downsizer in the making, Sally wasn't taken in by gorgeous gables or rolling sweeps of lawn punctuated by a rectangle of cool blue glistening in the sun; she saw large heating bills, an endless turnaround of bossy cleaners, grumbling gardeners and leaves on the pool. Indoor pools looked plain sinister and were always worse in the flesh, too, with their attendant whiffs of mildew.

The bingo-like screen of numbers blinked. Yellow and green for doctors, pink for the nurse. The pinks were at number 2. Good. She swapped the Country Life for a Vogue that had lost its gloss. It was this month's, though. Well, last month's really, the way magazines worked. She flipped the pages. More unreality. Impossibly skinny models in skanky pants and overpriced clothes, Photoshopped to bits. Great.

'*The new sexy is all about the offhand,*' she read. '*Out goes the lady, in comes the warrior woman. Think about unexpected contrasts – throw a parka over that skimpy dress.*'

The bag lady look, now there's something she wouldn't have to try too hard at. She turned the page. A perfume ad dotted with fluffy bits of old tissue flapped open like a used fly paper.

She chucked the magazine down so hard the old ladies jumped in unison.

Back inside Country Life, Cotswold sitting rooms were quickly dismissed until the beiges, greens and browns gave way at the turn of a page to Hockney blue skies, glass walls and white marble floors. '*Rare opportunity to acquire a magical paradise on the beach. Breathtaking views out to the Ionian Sea.*' And how far from a decent supermarket? Maybe the countryside would be a better option. Slowly crumbling away into the landscape, not worrying about hairy toes and bulging bellies, nose hairs and tits going south. There'd be views and fresh air, she'd be at one with nature instead of fighting with the rest of them in the Pilates studios and beauty salons multiplying all along the High Street. The properties gave way to the problem page.

*'Is it bad form to turn up to a pony club rally with a lorry rather than a 4 x 4 and trailer?'*

*'Multi-coloured saddle cloth or sheepskin numnah?'*

No, it'd never, ever work. She picked up another magazine. Look at the acres of empty space in those kitchens. Nonsense. But these pristine Aga temples were for families weren't they. Expanding universe families not contracting black-hole ones like her own.

A half-page ad made her sit up straight. Cottages with naturally big windows were rare, gardens with steps to the beach unheard of on the open market. Close enough to the sea to jump into it in the summer and hear its roar in the winter. That's what she and Dom had always planned.

Two bedrooms would do. Ami and Nick never visited together. Friends stayed one at a time and her old mum was too frail to leave the home now, even in a wheelchair. She looked at the front cover. June. Six months old. There. Well sold. Relax. But what a shame. She turned the page but flipped back. Leaning against a hedge in the garden was a bike. Black, with a baker's basket, unchained, its front wheel sticking out sideways like it had been left in a hurry.

There'd be no locks on the door either. She squinted at the tiny interior photographs. The open fireplace they'd always coveted covered an entire wall. What point would there be reading ghost stories beside a roaring log fire without Dom? She was lonely here though. Exactly! So there'd be no difference *and* she'd be away from all the sympathy glances.

Then again, supposing she got bored with primrosing around and ever fancied getting out there again? What chance would there be of a stray, suddenly-single Hugh Fearnley-Whittingstall type rocking up at the village, all sexy salty hair and rubber wellies, who'd be interested in her! Even if by some fluke – even if George Clooney himself were to leap on her from behind a bush she wouldn't be up for it. The thought of dating again was gross. Why would she want all that fuss, bother and trauma that poor Ami was going through? With added flabby bits?

Yes, that part of her life was over all right but somewhere deep down she hadn't accepted it yet. But then she hadn't accepted anything. Limbo made decision-making impossible. Living in the country would never work. Strange, lonely women were likely to be treated with suspicion. If they were too over the hill to be a threat they were practising witches.

Maybe if she got a dog then being a stranger wouldn't matter? Dogs were the passport to the universe, her *How to Win As A Widow* book said. The only English people who ever spoke to each other without an introduction were those out on walkies clutching their poo bags. Unlocked doors would work then. A whiskery mongrel, exhausted from its run, had been planted in front of the crackling logs when she felt a nudge.

'I think it's you, love,' said the woman next to her.

Sally looked up. The pinks had leapt from 2 to 6.

'Oh, sorry, thanks.' Damn. She closed the magazine and hid it at the bottom of the pile in case the two old ladies saw the cottage and decided to buy it ahead of her.

'All well?' said the nurse, not looking up from her computer screen.

'Very well.' Sally sat down.

'No infections or anything? No? Lovely.'

Click click.

'Now, roll your sleeve up and we'll take your blood pressure.'

The nurse pumped. The skin on her arm tightened. Sally stared into the middle distance and let the if onlys take over. If only Dom hadn't had blood pressure problems there'd have been life insurance. If only Dom hadn't produced the Frank Warner album as a buy-out and been on royalties.'

'Sorry?'

'I said that's all fine!'

The machine sighed, the squeeze on her arm vanished and the Velcro ripped open. She'd never fancied a holiday home anyway. There were enough scrummy hotels in the world she'd never get around to staying in as it was.

One home that she could love and afford would be plenty. A sensible 2 up 2 down in Twickenham, Whitton if she couldn't stretch to it, Feltham if it all went really belly up. Feltham with a shelf stacking job at the 24-hour Tesco. That'd be her. Then again, if she moved to a cottage nearby wouldn't it feel like hiding behind the bike sheds? How would she be able to resist spying on the new owners in her, their, home? Though Val would be giving her a running commentary anyway.

'Excuse me?'

'I said have you been through the menopause yet?'

'No!!'

Click click.

'Do you have the date of your last period?'

'20th December,' Sally said firmly.

'Would you like to go behind the screen over there, remove all of your bottom half and we'll get this over with.'

Sally meekly took off her coat, tights and pants, hitched up her skirt and sank onto the crinkly, paper-covered, bench like a flaccid, oily rag. Menopause indeed. She hadn't felt so humiliated since her dentist had given her an x-ray without checking if she was pregnant.

'Spread your legs for me, please?'

Sally stared fiercely at the poster of a Greek village, Blu-tacked thoughtfully to the ceiling. A white church perched on a clifftop against an IKEA-blue sky. Wouldn't Greece be better than sitting in a damp West Country cottage? If Nick had another overdose scare the dash to Newcastle wouldn't take any longer and think of all the visitors she'd have. Nick and Ami would be kicking the door down to come and stay. In the foreground a fishing boat rested on an impossibly translucent sheet of turquoise sea.

Photoshop again. Why wasn't anything real anymore?

'Take a deep breath, this might hurt a tweak.'

The cold touch of the metal pierced into her.

'Well *done!* Now, one mo I'll check we've got the sample.'

A thick rustle of the plastic curtain and Sally was alone. She stared at the ceiling feeling like a trussed-up piece of meat way past its sell-by date. Dom would have gone for that cottage though. Wouldn't you Dom? Dom? Where *are* you?

She wriggled. The metal felt cool against her, but quite nice.

Oh!

'No problems, that's all gone through,' the nurse returned and peered up Sally's skirt. 'Now, another deep breath please.'

Sally dressed with the slow nonchalance of the nurse's surgical, cool precision but as soon as she got outside she bolted, not stopping for breath until she reached the Green. Her heels squelched into the soft grass and her brusque stride turned into a crouched, unbalanced stagger. Her skin tingled with sweat. The nurse would be in her coffee break by now with that mealy-mouthed receptionist.

She could hear her slightly less formal, off duty, voice, 'Hey, you know that woman who ran off so quick?'

'What? Short legs, long brown hair? Dyed, obviously.'

'That's the one...' snide snigger, 'Pink paddle number 6?'

But, no, she was a professional, it was her job. She must get it all the time.

Blurred shadow figures sat hunched together at the tables behind the steamed-up windows of the Green Café. Convinced they all knew her, looking out at her from comfortable companionable cappuccino-land, Sally stopped, slipped off a shoe and pretended to inspect the heel.

*'What is she up to now'*

*'Floundering about in the middle of Twickenham*

*Green, poor thing.'*
  *'So sad, isn't it?'*

Pilates-erect and confident, Sally set off for home. She empathised with their empathising. They couldn't help their feelings of sorrow on her behalf. Why though? Why was it that only when she'd been part of the couple-land conspiracy round there had she got any real respect as an individual?

# CHAPTER FOUR

Sally prodded at the rice clogged together at the bottom of the old catering saucepan. It didn't look enough but rice never did before it cooked. Three cups would be plenty, she knew, but, sighing contentedly, she added a fourth to be sure.

'Table. Nick. Now!' she yelled up at the ceiling.

Ami leant on the dresser, reading, in the way she always had. One foot resting on top of the other, the book folded back on itself. She looked up, licked a finger and turned a page.

Upstairs, a door slammed.

'For Christ's sake!' Ami thumped her book down.

'I'll go.'

Sally went into the hallway and put her hands on her hips.

'Nick!' she called, unable to sound cross. The moment Nick and Ami had stepped through the door, the hush of loss in the air had lifted. The chilling dischord replaced by a presumption, a hope, of motion. Even the sunlight felt different, warming up the cushions on the sofa with bouncing cheer instead of the usual taunting hint of the world outside she wasn't a part of any more.

For how long she wouldn't ask. Ami said she'd be there three days, Nick, two, but that could change. Ami could stay longer. Nick could leave earlier.

No way would she go down the needy how long are you staying route. Her own mother's words echoed,

*'Can't you stay a bit longer?'*

*'Is that all?'*

*'What's so urgent?'*

*'You can change it, surely.'*

*'Oh.'*

*'I see.'*

Even when Sally had said her goodbyes and stepped out of the door.

*'Why don't you stay for tea?'*

When she was unlocking the car.

*'I got some nice scones in 'specially.'*

It didn't matter if she'd been there a day, a weekend, a week, it was never enough. Dementia had robbed her mother of all concept of time, Sally understood that now. All the same it was crucial that her children would never associate her with that kind of guilt. Her main job now was to pretend she was coping so they could cope.

When her dad had died, her mother was so devastated she'd had to look after her, listen and watch her grieve and give up on life. It hadn't been a sharing of it at all. She wouldn't make that same mistake. They were free to do as they pleased. They came. They went. As they wished. That way they came more.

The floorboards squeaked loudly in protest at the sudden whirl of activity. Nick bounded down the stairs with a hopping on the toes sideways step that always reminded her of Bruce Forsythe arriving on stage at the Palladium. She worried. His spirits were too high. He'd lost too much weight.

'Sister, relax, we still have beds,' he called to the

kitchen, hurtling straight past Sally.

'Only because I haven't started up there yet,' Sally said following him into the kitchen.

'Mmm, smells great, mum,' Nick took a flying leap onto the kitchen sofa and sprawled out with his eyes shut.

'Only tricking,' he leapt up.

'Not funny,' said Ami. 'Not remotely.'

'You're mucking in I see,' Nick said cuttingly, putting an arm around Sally and lifting the lid on the curry.

The spicy smell filled her nostrils. Determined not to fret, Sally stilled the moment to save up for later. A wonderful, ordinary moment of kitchen bickering and cooking. She knew only too well now that these ordinary moments were the most special by far.

'Where the fuck's the can opener gone?' Nick glared accusingly at the cutlery drawer.

Sally gave the rice a final prod to hide her flinch. Everybody said it these days. Fuck fuck fuck fuckity fuck. There, see. A word. Like duck and muck and suck. She said it herself sometimes. Get over it.

Ami laughed.

'What's so funny?'

'It's as simple as that,' Ami scoffed. She turned the book and read the title, '*Rooting Out Your Rubbish – Minimalist Living for the Soul* with Adela Brewster.' Adding acidly, '*It's as simple as that*!'

'It's been very useful,' Sally protested jokily.

'Anything that claims to be easy never is. You know that by now mum.'

'Nothing's ever simple,' Nick agreed.

'See? Even he knows.'

'I didn't say it was!'

*'The worst accumulator of Useless Things in the home,'* Ami read. *'All those items you don't need DON'T HAVE!'*

'That's us, right,' said Nick, taking a can of beer from the fridge.

'Don't be so needy,' said Ami witheringly. 'Look at all these capital letters. Dead giveaway. These books are so trash, mum.'

'You haven't stopped reading it since you got here, I notice,' said Sally. 'And it's helped me.'

'Sick,' said a passing Nick.

*'Don't be like the bits that fill drawers and gather fluff,'* Ami read. *'To let the successful future into your heart you must be empty, cool and uncluttered.* Mum I can't believe you're reading this gunk.'

'A life without miscellany drawers. That's what I've been working at.'

*'Empty, cool and open for opportunity,'* Ami read, 'As if a drawer could do that.'

'Charts and binbags as target fulfilment plans. It's incredible actually, once you start you can't stop.' A piece of paper fell onto the floor. Sally bent down to get it but Nick got there first. 'Getting down to that final little squished up bin-bag right in the middle is my goal. Every day I think I'm going to get there, but I never do. It's like playing pass the parcel with yourself.'

'Wire puzzle from cracker, handmade glass paperweight,' Nick read, 'oversized nail file; 2 mini rolling pins.'

'Writing things down helps you drop them, you see.'

'Refrain,' he tapped a rhythm on Sally's shoulder.

'Two mini rolling pins, night lights, Christmas tree pastry cutter, a jumbo, jumbo pencil with a bell on the end – a bell on the end, a bell on the end…'

Coke? Sally wondered. Or Ketamine?

'Hey. That was my jumbo pencil,' said Ami.

'Was, tough sister, long gone. Joss sticks?'

'Well rid mum,' said Ami.

'Purple ribbon, purple haze, purple ribbon; bunch of old keys, bike – man what's this – my *bike*?'

'In the kitchen drawer?' said Ami.

'It was rusting in the garage,' said Sally.

'Was?'

'Don't panic. It's still there, but not for much longer.'

'Cheers for checking.'

'The garage is your subconscious. I haven't got to that bit yet.'

Ami rolled her eyes and blew up at her fringe.

'Kay cool, throw it, I don't need that. Five halogen light bulbs, remote control, guarantees and handbooks, garden wire, gardening catalogues.'

'What's with the gardening?' said Ami.

'A short phase,' said Sally.

'Holiday brochures… that's it, you need a holiday. Hold it, listen Ami – sentimental rubbish from the kids, unsentimental rubbish from Mil, who's Mil?'

'Mother in law, Dom's mum.'

'Mil – peng, get it. Jewellery never worn. Bric a brac,' Nick looked up warily. 'Where's all this going, mum?'

'Bric a brac. Who in the world needs bric a brac? Broken, chipped, annoying word Amelia calls it. But this is the chapter that got me,' Sally took the book and flipped through. 'Now where's it gone?'

'That bit with the red arrows pointing all over it, maybe?' Ami went to grab the book. Sally held it high out of her reach and read, '*Change brings new life. YOUR LIFE IS MORE IMPORTANT THAN YOUR THINGS. Things are only things, you're bigger than that.*'

'More capital letters,' said Ami dismissively.

'I'm getting it getting it,' said Nick. 'This is more, like, you're into Michael Landy than Life Laundry. That's bare sick actually.'

'I've always been sick,' said Sally. 'Can someone lay the table.'

'Who's Michael Landy?' said Ami.

'This guy, you know.'

'I don't, Nick. That's why I'm asking. What guy?'

'Trashed all his belongings, you know. The artist. But then, no, you wouldn't would you, philly.'

'What's a philly?' Ami asked.

'What about his socks?' said Sally.

'Whose socks?'

'This Landy bloke. His socks. Did he throw them away?'

'Like I said, total. Photos, credit cards, passport. Yes, his socks. His dad's old coat was, like, the hardest thing to get rid of all of it.' Without realising what he'd said, Nick darted into the garden room with the cutlery.

Ami flashed her mother an anxious glance.

'I haven't started on dad's things yet,' Sally said quietly to Ami. 'Upstairs things I mean. But I'm getting there. With the binbag routine I'll do it. It's been long overdue.'

Sally could tell by Ami's face that she knew her

method. Saving it till there was nowhere else for it to go. Till there were no more miscellany drawers, cupboards, CD racks, garage shelves or spice racks to overturn.

'I said I'd help. We can all do it together as we're here.'

'I'd rather be alone. Really, I would. Sorting your bedrooms out is all I ask.'

'Don't worry about that. We're pleased you're getting on with it. Aren't we Nick,' she called. 'I said we're pleased mum's getting on with it.'

No reply. The cluttering sounds had stopped.

Ami grabbed her case. 'I'll put this upstairs. Oh, hold off, I nearly forgot.' She knelt onto the floor and reached for the zipper, her skimpy-soft, yellow summer dress falling above her knees. Effortless, Sally thought, looking at Ami's bare, colt-like legs. Real beauty was effortless. There was no other way.

'Here,' Ami handed her a thick-rimmed, silver Habitat frame. 'I wanted to get you flowers. Nick was in manic mode and wouldn't let me stop the cab.'

Sally took the picture into the hall, turning the frame over, searching for the new memory. Seeing a family photo she hadn't seen before shocked her. Like her memories of Dom had sprouted different corners all of a sudden.

Nick tore down the stairs and stood behind Sally with one arm dangling on her shoulder.

'What's this?' he sniffed. The joy of the energy she got from the feel of him turned to worry. A quick pee was it? Or a quick snort?

'Dune Park. Remember?' said Ami.

'Right yeah. One of those automatic theme park pics. Like you so want to know what you look like scared to shit.'

Sally couldn't work it out. 'Which one was Dune Park?'

Before the kids had arrived, she'd put up with the theme park rides to keep Dom company in his obsession, but as soon as Nick had been tall enough she'd stayed firmly on the ground.

'Orange Beach,' said Nick. 'That curry smells bare sick mum.'

'I haven't got any of the four of us together,' said Sally.

'That's what I thought,' said Ami.

'I love it. Thanks Aim. I can't understand what got me on that ride with you, though. Come on, let's eat.'

They sat down at the conservatory table in a silence riddled with formality.

Two chairs faced each other at one end, the scribbled names, drawings and initials etched into the wood covered with the yellow place mats from Provence. Sally had tried two chairs opposite each other and one at the end, but it hadn't been right. After arranging and rearranging, she'd settled on two chairs facing one chair, with the kids opposite her, where they'd always been.

'Are you sure it was Orange Beach?' said Sally still trying to remember.

'Z Force 1,' Nick said, twisting into the chair opposite.

'Nick, take your jacket off.'

To Sally's surprise, he obeyed her request, wriggling out of the sleeves and leaving them squashed inside out on the back of his chair. Seeing his pale, stick-like arms, she wished he hadn't. The contrast between the two of them was startling. Nick's thatch of freshly-dyed jet-black hair gave his reddish complexion the look of over-baked clay. His hyper manner didn't disguise the wary, dangerous kind of paranoia that fizzed at his every nerve end. The way his eyes darted about frightened her. Whereas Ami, with her hair cut into a short but silky blonde bob had the fake-tan healthy glow of a Blue Peter presenter fresh back from a spiffing adventure. Still, at least he was eating with relish.

The curry had kick. The first food Sally had properly tasted in a long time. She let the flavours linger and burn, playing with them with her tongue, slowly savouring each mouthful.

'It feels bigger in here?' said Ami looking around.

'Yup,' said Sally brightly. 'I'm really getting down to it. At last.'

'This is all about selling I take it?' said Ami going all boardroom.

'Sadly, there's not much choice.'

Ami opened her mouth to speak but Sally got there first. 'It's very sweet of you, but helping out with the mortgage when you don't even live here isn't the answer.'

'Her gear's here,' Nick pointed out.

'It'd only delay the inevitable. The good news is the agent said the studio's a bonus. Barn-like empty spaces are at a premium apparently.'

'They would say that,' said Ami dryly, 'they're estate agents.'

Nick stopped eating and stared at Sally.

'What?'

'Where are you going?'

'One of the cottages around the rugby ground I suppose. They're not as small as they look from the outside. Room for you both any time you want to stay, the attic rooms are really light and airy, some of them.'

She tried to sound convincing but knew she'd failed. At all the viewings Sally had turned herself inside out, desperately trying to ignore the little voices in her head asking "What would Dom have said? Will Ami approve? Would Nick ever want to visit?"

'You'll be miserable as fuck there, 'said Nick. 'Go for the beach house mum, live the dream, we'll be behind it won't we Aim.'

'I'm not going to do anything silly.'

'Them stadium cottages are silly,' said Nick, 'it creeps me out round there, it's weird, all that rugby.'

'There's nothing wrong with the houses.'

'The least silly option is to stay here,' Ami jumped in, 'if you won't let me help you, take in lodgers – or rent the studio out.'

'I've been through all that with Val.'

'Oh Val, of course you have.' Ami rolled her eyes at Nick.

Chewing thoughtfully, Nick looked around the room as if seeing it for the first time. He swallowed hard. 'Where've dad's bonsais gone?'

'Don't point your knife, please.'

'Where are they?'

'I gave them away.'

'Gave?' said Ami.

Nick glanced gratefully at his sister.

'If I'd kept them any longer they'd have died. They're

in a good home now.'

'What good home?' said Ami.

'Only next door.'

'I'd've had them!' said Nick to Ami.

Ami had her intimidating frown on now. The one that meant she was working out how to undermine whatever you said next.

'One died,' said Sally. 'I couldn't have any more dying on me, do you understand? Val's a good woman.'

'Scary woman,' said Ami.

'Still coming poking round every day?' said Nick.

'*Coming* round, yes.'

'Tell her to fuck off.'

'Ami!' said Sally and Nick together.

'Well it won't be for much longer now will it.'

'It is a bit much,' Ami said, 'considering what you used to say about them behind their backs.'

'And smarm up to their faces,' added Nick.

'Yes, and you know why.'

'The studio was always going to be sound-proofed,' said Nick.

'The parties weren't though, we got away with murder there,' said Sally. 'Anyway, there's no point in falling out with them now, before I move.' A stab of disloyalty pierced her soul as she said it.

They folded back into their own silences.

Forks clattered against china. The silence of loss had a hum, a buzz of its own which Sally kept on mistaking for something else.

It felt like she'd switched camps. She was back in her past with Dom, moaning about Val and Tony light-heartedly every once in a while. That felt more like reality, more *her*. Not anymore. In a day or so Nick and Ami would be gone, too. Back to their own lives, and she would be left here in hers. With Val.

If only they'd told Val and Tony to get lost when they complained about their planning application to build the studio, how different would things be now? Instead, they'd gone too far the other way, launching into a major charm offensive, inviting them in for drinks and schmoozing them like they were new best friends.

Sally had got on with Val in a distant, neighbourly way whilst Dom surprised her by really hitting it off with Tony. Like so many rock & rollers, Dom had always been a straightforward, homely man at heart and Tony had come along at exactly the right time. When they'd genuinely bonded over the bonsais, all objections to the studio had been withdrawn without question.

She remembered her euphoria. At last. At last an end to it all. Dom would be working in her sights away from all temptations. The era of the concept album had meant spending weeks, sometimes months, locked away with bands, booze, groupies and God knows what else in the depths of Wales, the Caribbean or the States. When Ami had come along so soon after Nick, he'd had to take on as much engineering work as he could, leaving her powerless to object.

Sally had been so happy that her marriage had been saved, she hadn't stopped punching her fist in the air for days. How could she have known they were signing his death warrant?

'That woman's taking over your life,' said Ami.

'Now she's got dad's trees,' Nick said to Ami so pitifully Sally felt terrible.

'Maybe I can get them back. When I've moved,' she said quietly. 'Let's see. How's Pete doing?'

Ami hadn't mentioned Oxfam Pete yet, which wasn't good. As Sally guessed, he was away again. In the field. Genuinely this time Ami insisted, on an immunisation mission to southern India. Nick made a disparaging remark and Ami launched into a torrent of defence so high on the moral ground it would have been pointless to back him up.

'He's not a proper boyfriend if he's never there is he.'

'Nick, don't,' said Sally. Poor girl. She didn't know what to advise. Even if Ami would have listened to her, experience was no asset in love.

'Simply because you change partners more often than your cacky underwear, doesn't mean the rest of us have to – and broadcast them to the whole of Newcastle,' Ami snapped.

'Leave it out,' Nick said over-lazily.

Sally looked hard at Nick.

'Has he not told you, mum?' Ami looked triumphant.

'What?'

'Nothing.'

'WHAT?'

'His Sunday late show,' said Ami gleefully.

'*Your* Sunday late show?'

'It's a slot,' said Nick.

'All about his love life,' said Ami. 'What did *Heat Magazine* call you?'

'You were in *Heat*!' Sally spluttered. 'Why didn't you tell me?'

'He didn't tell me either,' said Ami.

'Since when,' said Nick turning on Ami, 'did you start

buying Heat as well as The Guardian and the FT?'

'I don't buy the FT, I happened to…'

'I know, you happened to see it in the hairdressers. The listening figures are big, mum. If they keep growing, I'll get my own show, it'll go to mornings and the next step's national radio.'

'I can't believe you were in Heat and didn't tell me,' said Sally. 'What did it say?

Ami smirked, 'That he's the Shagger of the Northeast.'

'I talk about the arts, mum, what's happening, what's going on in Newcastle.'

'Arts? Tarts morelike,' said Ami.

'It's a big deal mum, personality-led.'

'Hysterical,' Ami looked to Sally for agreement. 'What did the headline say again?'

'Why should I give a toss? No-one else from the station's ever been in it, in any paper anyone's heard of. It's tasteful, subtle. I don't go into any under the sheets…'

'You so do.'

'I don't.' Nick smiled. 'If you ever listened, which I reckon you don't...'

'Strangely, we don't get Humberside Radio in Edinburgh.'

'…if you did you'd know it's films and books and…'

'Screwing girls,' said Ami. 'Faux falling for girls and broadcasting your undying love for them…'

'They're into it! And I do love them.'

'Until the next week…'

'They last months – sometimes…'

'Four weeks once.'

'Ah, so you do listen.'

'Then he goes onto the next, mum. Each time he makes out she's the one. The Big One.'

'It's all good. The listeners are in on it.'

'That's the crack, mum. He's so good at it, not only he believes it, the listeners believe it.'

Sally noticed the hint of pride in Ami's tone.

'It's not only dating. It's movies, books. It's called culture, Ami, not that you'd know.'

'I'll have to tune in sometime,' said Sally.

Nick looked at her imploringly. 'It's local radio, mum.'

'You can get it on the net!' said Ami helpfully.

'Ah so you do listen!'

'You'll totally cramp his style,' Ami grinned.

'I see,' Sally said brusquely, thinking style? God help the poor boy.

'Guess who I spoke to the other day – Ramone!'

They stopped bickering and looked at her blankly.

'Remember my 40th?'

'Way too long ago to remember.'

'Nick,' said Ami. 'Who is she?'

'I know – your party, right?' said Nick. 'Your old backing singer mate. Tarting herself about a bit wasn't she.'

'That was desperation,' said Sally. 'Looking for work, drugs, sex, anything anybody had to offer.'

'Ahh! The one that totally ruined your whole party?' said Ami.

'She was really angry that we couldn't give her any sessions here. One layer of extra vocals was all we ever needed, and they were in permanent residence.'

'So why did she make such a scene about it?' said Ami.

'Ramone makes a scene out of everything,' said Sally. 'I don't know what she's like now. I haven't seen her since.'

'Off her head!' said Nick respectfully.

'Anyhow, it was all a long time ago. I had to tell her about Dom, before she saw a review of The Maniacs' album and wondered why she hadn't been invited to the funeral.'

'And had she – heard?'

'Difficult to tell. She pretended not. I guess we'd have drifted apart whatever happened.'

'Don't tell me, now you're feeling guilty,' Ami chopped her rice into her meat with the side of her fork.

'Curious. It'll be interesting to meet up again. Going into town for lunch will make a change as well.'

'I liked her,' said Nick, going back to his curry. 'Bare fun.'

Ami took a pecky sip of beer and returned her glass noisily to the table.

'So, where's she living now,' asked Nick.

'Covent Garden.'

'Cool.'

'The same place she had when we were on the road together. It's a protected tenancy, low rent.'

Nick put his knife and fork together extra neatly. 'Peng curry, mum. Good as dad's that.'

'That's because it was.'

'What?'

'Dad's.'

'What do you mean?'

'He cooked it.'

Ami's fork dropped with a loud clatter. She looked down at her plate as if it had grown teeth.

'You mean – this was from the freezer?'

'I couldn't throw it away.'

'But…'

'It's the closest he could have been to us. Like he'd been in the kitchen only a few hours ago.'

Ignoring the exchanged sibling glance, Sally stood up and took Nick's plate.

'Now, does anybody want any more?

## CHAPTER FIVE

Val stood at Sally's fridge door in her stout, headmistress in assembly, pose – chin raised, chest thrust forwards and hands on the back of her hips.

'It's my target sheet,' Sally explained. '*How To Win As A Widow* says even if you have no intention of doing everything on the list, it's supposed to make you reflect on your problems without thinking about them.'

'Really?' Val whipped it down and took it to the window to read. Sally gave her a minute before gently taking it back.

'There,' she clonked it loudly in place with Ami's plaster-of-Paris sunflower magnet. Tipping her head to one side to check the alignment, she scanned it through to see how it read from Val's perspective.

*1. Don't do anything rash.*

*2. Don't let your worries about the future escalate out of control. Try and stay in the present moment. Meditation classes are good for this.*

*3. Look good for yourself, not other people. A small, effective way of doing this is to wear mascara every day even if you're not going out. Tears are not an excuse to look washed out. If you're still crying at unexpected moments, select a waterproof brand and buy a good make-up remover.*

*4. Treat yourself to some new clothes, even if you don't need them.*

*5. Exercise. Train for a short fun run maybe. Sociable – but you can always run away!*

*6. Drink 8 glasses of water a day.*

*7. Think about getting a dog. Not only for companionship and security. They get you out of the house and talking to people every day – dog owners are very sociable.*

*8. Think about booking a group activity holiday. If you're still feeling fragile, cruises come in all shapes and forms these days. The advantage of always having your cabin to retreat to cannot be overestimated.*

*9. Volunteer.*

*10. Join an evening class. Not so much to meet new friends with similar interests, though that may happen, but to give solid structure to your days. They don't only happen at night.*


'Lists,' said Val affectionately, 'That's quite a chunky one. Where would we be without them?'

'I'm supposed to post duplicates all over the house,' said Sally grabbing her leather jacket and keys. 'But I didn't want to look like a complete self-help loon. My bag's full of bits of lists as it is.'

'Now here's the plan,' said Val when they were charging along the fast lane of the A316. 'You won't want me at the estate agents so when I've done my bobs I'll be in the library. We're meeting Tony in Carluccio's at 1, he's reserved, he's going to the computer supermarket so don't expect him to be in a good mood, hopefully your presence will calm him down. Maybe he can persuade you out of it.'

'Persuading doesn't come into it.'

'But I don't know if you're doing the right thing selling now?'

'I've got no choice.'

'The market's so volatile. What about those royalties you were expecting?'

'The album crashed. Bombed. Took a dive. Didn't register on the radar.'

'But I thought everybody loved it?'

'That was the other album, the Maniacs.'

'And Dom produced it, no? He did, Sal. I saw him on the television.'

'It was a buy-out. He got a one-off fee instead of royalties, to give him a negotiating percentage next time round, except there isn't a next time round is there. We needed the cash at the time. Biggest mistake of his life, apart from –'

'Is this a forty-mile speed limit or a thirty? It looks like a forty but it's a thirty, see that?' Val clicked her indicator and peered into her rear-view mirror. 'Nobody pays a blind bit of attention do they, how am I supposed to get in the correct lane, whoops. Couldn't you hold on a bit longer, Sal. You don't know what's going to happen. I mean, things might come right.'

'I found the party really difficult this year.'

'You did very well.'

'Did very well! See? It was meant to be a party not an endurance test.'

What a nightmare. Little groups parting in her wake whenever she tried to move anywhere. Last time they'd all been together, they all wordlessly said, Dom had only a few short days left.

'Though it would have been harder staying at home, listening to all of you lot raving it up and down the road.'

The Bushwood Avenue New Year's Day parties had been a fixture for decades. Bloody Mary's at number three at twelve, followed by a buffet lunch at number twenty-four and resolution-busting puddings at number eighteen. As the kids had grown into teenagers they'd criss-crossed with the adults, off on their own combinations of noisy parties and quiet bedroom spliffs. Anyone drunk enough and ready to party on had always ended up at the Lightfoots' for the hard liquor and a communal jam out the back in the studio.

Nobody had really known how to deal with her. She hadn't known herself. The slightly eccentric woman in sparkly jeans and Hawkwind T-shirts who ran Strawberry Studios with panache and flair had gone. She was a widow now. A winner who wasn't winning any more.

At least she'd faced up to it. Though she'd never forget all those concerned eyes swapping mute notes of knowing, followed by that awful half beat pause before they all spoke at once, loudly and over-animatedly, with a What mood's she in today? sentiment lurking behind every word. She'd considered getting a placard on a stick in the style of a Christian fanatic, saying 'talk' on one side and 'don't talk' on the other. Because sometimes she wanted to talk about Dom, but at other times she didn't and how were they supposed to know?

Being alone was horrible. She detested every moment of it.

'You looked lovely, though. I thought.'

'Thank you!' said Sally, surprised by the compliment. She felt a surge of warm affection for Val. Better blunt and tactless or patronising praise sometimes than having to face strings of words deliberately mentioning Dom or deliberately avoiding Dom. Every word wrapped in awkward sincerity.

'Good to see you out of those old jeans and T shirts.'

Sally opened her mouth but, realising there'd be no point, closed it again.

'You looked really pretty. Really young I thought. Other people noticed it as well.'

'I wasn't trying to look young, I was trying not to look fat. And old.'

'Oh come on, you're not old, Sally. Only ten years ago you were still in your thirties, think of it that way.'

'And in ten years' time?'

'Oh, I wouldn't worry about that, once you get to sixty you start shrinking again.'

'How do you know? You're only forty-seven, Val. You wait.'

'Perks are perks, they're not to be sniffed at. There's more to it than buses and trains you know.'

Val, Sally thought, had probably been born for middle age. That earnest look would be there in her school photos, along with the gingery hair that tended to frizz in the rain, swept back off the grey, discerning eyes, squared off nose and firm jawline. The freckles would be exactly the same, and the matronly Playtex cross your heart bust shelf.

Sally could see no advantages to hitting fifty. Everybody had insisted she must celebrate her Big day knowing full well that taking centre stage had never been her thing, even in her own life. The invitation to a mammogram that had dropped through the letterbox along with all the 'comedy' birthday cards had, despite the clear indication that death might be closer than she thought, been a welcome nod to normality through all the fuss.

'One thing to remember is to keep your mouth shut when you're standing up or sitting down, does it say that in your book?'

'Excuse me?'

'Grunting. My poor old mum never let up on that one. One of the worst habits to fall into and the easiest to put right she always said. Apart from that, it's all about attitude at the end of the day. If you don't like your age, change it.'

'What's the point of that!'

'Oodles of points. Why would people ever bother otherwise? There must be ten good reasons, at least, to lie about your age. Make up a different number, nothing too outrageous, but be sure to stick to it or you get into all sorts of pickles. My sister had her store card taken away. Can you imagine the embarrassment? She'd put a wrong date on a form that's all. Got the third inquisition. Make up a date, keep it somewhere safe in the pin part of your brain. Pin, password, second date of birth.'

'That's lying to yourself.'

'All part of the way people perceive you.'

Sally knew how people perceived her all right. They saw her and missed Dom. When they looked at her they saw his absence. In all purity, that's what she'd become:

the absence of him.

She had to take and absorb their own sense of tragedy, their own feeling of desperate loss, on her own chin. It was no wonder that Indian widows used to throw themselves on the bloody fire. Still did in some parts apparently.

'I'm always going to be seen as that woman who isn't any more.'

'A little twiddling with your personal numbers is one of the easiest things to put right.'

'Blowing up like a self-inflating mattress overnight doesn't help. Now my chin's decided it would rather be part of my neck. If I could afford it I'd have a facelift tomorrow. For my own self-esteem.'

'Nonsense.'

Sally leant forward and looked at her feet, 'What's this then?'

'Well – don't look down.'

'You wait. Hitting fifty is a pile of sh… cack, Val, it really is. I could do without it.'

'But you can. So long as you're a little bit – subtle about it and not, you know, too ambitious with your numbers. Why are you looking at me like that?'

What an idiot! How had she managed to get so far through life and yet still believe everything that people told her? She still felt like she hadn't grown up yet, let alone old, that was why. She still thought big sunglasses made her look cool and sexy. That she should know which bands and clubs were in. That she'd lose that stone in weight one day. That if she drank too much it was to make her feel better there and then, not worse the next morning. That she'd have that villa in Provence or the whitewashed shack in Greece one day, as soon as she'd worked out if she would be rich or poor. She still summed people up she knew nothing about far too quickly and was still permanently in awe at herself for having a headmistress, even an ex-headmistress, like Val as a friend, even if they were friends in, as Tony would crook his fingers in the air and go, "quotes".

Right after they'd moved in next door, the first time they met, Dom had remarked on it. They'd both seen teachers as people who stood at the head of classrooms or paraded in the playground before dissolving into the ether when the bell rang at 4.

'All right, Val, out with it, how old are you really?'

'Now what have I been trying to explain to you?' Val said blowzily, blowing one of her noisy huffs of finality.

Sally looked long and hard at Val. She was ageless, she'd probably settled into that stockings and polyester look when she was still a teenager.

Val turned to look at her.

'Keep your eye on the road!'

'My sister started it. Took fifteen years off, cheeky thing. Highly annoying, your big sis ten years younger than you in a flash. So, what could I do? But, you see, she kept her cosy little admin job till she was ready to retire. When *she* was ready not when they told her to. It does no harm to anybody. Like my new coat. I'm a size fourteen but sometimes I'll buy a sixteen to give me a little bit more fabric, a bit more room – it doesn't mean I *am* a size sixteen does it? Any more than anybody thinks you're a natural brunette, Sally. All that matters is that you're proud of who you are. Did you listen to Gardener's Question Time yesterday?'

What else was there to do on a Sunday afternoon? Sally thought, checking her seatbelt.

'What did you think of Bob's sapling advice? Bit on the radical side we thought.'

Sally searched for something to say but failed.

'You did tune in?'

'I had it on, but I don't always listen,' she confessed.

'What's the point of that!'

'If I'd wanted to get into the whole gardening thing I'd have done it before now. It's the voices, Val. The tones going up and down in the background, they're easier to listen to than music.'

'But you're a super cook, Sally. Good cooks make marvellous gardeners, everybody knows that.'

'I don't cook any more. It's bad enough having to eat. Sensibly,' she added to Val's pointed glance. 'Keep your eye on the road will you! I'd be a rubbish gardener. Why do you think we had it paved over in the first place?'

'That was Dom's idea! To build his studio!'

'To build our business,' Sally corrected.

'And if you really want to know, I've gone right off Bob as well.'

The car jerked forwards.

'You haven't gone over to Titch…'

'No.'

'You were, you were so enthusiastic, I'd never seen you so animated since, well – since.'

'Let's face it Val, gardening's more about killing than growing. Killing and fighting never-ending, losing battles with slimy things and itchy flying things. My affair with Bob is no more.'

Back in the early summer Sally had heard a kindly

voice coming from Val's kitchen radio explaining, with musical highs and authoritative lows, how to feed Epsom Salts to the roots of tomato plants. Momentarily mesmerised, she'd shushed Val to listen. Months after losing Dom, Sally found herself sharing Val's passion for the voice of Bob Flowerdew. A ray of barely remembered contentment fell over her on Sunday afternoons as she reverentially tuned in and planned the future garden she'd have when Dom's *Hard Drive* album got the airplay it deserved and got picked up for a Vauxhall ad.

'People go off people sometimes, Val.' Sally said pointedly. 'Think of Monty.'

'Leave Monty out of this.'

'You almost forgot Monty Don had ever existed when Gareth from *The Choir* programme came along.'

'Almost, Sally, almost.'

'Almost hah! I've never seen such a fast turnaround of affections. All right I'll tell you. I read an article about Bob in the paper.'

'And?'

'Did you know about his plait?'

'Of course!'

One glimpse had been enough to make the glue of Sally's one post-trauma erratic erotic bonding moment, as *How to Win* had wordily labelled it, lose its stick. Their shared girlie crush on the voice of Bob Flowerdew, probably the nearest she'd ever get to fancying a real man ever again, was no more.

'Oh, save me – a man with long hair. Really, Sally, with all the comings and goings there used to be at yours. How can you of all people worry about Bob's long hair when your house had more big hairy men and little hairy men passing through it…'

'Not any more eh.'

Val purpled, 'Oh, sorry Sal.' She crunched into first gear, turned left into the main road and stopped.

'Great,' said Sally looking at the queue of cars stretching away into the distance.

'Nothing we can do about it,' said Val resignedly, tapping at her steering wheel.

'It's not even a dinky little pigtail plait,' Sally persisted. 'Which, if cancelled out by other assets, a job as an Italian movie producer with a name like Berterollini or something, I suppose could pass as eccentrically charming. It's a great big long rope, Val. An Angela Brazil job!'

'All part of his character. Part of who he *is*, Sal.'

'All right, did you know his wife plaits his hair for him?'

Val's lips thinned.

'That he thinks it might be some kind of aerial that influences his dreams? Take my advice, Val, don't read this article. It's OK, I'm over it now. Let's face it, I'm not a real gardener anyway. If I was I'd have known about Bob's plait.'

'But –'

'You carry on enjoying his kind, purry voice eh?'

'But – oh what the heck. I'm not supposed to say anything until we have it all on paper. It's as much as settled and – Tony was going to tell you at lunchtime today. He'll throttle me when he finds out he's not here to see your face.'

'Tell me what?' said Sally darkly.

'But you know how I am with secrets… Oh heck it I can't keep it in now can I – you're in, Sally.' Val inched the car forwards.

'In? In what?'

The fait accompli beam that accompanied Val's next statement rendered Sally speechless. There followed a conversation she didn't think she'd need to be having for another ten years at least.

Carluccio's was bustling and loud in its happy Italian, sunlit blue and grey way but for a dark cloud over a small, round table for three by the window.

'I must say, this isn't the reaction I expected,' said Tony sharing a wounded look with his wife.

'You did *say*, Sally,' said Val.

Asking them to put her name down for an allotment had seemed harmless enough at the time. A positive step where even a list to join had felt like progress. Another small way of helping them through their sadness and guilt.

'It was always more the sherry, shed and bonfire thing for me,' she said fiddling with her place setting. 'A few chickens maybe like that writer in Hampstead, you know, way in the future, not now. Not for real.'

'It can be for real!' said Val, beaming.

'It can't! There's a ten-year waiting list. Everyone knows getting an allotment's harder than getting into the Groucho these days.'

'You're already in the mail merge,' said Val as if that settled it.

'Well you can damn well take me off again.'

Sally made her excuses and left, knowing more than ever now that a more permanent escape was inescapable.

# CHAPTER SIX

Sally was struck by how the usefulness of the High Street, with its shops full of clothes she couldn't wear and food she shouldn't eat, faded with each visit. Resisting the lethal triple cluster of Paul, Cafe Nero and Hotel Chocolate, she speeded up to a fast clip. The blow-out lunch had made her faithful black skinnies tight enough already.

The fashionista who'd said that women over forty shouldn't wear denim had always been an idiot in her opinion. Her uniform of straight jeans with baggy dark T-shirts or loose-necked jumpers had been her core look. Her long brown hair, a few good, funky accessories like her pink dayglo metal lightning earrings and silvery heels for parties had seen her fine.

Until now. Jeans were only the start of it. Her trustworthy stash of American Vintage Galeries Lafayette T-shirts had started sticking out in a squareish old-woman way at the tummy and even her old faithful black leather jacket clung rather than dropping to a casual hang at the bum. With the house on the market, the 'all elusive' comfort and style was her aim now, even if no woman on earth, apart from Helen Mirren, appeared to have cracked the look yet.

She passed Next, Wallis and the bank that held her overdraft. All of them indicators of a groomed, efficient life that bore no resemblance to her own. Groomed had worked once upon a time when she could enhance her Kylie-petite figure even further with the clingiest silks and lycras with a stage to show it all off on. With the prospect of money in the bank again, her main hope now of salvation from the dreaded stretch denim was a pair or two of well-cut Sweaty Betty trackies.

At the estate agent's she screeched to a standstill. There, in prime position, was a photo she recognised. She read the description underneath.

*A handsome red-bricked Edwardian house on a corner plot with high ceilings, arched Gothic windows and oak floors.*

If they could get it up that quick maybe they weren't exaggerating about its prospects. What if it did sell quickly? Who wouldn't want it?

One thing for sure, she was doing exactly the right thing. The insanity had to stop. Val and Tony were only trying to be kind. She'd had to go along with them to some extent, and had wanted to. But enough was enough. If growing older was all about trading danger for stability, she would bloody well trade stability for danger. She couldn't suffocate behind her own mask for a moment longer.

Where to though? There'd been invites from Kate and Dave in Yorkshire, Debs and Stu in Brighton, even Dom's old record company bosses Tonee and Andy in the States. They were all good old mates rather than random neighbours but would it be any better in the long run? There'd still be all that obligation. More. She'd be a permanent gatecrasher in their lives. She'd either have to keep on stating her independence or not let the feelings of being in the way get the better of her.

At least, having caused it, however indirectly, Val and Tony were a natural part of the hell of it. Blatant was better. On the table and dealable with. Not her choice in life. But then nothing was her choice in life any more.

Noticing a group of charity salesgirls on the pavement outside *Bibs to Booties*, Sally doubled her pace. Chuggers were a curse not to be graced with any acknowledgement. Everybody knew that's how they pulled you in. A tall girl in a Zorro mask cut right across her path. Keeping her eyes fixed determinedly into the distance, Sally scooted past.

There!

The girl hadn't tried to stop her. In fact, Sally mused, she'd stood right back to let her pass.

Outside Tesco Metro she slowed and turned back to see the girl darting towards everyone that passed. 'Hey, have you got a moment?' 'Gowaaaan.' 'Sorry to trouble you?'

What had been so wrong with her own moment that it couldn't be troubled? Sally thought, prickling with indignation.

She turned and ambled back past the girl.

Amazing! She might as well have been wearing a Harry fucking Potter cloak.

Hovering at the bus stop, she watched them for a moment before retracing her steps one more time. This time she stopped and looked Zorro-mask straight in the eyes.

'Hello.'

'Hi there!' the girl grinned toothily.

Sally stood her ground and waited.

Nothing happened.

'What have you got there?'

'We're giving away free chocolate today.'

'Oh!'

No response.

'Can I have some then?'

'Sure!' A black gloved hand placed a silver-foiled bar in hers, and in a flourish of a cape she'd gone. Off to accost a couple of fresh-faced young pram-pushers.

Quite a big bar for a *Bibs to Booties* marketing ploy Sally noted. It looked, no, she turned it around, it couldn't be… but it was. A chocolate – a chocolate cock? She slipped it smartly into her pocket and gave the shop a second look. *Bibs to Booties*, she realised, didn't have an aggressive marketing ploy. *Bibs to Booties* had gone. The 0-7 white, pink and blue baby-gros had been usurped by a row of faceless semi-naked mannequins, strutting their stuff in red g-strings and tinsel bras.

Sally peered into the broad, open foyer. How had that happened? Did Val know? She could already hear the conversation playing out the next morning. How come McDonald's up the road had been forced to disguise itself as an old country cottage? A joke old country cottage. How come the iffyness of real live dead bodies next to the Body Shop had kept the funeral directors way out on the edge of town? Yet here is *Panty Parlour* right by the bus stop where death and hamburgers have failed to get a look in?

'Come on in, have look around, give yourself a treat today why don't you,' a devil-girl stood in front of Sally and held her arm out invitingly.

Feeling ridiculously pleased to be acknowledged, Sally beamed widely at her.

'Here we are, get that in you,' the girl offered her another chocolate.

Sally thanked her, slipped it into her pocket and scanned the High Street for familiar faces. The age of invisibility had to have some compensations. A final glance over her shoulder and she found herself inside, looking vaguely around with the exasperated expression she used for the supermarket when it suddenly moved the eggs.

Scared that the girl would morph into a chatty, Disney Store new best friend, Sally took cover beside the underwear carousels in the middle of the floor.

Her love life might be over but she did need to learn to love herself a little more, she thought, shoving a few hangers along the rail.

She stopped to admire a white lacy combo. It really was very pretty, and sexy, and very wearable if you were already a pretty and sexy size zero. Was she really ever that size? It was unfathomable. Young people were getting smaller, that's what. But even if she had been of midget proportions, this wasn't meant for her anyway. What she wore didn't matter any more. It didn't matter if she lived in London, Swindon or the Outer Hebrides, no Clooney clones were going to beat a path to her door and give her that tingling rush of affirming life-force ever again.

Further in it got trickier. The back of the store was a very different place to its girly Top Shop-like beginnings. Sally casually scanned the shelves of spanking paddles, leather collars, vintage lace blindfolds, sex manuals and glittery nipple covers. She took a bottle and squinted at the tiny print, impossible to read even with her contacts in. Flavoured lubrication, she assumed. It wasn't going to be salad oil was it. A bit trickier to cope with on your own, that one, unless you were Madonna. She moved across to a row of shelves against the wall furthest from the till which appeared to contain pasta. She studied the tiny shapes. There you are, silly Sally, pasta shapes, ha ha. Who buys that? Who cooks pasta penises? Who eats pasta penises?

A black vinyl pencil case caught her eye. She opened and closed the zip vaguely, wondering where on earth pencils came into it all.

She took her first furtive glances at her quarry.

There they were. Rack upon rack of them. Some, in their see-through plastic packaging, hung on carousels like petrol-station liquorice allsorts; others had escaped from their shrink-wrap and stood erect in all their pink flesh glory, marching across the shelves below.

At the till, a girl with purple lips and vacant eyes fiddled with a strand of purple hair. Look, Sally told herself. This girl had customers going up to her all day, every day buying all of this. Lubrication creams, titless bras, crutchless pants, and willies. Fat willys, thin willys, black willys. All normal. All fine it was fine fine FINE. This is a WILLY SHOP. A shop for people who didn't have willys, but who would like to own a willy. All she had to do was grab one and get out of there. But if she took a really, really big one, wouldn't it appear greedy? The black ones were less – ugly pink – but wouldn't that make her look a bit – pervy? PINK WOMAN BUYS BLACK WILLY, she could see the headlines. Why go for a small, modest-looking one? She'd never gone along with the size doesn't matter argument. She hadn't had to, had she? This was, after all, Dom replacement therapy. What about those tiny stimulator rabbit thingies, where were they? That would make the till moment a bit easier, like buying Lil-Lets instead of Tampax from the local newsagents, as she'd had to do once in her teenage years, sandwiched between two Turkish Delights. But she isn't even off the nursery slopes here. No way would she get into a John Lewis-like discussion about what was in stock. She turned away. This was hopeless. The imagined going over the top burst of courage was not going to materialise.

She noticed a young couple next to her looking at the pencil cases.

'What you reckon?' the girl said to her lanky, pock-marked boyfriend.

'Could do,' he said. 'Places for your spare batteries an all.'

Sally dropped the case and made for the door. What was mail order for, anyway?

She may as well stop it and get off right now, she thought miserably, all the way home on the bus. The world was rolling away without her. She was a prude. An ancient, prune-necked, allotmenty, forgetful, past-it prude.

No, you are not! came Dom's voice, clear as a bell in her head.

Yeah, you stayed away didn't you!

Just as well, he'd have creased up with laughter.

*Backing singers may sing in brackets but you know all*

*about living on the front row of the fast lane. Start living again, Sal. Give yourself a good time. You deserve it.*

'Where are you now?'

*Don't forget who you are Sally, you're still my old lady, the best lover and the best singer on the planet.*

Old lady, you said it.

*The original Cosmo girl you were.*

Cathy & Claire if you don't mind.

*A fully paid-up veteran…*

Veteran?

*All right, insider. You were there Sal, on all those tours. Travelling the world, screwing half of it, I seem to recall, before you met me I mean. Remember, you've been there and done that like all the kids these days, fiddling with their sad bits of electronic fuck gear, will never know.*

Sally stared fixedly out of the window not seeing anything. The tears were back, blurring her sight. It wasn't the physical act she was missing but the physical presence. Her man being around, being loud and bossy and funny and annoying and untidy and loving and needing and smelling and giving and taking and cracking open another bottle of wine when they shouldn't. Masculine assuredness, that's what she ached for. That alpha arrogance. Being taken. That whole affirmation of being female.

*You managed before you met me.*

So long ago, Dom. So long ago.

Boz Scaggs, Boston 1974, her last moments alone before Dom. Before she spotted this chunky, blonde hunk on the mixing desk. A flash of a thigh, a double-take, confirmed with a grin and in one more flare of the eyes her future had been fixed.

*Remember how you were before? Go on. There was a time, remember it.*

Are you trying to get rid of me?

*You got to live, Sal, you go to carry on.*

Before? Aladdin Sane, 1973, her first American stadium shows and her last tour as a single girl. Radio City Music Hall, Philadelphia, Nashville... still there in the music. Lady Grinning Soul they all called her, with her tiny skirts and long suede boots. The adrenalin-fuelled shows followed by the tedium and stink of the tour bus. The once-removed from the rest of the world feeling, the chance meetings, the in jokes, the collective sense of purpose, the one night stands.

Sally smirked to herself. There'd been no need for toys. Having a good time was part of the job description. Apart from a few caterers and hairdressers, those tours were all-male domains. The bands could pick and choose from the groupies, but the backing singers could pick and choose from the band.

She stared happily out of the window. Ramone would have had no problem back in that shop. She'd have had every assistant padding around after her, getting them all out of their boxes and demanding demos.

*Why couldn't you get past a few teenage shop girls if that's what you wanted?*

Because, frankly, Dom, they looked disgusting. All those plugs and plungers ....

*You know why? Not your style, babe.*

You'd rather I found one with a bloke on the end of it would you?

Silence.

Dom?

Ringing silence.

Dom! I'm messing about! Remember how we used to joke?

Nothing.

She watched the houses going by.

What if he'd never existed? If she'd never married and stayed in the city, would she still be like this? Since Nick and Ami had arrived she'd been hardwired to give. Running the studio, catering, accounting, and filling in on a few sessions here and there. Too busy to think most of the time. Now she did nothing but. She couldn't help it. As men and career women projected the central image of themselves through their work, mothers filtered it through their family. Anything before disintegrated into nothing more than preparation. Anything after the residue of what had been.

Ami and Nick's lives might be all about their futures but hers was all about her past.

Back home, determined to be get it done, once and for all, she went online.

*Get the whisky.*

'Oh thank God, you're back! Please don't leave me like that ever again.

*Get the whisky.*

'If I start on that I won't stop and my cheeks will be red for weeks.'

*G&T, go on.'*

G&T's a faff.

*With ice and a slice of lime the way I used to make it for you. You deserve it. Look after yourself, love yourself! Pretend you're making it for me if you have to.*

73

*Make one for me as well and drink them both, go on!*

The alcohol made no difference. No more could she click on the little shopping basket icon and quote her credit card number than she could have taken one of those demo cocks in Richmond High Street.

What if Ami or Nick were there when the brown paper parcel arrived? They probably weren't brown paper any more, but as luridly transparent as the packages on those racks: her sad frustrations advertised via the postman's bicycle basket to the whole of Bushwood, one tiny click away.

Another image appeared. As high definition as the porno ads now multiplying all over her computer screen. Nick with the post, looking innocent for the one and only time in his debauched drug-filled adulthood. 'What's this, mum?' and settling back, Converse up on the table, to watch her open it like it was Christmas 1985.

Her own non sex life was a dark, not-to-be-mentioned, forbidden-of-the-forbiddenest places. What would they think of her if they knew she was doing it again? Even with herself.

# CHAPTER SEVEN

'Tea, or coffee?'

'Tea, thanks.'

Sally stood in the door arch of Ramone's tiny cupboard of a kitchen watching her slickly slotting plates into a wobbly over-sink rack.

'Mug or cup? Cracked or stained?'

'Um.'

'Stained mug it is. Hippy or builder's?'

A merry whistle sounded from the kettle, followed by a thump and a curse. Sally stared intently down at the cracks in the lino, the effort to keep up, without warning, overwhelming her.

Ramone turned and waited.

'Whatever you're having,' she said weakly.

Through lunch the old rivalry had been bouncing between them like they'd never parted. Sally felt a perkiness in her old friend, an energy she hadn't been around for such a long time. Not since having a houseful of teenagers. They'd been a generation removed and over there, though. This was right here and beckoning her in. So why was she feeling so tearful all of a sudden?

With a slick, slender-heeled twirl, Ramone pulled down a packet of English Yorkshire from an open, splintery shelf. 'Cry over me much as you want, you know that, we've traded enough tears over the years.

But do me a favour, stop hovering, shoo that cat away and sit yourself down. I'll be out in a second.'

Sally obeyed, analysing her feelings. It wasn't missing Dom or worrying about Nick, it was the choreography of her old friend's movements that was setting her off. The automatic, subconscious dance of belonging.

Pushing aside a crumpled pile of Heats and Hello's, she perched on the faux Louis XV sofa, the same one she used to sit on all those years ago. Washed-out pink rather than scarlet now, but it had faded well, clashing with the yellow, purple and green plastic tendrils spiralling down from the central light fitting. The high ceiling that gave off the same old feeling of white, echoey space, or was it emptiness? Nestling in the bay window were the same collections of beaded lampshades, tall, spindly candles and white rattan chairs, set in the dust. The same dust, probably. It smelled of sunshine, time and regret.

Sucking her teeth to her top lips, Sally made the human cat noise at the slinky black cat furled into a ball next to her. An emerald eye opened but as she went to stroke it, a paw lashed out and the cat leapt to the floor. She watched it stalk snootily away across the splintery white floorboards, flashing its arse at her. The fireplace was filled with church candles clustered with drips. A full ashtray bulged onto the hearth. A sardonic smirk crept across her lips as her eyes rested on the zebra striped rug, the very same carpet she'd once screwed Will Urlong from *The Pixons* on. The whole place reeked of the glamour of possibility she'd forgotten had ever existed.

Could ageing with attitude be for everybody, Sally

wondered. Or was it only for the few, like Ramone, like Madonna, who already had flair in spades anyway? Ramone plonked the mugs on the floorboards, sparked a cigarette and pulled up a white leather beanbag. The cat raced in from the bedroom meowing at her.

'Sorry, I felt myself getting a bit teary then.'

'You been having a rough time, girl.'

'It sounds a bit mad, but it does get to the point where it stops mattering. Most of the time. You've been through all the fears and dreads. The worst has already happened. You're not sleeping or waking up in the middle of the night with cold sweats. You kind of accept that every day's going to be crap in some form or other, and it all stops being such a worry. The light still shines for some people somewhere I guess.'

'It'll glow again for you Sal it will. Look, how do you think – how'd Dom be coping, you know, if it'd been you that'd, you know...'

'Died?'

'GO!' Ramone growled at the cat in a cloud of smoke and it fled.

'Like me, he'd've fallen apart.'

'But a freshly single hunk of life-force in his forties?'

'What are you saying?'

'What I'm saying is how long do you think he'd have lasted on his own? What I'm saying is he'd've caved in to some leggy redhead launching herself at him eventually.'

'Leggy redhead? What's that supposed to mean?'

'Petite brunette then! Or big-boned, loud-mouth diva that never was come to that.'

'I suppose you're right, he'd have been off into

another life by now, manufacturing the next family module. My book says that over half of widowers are remarried or engaged within a year. A year!'

'What's new, not as many guys to go around.'

'Men feel like they've lost part of themselves, apparently, whereas women feel abandoned. Do you think that means abandonment is harder to get over than losing a part of yourself?'

'Depends which part.'

Sally laughed, 'And who wants the farty wheezy leftovers?'

'The tasty ones have to be dug for, like truffles.'

'Abandonment would be progress. I've still got to get over my delusions that he's still alive and kicking about the sodding planet somewhere.'

'Awww, come here,' Ramone leapt up and engulfed Sally in a musky patchouli-scented hug.

She pulled away, held onto Sally's shoulders and looked into her eyes, 'You know what? Every door marked exit is an entry to somewhere else. You'll move on. You will.'

'Feeling like I belonged somewhere in the first place would be a start.'

'Bah, nobody belongs anywhere,' said Ramone falling back down on the beanbag with a loud crunch. 'We all came from somewhere else originally. Have you been on the net, checked out the talent?' Her hand flew to her mouth, 'Or is it too soon? Sorry, Sal, I'm being a crass fuckwit here aren't I.'

'No!'

'I am. I'm a whore-mouthing, bitchin bitch insensitive…'

'You've no idea how refreshing it is, Ramone. Everybody pussyfooting around has been driving me insane. They're only trying to be kind as well, which makes it worse. But no, as I said, I don't want a relationship again.'

'You said you did!'

'I didn't.'

'You did, girl! Fuck, I'll get a recorder going in next time you're coming round. You said it right over our lunch there, you were a woman who needed a man, you were a woman who had a man and now you don't…'

'I had a man for twenty-five years, but now I haven't. He was there and now he's gone and I'm still not dealing with it. Being here, that's good enough for now.'

'Honey, I know I have my butch side but…' Ramone slapped Sally's thigh affectionately. 'We got to get you out there again.'

'I am out there. This is it.'

'You're a one-man-woman. Nothing wrong in that. You need to find a new one man.'

'I don't.'

'That's what you said.'

'I need to find a new me. I've got to get rid of this feeling, this preoccupation, that I'm on my own the whole time when everyone seems to be with somebody else. I know it's not true but it's like this alone aura thing that clings to you.'

'Listen, there's this site right…'

'Oh No no no,' said Sally holding up her hands. 'No internet dating. No way.'

'Have you looked?'

'Of course I have and it sucks. Don't tell me

everybody does it now because I know that and it doesn't make any difference. Ami got her bloke online. Nothing but trouble and she had a choice.'

'So do you.'

'Hah. You try typing in men between forty-nine and fifty-five and see what you get? Shall I tell you? You get men between, quote, forty-nine and fifty-five, who are probably between fifty-six and ninety-five who are looking for girls between eighteen and twenty-nine. I quote "thirty year-olds need not apply".'

'You look hot, so why ruin it? Lie!'

'Like those losers. Great.'

'Hit nineteen – twenty-five then, go for the pervs.'

'Pervs?'

'Young guys who want older women. They're out there, believe me. There are websites.'

'I bet there are.'

'Here.'

Before Sally could stop her, Ramone was tapping into her iPhone.

'Toyboywarehouse UK,' she read, 'online dating for gorgeous women and younger men.'

'As if I haven't got enough insecurities!' Sally chucked the phone back, laughing.

'There's this totally happening bar opened in LA. Young guys, older women.'

'A pick-up joint you mean.'

'Don't be a priss, what's there not to like about it? It might even be worth the trip, though they've been going in Italy for years of course, and who cares about the language barrier? That's not what I'm saying anyhow.'

After a couple of touches to the screen, Ramone handed

it back. 'This is different.'

Sally looked at the stream of grinning, golden mug-shots sliding across the screen, 'This is fantasy, pure fantasy!'

'Forget about them, they're only the hot picks, here, look at...'

'No!'

'What's it called?' Ramone commanded.

'I don't want to know,' Sally handed the phone back. 'I'm going to see someone I know on there in a minute, the kid of someone I know I mean, and it'll freak me right out.'

'OK there another one called Mysinglefriend.com OK? So I put you up there, tell the world what a great catch you are and you sit back and wait for the e-mails. How easy is that?'

'I'm not a catch.'

Ramone shrugged and closed the phone, 'You said you been looking online.'

'That was years ago. Out of curiosity.'

'Years?'

Sally shrugged. 'Like I said. Curiosity.'

'When he played away from home?'

'It gave me the creeps then and it gives me the creeps now.'

'So you're going to wait until you fall in luuurve again before you get any action?'

'It's not going to happen.'

'Letting all that falling in love bull get the upper hand, big mistake.'

'That's why it's called falling. That's what falling means, Ramone, you can't help it. You don't step into love, do you. You don't buy it in a sex shop or move into it. There are no lawyers ready to exchange contracts and wait for completion.'

Ramone pushed her hair back from her forehead over and over until it lost its spring, put her elbows on her knees and looked up. 'Sorry.'

'S'okay.'

'What would I know about love anyhow?'

Sally couldn't think what to say. Seeing her friend crumble so fast jolted her. Without the tumble of Afro curls framing her eyes, Ramone looked older and washed out. All her fault, she thought guiltily, bringing her down to her self-pitying level. 'I'm the one that should be sorry,' she said softly, 'I appreciate your concern, really.'

'Sure?'

'Sure. It was mean of me to ask you not to play any music. Please, put something on.'

Ramone sprang across the room. 'You know what?' she yelled above the sound of a soulful American funk intro, 'This big mouth of mine needs a good zip across it sometimes.' She shimmied back to Sally, her lime silk chiffon trousers and deliberately mis-matched turquoise and beigey brown fingernails all making perfect, beautiful, crazy sense again.

Sally resolved to match Ramone's upbeat mood. 'Hey, Dom's dead. Sex is everywhere, I think I should start doing my bit for death. OK I'll go with you a bit. Supposing I were to meet a Clooney clone somewhere not on the internet who I was really, really attracted to, and they were to me, ha ha.'

'You're fifty, not dead, woman!'

'OK, suppose I'm out there sifting through this imaginary world full of eligible, uncreepy men wanting to know more about me…' Sally smiled to herself. The shifting eyes of Strawberry Hill felt a long way away.

'Go on!'

'Even if I got that far – this is all complete supposition you understand – it's not what happens at the bottom end, the going all the way that worries me so much as the beginning.'

'Beginning of what?'

'The top.'

'What top?'

You know, the kissing bit. Snogging.'

'Sucking face?'

'Oh please – but yes, all that – well, suppose I got a – a slobberer or… a furry tongue or…'

'A dry kisser with chapped lips and sandpaper tongue?'

'Don't!' Sally screeched.

Here, wanna practise?' Ramone planted her bosoms in Sally's lap and puckered her expansive orange lips.

'Get off!' Sally pushed her away.

'Please yourself.'

'Kissing has to be in real. All-consuming. All mushed up in the love of it. When you don't know if you're giving or receiving and it doesn't matter in all that desperate need to be a complete part of each other. In every single way. Especially in that way.'

'What's this book you keep going on about?'

'Oh a widow's handbook thing?'

'How's that helping? Apart from giving you wrist-slitting statistics.'

'It's given me an action plan, here,' Sally reached for her bag.

Ramone took the list, read silently and gave it back without comment like a disappointed teacher.

'It's the small things, you start with the small things,' Sally explained, folding it up and putting it back in her bag.

'By drinking *water*?' Ramone implored.

'By getting into small habits.'

'Forget the small things girl. The big decisions are the ones that get you moving.'

'It's not that simple.'

'Consider. Decide. Do. That's all there is to it. Forget water. It's a champagne habit you need girl. Wine at least. It's that book of yours that's too simple. No wonder you're – look, I'm going to be blunt here, and it's what I've been trying to say all over lunch in a roundabout way. Girl, you need to get out there again.'

Roundabout way! Heaven help me Sally thought, but reined herself in. 'It's a start, that's all, a start.'

'Hey, let's sex this thing up a bit,' Ramone said, moving next to Sally on the sofa. 'It's a copy yeah? I can scribble all over it? This drinking water crap can go for a start.'

Sally found a pen in her bag.

'Oh neat, red pen, thanks,' Ramone scribbled.

'I'm not drinking eight glasses of champagne a day.'

'Half a bottle – *shared*. Or wine, good wine. No cheap dross. Don't drink at all if you can't drink the best. Which reminds me...' Ramone got up.

'I'll have to be making a move soon,' Sally said taking the hint.

'You stay right there,' Ramone ordered, dashing into the kitchen.

'Now, what's this,' she said when the wine had been poured, '– *don't do anything rash!* Bollocks! Consider. Decide. Do. Let's simplify that. Number 2: Do It. Act before you think. Thinking too much, always been your problem Sal. Now what have we? *Wear mascara every day even if you're not going out.* Oh babe oh babe. Mascara's an afterthought not a magic wand.'

Sally watched Ramone's big spidery writing scrawl all over her list. If this were anybody else she'd be irritated beyond belief. But she was glad to see Ramone getting off on trying to help her. Grateful for her old friend's spirit and generosity.

'Get yourself some sexy heels and a killer haircut and the rest will follow.'

'I'm not having short hair.'

Ramone looked up, 'Did I say that?'

'I've seen too many lives ruined by that one wrong cut that changes you forever. If you have long hair you can't look old.'

'Oh, Sally Sally.'

'They don't! Old people don't have long hair.'

'Nothing wrong with long till it starts matching the way your teeth are going.'

'Plenty of older women have it... Twiggy, Goldie Hawn, Jerry Hall!"

'Nobody needs hair past their shoulders. So do me a favour, get your plastic down to Michaeljohn and get Charlie or Fred to sort you.'

'Oh sure,' Sally scoffed.

'So, it costs twice as much as High Street Helen –

halve the visits!'

'Like once instead of twice a year?'

'No brainer, Sal, top and tail, hair and heels.'

'There's a very thin line between cool and sad Ramone. You've got it sussed but no way am I ever going to be hobbling around the house feeling half an inch taller. Heels are for parties now, not staggering around Sainsbury's.'

'See these?' Ramone waggled a slender purple diamante cuffed ankle boot.

'Love'em,' said Sally, 'and they make you look even more sexy and gorgeous than you already are but I'm not squashing my feet into anything like that. Not for anyone or any thing.'

'Footwise, Ken Church Street. Sexy fashion heels made for comfort, they can x-ray your foot and everything. I'll write it here, and while I'm at it, number 5: you need a new dress to die for.'

'I don't wear dresses.'

'I'm talking a serious animal of a dress, that's got a life all its own. Westwood, Miyake. Vivienne Westwood said clothes are so empowering they can change the way you think and that's the solid, cast iron truth of it. You gotta house for sale, you gotta do it for yourself.'

'I'm selling because I'm broke, Ramone. I need everything I can get to keep going. We had no insurance, the business is over. I've got a whole pile of practical problems to sort...'

'Tuh tuh tuh –' Ramone silenced her, 'how can I put this in your language? Think of it as a new boiler. If the house boiler crashes what do you do? You FIND the money.'

Sally exhaled noisily. So she was an old boiler now. Ramone was trying to help, in her Ramone-like way, but the past played its part here. When they'd been on the road together the attitude had always been that life was one big game which one of them would win and one of them would lose. Like Ramone had always wanted to be the lead singer. Sally would argue they had the best of it from right where they were in the back row. Ramone vowed she'd prove otherwise. Subtle and safe or upfront and dangerous, only one of them could win.

'I might quite like being an old boiler,' Sally said buffering up her position. 'Even if I didn't, I don't even know what I'm going to do for work...'

'I'm getting to that.'

'I'm not blowing a fortune on any of these things, Ramone, especially not a dress I'll never wear.'

'eBay, vintage, Portobello... You got to be real picky though. Second hand's trickier to pull off on older skin. The Westwood sale's over but I'll flag you the next sample sale. I'm writing this down because this is more important than a leaky bathroom, Sally, this is you. The rest of your life. What's this – *Get a dog*! Joke. Right?'

'It's not replacing people with dogs, it's so you can go out every day and speak to people, other dog owners, you know...'

'A *dog* to talk to people?' Ramone's scribbling got more dramatic, her script more flourishing.

'And, with the money you save not getting a dog and all its little doggy bills – you haven't got one yet I'm taking it?'

Sally shook her head, laughing.

'Group holiday? Is there anything worse in this world?'

Ramone scribbled happily. 'Holiday alone. That way you have to speak to strangers. Hey I like it. They're running into each other. Like they're meant to be.'

'Wherever you go you take yourself with you, at least I'm old enough to have learnt that one.'

'No excuse.'

'I'd be worrying about Nick even more if I was away.'

'What's the difference. Worry somewhere else instead. This leads into number eight, you'd better do something about that tummy before you go.'

'Thanks.'

'You have to be tough to be kind sometimes,' Ramone looked sniffily at Sally's thighs.

'Before you say anything, these jeans cost a bomb!'

'Hmm you're sort of getting away with your grungy old style, but getting away with it's not enough any more. You want to be carrying yourself like a torch, out there and proud. It's going down.'

8. *Twenty sit-ups three times a day.*

'Sit ups do my back in.'

'You got the angle wrong. Get yourself one of those balls from Argos. Now we're getting to the meat. Volunteer? Fuck volunteering, get a job!'

Sally grabbed the opportunity to turn the questions, 'What did you say you were doing at the moment?'

'I told you. Sweet FA. The music business is dead as fuck, you know the crack, all my contacts going out of business. Now you as well. Not that you ever put any sessions my way.'

'You know how it was.'

'Joke. But yeah, dire and getting worse. I got one or two producers still hanging in there, but listen up – I think I got an agent.'

'They're hiring backing singers?'

'No no no,' Ramone grabbed Sally's arm and whispered. 'Musicals. Can't you see it! Ramone Rockett, the new West End sensation? Me neither but I might get a regular gig out of it. I'm so over all that diva business, Sal, it was never meant to be. Imagine it though.' Ramone narrowed her eyes and looked into an imaginary, sparkling distance, 'a steady gig in a chorus – showtime every night, pitching up for regular hours, regular time off. They got union reps that look after your rights. Heavies! Sick pay!'

'This doesn't sound like you.'

'Not knowing where the next gig's coming from. It's no life. But hey, gigs turn up and there's plastic for when it doesn't.'

'An agent eh?'

'When I've got myself sorted I'll put you onto her.'

'That's really kind.' God! It was kind. Friends could be so incredible when you were down. 'But I'm not singing anymore.'

'You're not singing because you haven't got a gig.'

'I mean I can't sing,' Sally paused for a moment, she could feel herself spiralling down to the dark place. She blinked hard. Don't blub. Not now. She kept her voice slow and steady. 'I can't listen to music even. Most music. That's why I didn't want anything on earlier.'

Ramone made to move but she stopped her. 'No this is fine, honestly. James Brown goes with the flat, with you, I might even try him at home, but I haven't sung since the funeral.'

'Most music. So, what can you listen to?'

'Heavy metal?'

Ramone raised an approving eyebrow.

'It has to be at full volume, when I'm feeling really low which I'm not at the moment so it's fine, but Van Halen's about the only thing that's doing it for me at the moment.'

'Not forever, Sal, not forever. The agent's going on the list anyhow. Number nine, the magic number. Right, one left. That book of yours isn't all crap, you do need to plan some things more than others. On this whole getting over Dom thing I reckon you need more than a list can give you. More like a schedule, a plan of action.'

'I've already said, Ramone...'

'This sad alone feeling you're hauling around with you like a lead balloon and hating yourself for isn't doing you any favours, is it?'

'No,' tight chin, don't blub, don't, don't, DON'T.

'What you are Sally is, technically, a born-again virgin.'

'Come again?'

'You might well say,' Ramone reached for her cigarette, took a quick drag and exhaled smoke slowly out of the side of her mouth. 'You've gotta be bold about this, lose your wididity, that way you'll be ready to move on to the next stage.'

'My *what*?'

'Take it in two phases. Get the sex out of the way, move on.'

'It's not about that.'

You were married for – however many years – you're

bound to be –'

'Rusty? That's one way of describing it I suppose.'

'I was going to say gagging for it...' Ramone rested her cigarette carefully in the groove of the ashtray.

'But I'm *not*. I don't like being on my own all the time, that's all.' Sally watched the smoke wisp into the air.

'Work at it. I know it's tougher than drinking a few glasses of water but it's going on the list. Number 10, Lose Your Wididity. Get the first guy out the way. Then when someone who does matter comes along. Bam! You're back in business.'

'You're insane.'

'You only go there if you want to go there. If the chemistry's not happening, it's not happening but you got to give it a chance.'

'That's *not* what you said, you said go out and screw the first...'

'If you don't look you're not going to find. Don't go for anything unless you want it. No man ever goes for anything unless he wants it, right?'

'Because they're less fussy,' Sally picked up her mug from the floor and leant back. A quiet, contented grunt emitted from her mouth. What a relief to be talking about her needs rather than her losses. This could almost be the future. A future life that she felt a part of again.

'Takes some finding but it is out there. Submission's what it's all about.'

'Oh yes. There's something incredibly sexy about that moment when a guy's been chasing you and you finally give in to his demands…'

'No no no Sal, you get them submitting to you.

Always ALWAYS keep the upper hand.'

'It doesn't work like that, It's never worked like that. Not for me anyhow.'

'It can. Know where you stand and what you stand for. Don't let people push you around. It'll take time I'll give you that.

'But is it all worth it, Ramone? I mean there are alternatives these days. I had a sneaky peek in the new sex, um accessory, shop that's just opened in Richmond High Street the other day.'

'You devil.'

'*Richmond High Street!* I was way too embarrassed to, you know, look too closely. I should have had you with me I was thinking at the time…'

'Ah, I may be able to help you there. Come with me.'

Ramone led her into the bedroom.

## CHAPTER EIGHT

Sally stood gawping. At first she thought they were statuettes. Or trophies from Ramone's secret life as an undercover ice skater or darts champion, displayed as they were, so majestically on the bedroom mantlepiece.

Ramone stared fixedly at Sally in drop-jawed amazement. 'You're telling me you *don't have one*?'

'No,' said Sally in a small voice, 'I don't.'

'Haaaaa aa a a a ha.'

'I had a *husband*, remember! Sex and toys had separate functions in our house.'

'Sally Screwball Aldridge! And you don't even own a vibrator? 'Yezzzah, girl! Where have you been?'

'It's not so strange. We didn't need it.' Sally ran her eyes across the forest of glass dildoes, wooden dildoes, large ugly pink dildoes, fat dildoes, gold dildoes, double ended dildoes. 'Why so *many*?'

'Remind me of the old days maybe. Like when we used to pass lovers between us like so many joints.'

'A long, long time ago.'

'Crazy times,' Ramone said fondly. 'Hey, look what I found the other day,' she turned to the cluttered shelves by the unmade bed and pulled out a garish album cover. Sally looked at the picture of a grossly overweight woman with a fleshy, taunting leer surrounded by food, her naked body dripping with melon, bananas, grapes and every kind of soft fruit.

'Recognise this?'

'Vaguely,' Sally said, wishing she didn't. It was grotesque. The blatant sexism of those days still amazed and horrified her.

'Juicy Lucy. Our first gig together.'

'Not Juicy Lucy – we did Atomic Rooster, Croydon Greyhound before that. Then the ELO Radio 1 session then Juicy Lucy.'

'Ah well, near enough,' Ramone said, squeezing the cover back on the shelf.

'Hell, we were a tight unit back then weren't we.'

'We should've given ourselves a name, Sal, gone out there as an act. I'll always regret that.'

'Girl bands didn't exist.'

'Why I'm still so hacked off we didn't go for it. Think where we'd have been today if we'd grabbed hold of a couple of guitars and followed that gut instinct of mine.'

'I'd rather have done the glitzy stadiums than headline the sticky college unions and Top Ranks for years on end,' Sally said, moving the subject swiftly on. She and Penny had ganged up behind Ramone's back and together chucked every scorn at her idea until it died. Even if they'd taken off, she and Penny would still have been backing singers. To Ramone.

'Not so bad, I guess, being the only chicks on the scene. Penny! What happened to her?'

'Married that Swiss chef guy she met on the Slade catering unit, remember. Maybe she's still living in Geneva.'

'Bored out of her mind.' said Ramone solemnly. 'All that lake.'

'We all thought that was such a sophisticated move.'

'Now, Sal, look at these guys I got here and remember how you were. Is my wididity idea still so crazy? Isn't the old Sal still in there somewhere?'

'I'm a different person now, Ramone. I'm not going to go off and shag a stranger or anybody else for that matter.'

'We were all strangers once, and I've been on the road with you, remember.'

'And I've been on the road with you.'

Ramone sighed. 'Who'd have thought it'd ever end the way it did?'

'With all of this,' Sally shook her head at the display.

'We lost so many people. But hey, it's all different now. We're condom-smart and we carry on.'

'You might.'

'Don't get into this old maid vibe Sal, please. How many of those guys we screwed did we ever do the dating thing with?'

'Dating didn't come into it. We were being – friendly – that's all.'

'Sex was there to be enjoyed, right?'

'It was the 70s, that's how it was.'

'And this is the noughties and guess what, some of us are carrying on the good old rock & roll traditions.'

'But all of this, Ramone, it's such a pointless...'

'Now pointless these babies aren't, I can guarantee you that. Maybe it's what you need.'

'Listen, thanks for today. I owe you one.'

Ramone looked bashful. 'To be honest I've had a ball. It's been cool catching up. Feels good to be useful. Makes a change.'

'It's not fair, concentrating on me and what I want like this when I know you got problems we haven't even talked about.'

'You're in a fix honey. I want you to get In Control, take hold of the levers hmm? Much as you loved your man this is your time to shine. Here, feel this,' a disturbing manic glint appeared Ramone's eyes. 'Real soft and springy hnn? It's a new material called Elastomer. And this little baby,' she proudly held up a pink rod with bobbles all over it, 'is the Pixie Plus, isn't it cute? Like a pinky little sea urchin.'

'I wouldn't call that little.'

'Yup, it packs a punch that one, hundreds and hundreds of little tickly bits all going off at once. Keeps you young that one!'

'I'm sure it does stop your hair going all wiry and your ears growing, but…' Sally looked anxiously at the door.

'Look at this, medical grade titanium, designed by aircraft engineers. The parts are guaranteed for life, as well. Now, hold it right there,' Ramone pulled a drawer out from underneath her bed and poked around inside it. 'Ah.' She emerged with a box. 'Here. Give it a try. Learn about loving yourself.'

Sally pulled a face.

'Not *now*, I'm not saying now. A girlfriend bought it for me for Christmas, but I'm already doubled up on that one. I was going to take it back but never got round to it. Here, have a look at mine.' Ramone darted for the mantelpiece and came back holding up a whopper to the light like a glass of rare claret.

Sally giggled, 'It looks like a stray from the limbless hospital, or a warped table leg.'

'Here we go my little beauty,' Ramone clicked it on.

With a barely audible whine, the bendy end started to rotate.

Still laughing, Sally sat down on the bed, 'Now it reminds me of my food mixer.'

'Here, feel it,' Ramone placed the revolving pink giant slowly and reverentially down onto Sally's lap.

'No!' Sally leapt away like she'd been handed a spider.

'That's what you're missing isn't it?'

They both stood watching it loping around the pillows like a mutant insect.

'Think of it as yours,' said Ramone.

'No, I couldn't…!' Sally went for her jacket.

Ramone packed it back in its box all the same. 'I know I know, hugs and masculine presence. But in the meantime, this is your baby.' She dropped it into a Sainsbury's bag and shoved it in Sally's handbag. The gesture reminded her of the way her mother used to pack her off with the leftover pieces of chicken after Sunday lunch, covered in leaky greaseproof paper and a brown paper bag.

Hugs and masculine presence? The bleak horror of acceptance crept all over her skin like a cold, clammy sweat. Dom wasn't coming back. Ever.

'No. Thanks, but no. I couldn't carry it on the tube. Supposing there was a bomb scare? A security check? I'd never be able to look the Strawberry Hill ticket man in the eye again.' Sally placed the bright orange package back down on the sofa.

'Now no more questions. A woman's relationship with her vibrator is strictly between her and her nerve endings.'

'I suppose it's as close as I'm ever going to get to…,' Sally demurred. 'It might as well be a bit of old plastic.'

Silence.

'No-one can replace him can they...'

'No.'

'A woman, maybe?'

'God! No!'

'Now now, don't knock what you haven't tried.'

'How do you know? Look, I really need to be on the tube before dark.' Sally slipped on her jacket.

'You're still the old silly Sally aren't you. What are you saying, it's dark down there anyhow!'

'You know what I mean.'

They hugged goodbye.

'You come back soon, yeah? And I don't want you changing your mind! I know all your old tricks, remember? And I'm not having it.'

'I won't,' Sally promised.

'Including that one.'

'What!'

'Saying things people want to hear.'

On the doorstep outside, Sally paused to collect herself.

It was a fine evening. Office workers criss crossed each other in front of her at a pace that would really hurt if they were to crash into each other. But they were all so in tune with the race to get themselves to wherever they were going it never happened. They were up to speed. She'd get there. If she didn't keep up she'd fall right off and the world would roll on without her. As it did to everyone eventually. But not for her. Not yet.

With Ramone's voice still ringing in her ears, she

shoved the orange parcel to the bottom of her bag and gave the, now crumpled piece of paper, a quick look.

*Don't do anything rash. Consider, one minute max. Decide, one minute max.* **DO. Done! Keep on MOVING....!**

*Don't let your worries about the future escalate out of control. Stay in the present moment. Meditation classes are good for this.* **Fuck thinking about nothing, GET ON WITH IT.**

*Wear mascara every day, even if you're not going out.* **Mascara's not a magic fucking wand. HAIR and HEELS – top and toe with style and let the rest take care of itself.**

*Get some new clothes.* **LESS is MORE with clothes, get a killer dress. EVERY woman should own a Westwood.**

*Exercise – train for a Fun Run.* **Whoever wrote this needs to run away from themselves. Running round in circles every day is for nuts. Get an exercise ball and let it do the work – 20 sit ups 3 times a day, 10 minutes max and you're done.**

*Drink 8 glasses of water a day.* **Make that one bottle of champagne a day. OTT? A couple of vodka sharpeners then, or GOOD wine.**

*Get a dog.* **Speak to strangers NOT their fucking**

**dogs.**

*Go on group activity holiday or cruise.* **NO GROUP TOURS – ALONE is the way to meet people that are WORTH meeting.**

*Volunteer.* **Get a JOB, SING girl SING!**

*Join an evening class.* **Life's too short for papier mache clubs, get ON WITH IT, GET DOWN AND LOSE YOUR WIDIDITY *** NUMBER ONE TASK**

# CHAPTER NINE

That evening Sally locked herself in her bedroom, reverentially unfolded the thin white gossamer covering and slipped her new toy out of its plastic tray. She found the on button hiding behind a plastic bollock.

On off, she giggled to herself, so like a real man. Squeezing her eyes tight shut, she pressed the end against herself. Guilt. Does Ramone feel guilty? No way.

Push and be proud!

This is normal behaviour.

Everybody does it.

You can bugger off as well, she scowled at her imaginary husband, hovering below the ceiling, arms folded across his chest, laughing so hard his shoulders were shaking.

Had it really come to this? Oh well, here goes. She closed her eyes and pressed the on button. Nothing happened. She tried again.

Dammit!

She leant down for the box on the floor, 'Ouch!' Sudden shifts sideways not good idea, not in instructions. Where were the instructions. She hunted in vain, examining all the writing on the box. A happy, orgasmic woman grinned madly at her out of the graphics.

There she found the dreaded Christmas morning words 'Batteries not supplied.'

'Curses on you Ramone, don't you know you're supposed to tape the batteries to the outside?'

Why should she. That was a yummy mummy habit for Thomas the Tank engine sets and dolls that cried and wet themselves. Not Ramone's world. So much for appreciating her friend's generosity.

Ungrateful bitch, Sally. Seedy, ungrateful, lonely, sad sad… this was all too sad.

Guilt. Disgusting thing. Don't look at it. Hide it under the covers.

She put on her glasses and examined the small print on the box until she found the magic sign 2 x AA. Feeling like a thwarted child, she put the box back beside the bed and stomped around the bedroom, picking things up and putting them down at random.

Life, she decided, was full of nothing but soul-less unfulfilled mono-sex where everyone in the world had become so selfish they had to screw themselves.

Her eyes rested on her alarm clock. Her battery alarm clock. Her alarm clock with 2 x AA batteries inside.

A vain search through her cleaned-out kitchen drawer produced nothing more screwdriver-like than a potato masher. The chances of finding a miniature sort with a starry end were nil.

'How like stuffing Christmas this is,' she mumbled, going to the bathroom. 'Christmas without the stuffing in my case.'

In the bathroom cabinet she pounced on the tweezers. Tweezers had worked a treat on Nick's Furbie. She prised them open and slotted the side of one edge into the tiny groove of the screw. With all her force, she pushed and turned. It gave. A few more turns and the casing fell open.

The batteries slotted smoothly into place, her breathing quickened as she tightened up the casing. She leapt back onto bed and pulled the covers over herself.

Bzzzzzzzzz.

Blinking heck! Her eyes widened as her body began to shudder. Here we go, she lay back and let her legs flop.

'Oh?'

It turned.

'Oh my…!'

Sally lay there, juddering. Nerve messages tore down her legs and up her spine.

'Aargggh!'

'Oh?'

So.

There you go then.

Now what?

She could do it again now.

And again.

But she didn't want to.

However many times she did it, there'd be no cosy cosy post-orgasmic flop of satisfaction with the world and everything in it. This feeling hovered somewhere between tacky guilt, hollow loneliness and sad, maiden aunt in an old Robert Morley movie.

*Put it behind you, Sal. Put it behind you, love.*

'Where are you!' she screamed at the ceiling, 'Where THE HELL are you when you're needed?'

## CHAPTER TEN

Sally saved the worst job until there was nowhere else for it to go. Until there were no more miscellany drawers to clear and no cupboards unturned. No CD racks full of newspaper freebies she'd never watch and no garage shelves full of tools she'd never use.

Her hands felt numb, like they were removed from the rest of her body, as she took down the coats, jeans and t-shirts, as crusty as dried flowers, burying her face into the armpits searching for the lost odour of his skin. But all she got was the smell of old wood and charity shop.

*Megadeth* blared full strength out of the iPod speakers. After each bin bag filled, she sat back on the bed, still and attentive. Listening as closely as if it were Bach, she forced her concentration onto the sounds of the shrieking men, throbbing basslines, frantic guitars and lingering feedback, separating each component as if it were a track in a recording studio, so she only heard the single notes whilst they were there.

As a method it worked. But then she reached the sock drawer. Tucked behind the little round furry bundles of soft black cashmere; behind the thick, virgin white tennis socks he never wore, she found a little Angel's feather.

She put his suitcase beside the bed and sat down heavily, fingering the red silk handkerchief Dom had stolen from one of Nick's magic sets. The glaze over her eyes gave way. The tears fell silently.

Trying to keep her contacts in place, she blinked hard, crammed the stale hanky in her mouth and waited for the choking. None came. The guitars fizzled out into reverb. The hush enveloped her.

Letting the tears fall unchecked, she reached into the back of the drawer and took out the blue Rizlas and a squashed, half-full packet of dry, crumbling 10 Benson & Hedges. She moved fast, tying up the bags and carrying them down to the hall. After a quick detour to the music shelves followed by the fridge for wine and chocolate, she was back upstairs.

Lick, stick two cigarette papers together lengthways and one at the end. The CD case wasn't as spacious as an album cover but with careful balancing she managed. A couple of puffs and she was away. Floating in the dry smell of the past, where joints had been as much a part of her daily routine as her eight glasses of water were now.

She swapped *Megadeth* for *Aladdin Sane*, lit her whole precious collection of Diptyque candles, and poured a whole half bottle of Usiku under the bath tap.

*'I knew that stash'd come in useful one day.'*

Sally froze. 'Dom?' she whispered.

*Reckoned you'd be needing that, Sal, after a difficult day, aye?*

'Where are you? Where have you *been*?'

Silence.

'Come back!' she screamed. 'Where did you go, Dom? I can't do this. I can't manage it. Please – please come back to me.'

How could he disappear? There wasn't anybody else like him, anywhere. And wouldn't be again. She lowered herself into the hot, scented water and sank back into the past. To the macho world of the 70s rock tours where everyone had been so cool and self-possessed. Dom's tender, protective ways and fierce possessiveness of her had taken her by surprise at first but she'd soon come to expect it. When he was around her worries dissolved and that feeling had never changed, right up to the day he died.

The adrenaline rushes of the shows clashed psychotically with the long, boring stretches of motoring between gigs. They'd always said the closest equivalent job would have been a long- distance lorry driver on regular acid trips. It had all been such a once-removed existence. A bit like now.

She looked at her tummy. It was the tummy of a middle-class woman in the middle of her Middlesex life. Without any sex but with a middle that was too big to be a good middle, stoned senseless and listening for the voice of her dead husband.

This was it, she was going the way of the crazy. No wonder Nick's favoured communication channel was in less than one hundred and forty characters via Twitter. No wonder Ami lived in Scotland. It wasn't anything to do with finding that fast-track graduate job. But that's what they'd both wanted for them. Their kids were as independent and as free as she and Dom always wanted them to be. But why didn't they visit more? Was she becoming too crazy now?

Paranoia. She was being paranoid. Dope always made her paranoid. What was she doing smoking hash at her age? What right had she to want Nick healthy and well when she behaved like this?

Never again, that's all. It was an experiment that had failed. No way did she have even a fraction of Ramone's cool, spirited aplomb to do any of that growing old disgracefully lark. She popped a Revel in her mouth.

Worrying about her middle wouldn't do any good. It was a natural middle. As nature and Gok Wan intended.

She needed to – *had* to – cultivate Val's assured contentedness on this one. Accept the inevitable and grow into her saggy cardies with refined, understated grace. That was the cool way to go.

*Gowan, you know that's not you, Sal. You can do it, you're a beauty.*

Sally shot bolt upright, sending a tidal wave crashing onto the floor. The voice didn't come from her head this time, it was out there.

'Was me, Dom,' she replied out loud.

*I want to see you happy, Sal. You're too good to waste away. Think about the last guy before me, go on truth or dare now I can take it! That lead guitarist wasn't it?*

'An easy guess but which one?'

*'Which one? Listen to you!'*

Lead guitarists had been Sally's weakness. Some girls had the same hankering for singers, others for the mental drummers. Drummers were always mad. What's the difference between a drummer and an equity policy? The equity policy will one day mature, went the old Dylan joke. No, for her it was the strutters. The unobtainable, arrogant pretty boys.

Raphael had been one of those. Prettier than all of them with a low-key arrogance that only surfaced on stage. Less than a week out of England and she'd been the first to get him. Once the others knew he had no old lady in tow, she knew they'd be all over him.

She took a big sip of wine and slipped down into the bubbles. Room 103, she always remembered special room numbers. Room 103, Des Moines Airport Holiday Inn, 1973. Four in the morning, wide awake, lying there, looking at him. She couldn't sleep, he really had been the prettiest star. Too magnificent to sleep with. Or had it been the speed that kept her buzzing?

She gazed at his profile on the pillow. What a waste! They hadn't even made love, not all the way. The girls wouldn't believe that. Maybe she shouldn't mention he passed out when he hit horizontal.

So quiet and still. The electricity had to be in him somewhere, all that energy gone into recharge. She'd half imagined raucous riffing snores, maybe, a windmill arm whirl, a strut of breath, a finger-slide wail of painful, face-screwing reverb. Her eyes pinned on him, she stretched her naked little body out contentedly and laughed at herself, daft.

He was even more ravishing offstage without all the glitter. A down to earth northern boy, as gobsmacked as she was at where they'd ended up.

'Who'd have known it, me, Sally Aldridge, the kid from Croydon, on a tour of America,' she'd said to him when they first started chatting at the twenty-four-hour hotel bar.

'And me, Ralph from Rochdale.'

They'd sat talking till 3 in the morning about the mundanest of things. Mowing the lawn for his parents. The shock of seeing Woolworths in America, selling towering salami sandwiches ten times the size of Wimpys and their shared favourite pick n'mix, iced caramels with soft, chewy centres. The unreality of life on the road made talk like that something special.

The next thing it was dawn and she was discovering there'd be no need for any pretending. The soft strokes of his hand on her leg and his kisses on her neck and behind her ears, and she was melting into the sheets. Half-awake, half-asleep she turned to him, elegant blonde god. She snuggled into him. The love me tender of the night before had gone. He was mentally preparing to move on now, she could feel it. She was getting what was known in backing-singer talk as a good seeing to. Those soft words of last night might as well have never existed. The mundane 'I'm an ordinary bloke' chat a thing of the past. Because he wasn't. He was back strutting his stuff, and she felt lucky to be the girl who was being played. She gave into him like a woman, feeling herself being turned, used and objectified. Backing singers were fair game. And they knew they had the best of it.

Fair Game. She didn't want to marry the guy. She didn't even want to spend the rest of the tour with him. What? Trying to hang onto this with all the screamers pawing and clawing at him let alone the rest of the crew? Forget it. No, this was it. They were moving towards their second climax when the phone went. She hated the American ringtone. Long and singular. Persistent and threatening, like a horror movie.

'Leave it,' she said, holding him close to her, but he moved her with him as his tanned, fair arm reached over. She breathed in the sweet marzipan smell of him.

'What?' he said. 'It can't be.' Silence as he listened. 'You'll have to wait. You heard. Listen, man, I'm in the middle of a FUCK!'

He banged the phone down and turned back to banging her. Being the lead guitarist had its compensations. Knowing they were late made it even more intense, knowing there was an army of people downstairs, sitting on the bus, tapping their feet, waiting for the two of them who were too far gone to stop.

Afterwards he'd escorted her to her room. Touching, she'd thought. He needn't have bothered. He could have gone down on his own. Sweetly, while she quickly packed, he lined up two rows of coke on the dressing table.

For a moment they were like a real couple, heaving their suitcases into the lift. But once the doors slid shut they were snogging again and she was getting the wham bam thank you mam vibes.

Out of the air-con into the rush of sticky, warm Iowa air and it was all over. She was pulling herself together, readying herself for another town, another night, another – who knows? She looked for Ramone and Penny through the bus windows. The good old tour bus with its tables and lamps and navy-blue airplane seats that reclined. She couldn't wait to see their faces.

There they were, half way down on her side, both noses squashed to the window like pigs. She jumped up and down and waved at them. Talk about the cat that got the cream, she was a bitch sometimes, she couldn't help it. Their expressions though – priceless!

Raphael, gentlemanly Raphael again, stepped back for her to climb up first. He gave her bum a final pat goodbye as she made her way down the narrow aisle, grinning widely. The whole bus, cracking with laughter, slow handclapped when he appeared. All except Graham, the manager, and Will, the bodyguard, who both stood beside the driver at the front of the bus, their arms crossed, frowning like a pair of St Trinian's headmistresses.

How brilliant had that been?

Giggling to herself, Sally turned the tap on with her toe.

Lukewarm turned to hot. She squashed the skin of her left knee together and poked at the gungily soft flesh with her finger. Humming softly she slipped low into the bubbles, so stoned she didn't even realise she was singing again.

After her bath, wrapped warm in her towelling robes and fluffy slippers, she called Ramone.

Ramone was speeding and full of news. 'I got called in only yesterday, but can you believe it, I got the gig! Guess what the show is.'

'Go on.'

'Only Montana Mountain.'

'Um...'

'Oh Sal, you know, the cowboy musical the whole of London is talking about. Narina Ferina's the lead.'

'Wow. But that's fantastic Ramone.' Who was Narina Ferina?

'All the glitz with job security, union rules the whole show.'

'Brilliant.'

'Brilliant? It's fucking great. My dreams have been answered. I should've done this years ago, rock's so dead on its arse.'

'Well done Ramone, I'm really pleased for you.'

'Once I'm in there I'll be putting the word in for you. It'll be like the old days, both of us up there, on stage where we belong, hey?'

'I don't think...'

'No thinking, Sal. Do, remember? Soon as there's a gap I'll be putting you up...'

'Listen, get in there and enjoy it, OK? I'll be cheering from the stalls, believe me, but when I said I can't sing any more I meant it. The music's gone from me Ramone...'

'I'm hearing you. I'm only trying to snap you out of all that boring – wife – business.'

'I may be boring, but I'm not a hon and I'm not a wife – I'm a widow, OK?' Sally clicked off her phone and threw it across the empty sofa. What the hell did Dom think he was doing, cruising with the angels, leaving her to cope?

# CHAPTER ELEVEN

The news that the house would be going to sealed bids fell into Sally's life like an unwelcome disease.

'The market's supposed to be slow around here!' she'd protested.

'It's a very popular road, Mrs Lightfoot,' the baffled estate agent had replied.

Sally clicked her phone off and swore.

Sticking out for the full asking price, keeping the bank on side but stretching her time there to the other side of the summer at least, was the plan. Instead there she was in early May with three sets of buyers gagging to get in. Each of them already behind her front door in their imaginations and each with their own ideas on how they were going to rip and knock, paint over and redesign her already fragile existence into oblivion.

She turned to the stereo.

*Van Halen* and *Metallica* were still her music of choice but as the days warmed, the brute force of the colliding guitars and vocals added to her gloom rather than detracted. Joni Mitchell, Nerina Pallot and Elbow all failed but Erik Satie seemed to have as many empty spaces and holes in it as Sally and the house.

Classical music again, Sally, she thought slipping the CD once more into the sound system. Why had it taken so long?

Accompanied by piano music so slow it sounded like it might grind to a halt at any moment, she drifted upstairs. How the hell did she let go of all of this?

She ran her fingernail along the glass shelf over the bath. After decades of hosting little more than ring-marks, Nivea and soap-scuzzed Wash & Go, the deep blue Neal's Yard bottles gave it a shining glamour. Professionally cleaned windows were another revelation, banishing those murky outside bits in the middle she'd never reached herself. She had a clear view now of the back alley to the allotments, bulging with lovingly cherished produce.

She should have known the house would go quickly. Bushwood Avenue was the kind of friendly, family-heavy street that fanned out from every popular state school in London. One of those leafy, communal roads where the Ocado grocery and organic veg-box delivery drivers waved cheerily to each other several times a day.

From that day everything sped up and slowed down at the same time. When Sally wasn't out dismissing yet another cramped cottage with squat Velux windows, shiny laminate flooring or dank, windowless bathrooms, trying desperately not to care how much Ami would hate this, or Nick that, or Dom everything, she wandered her home obsessively. Going from room to room, as if by making her presence felt in every part of the place she'd bounce those festive viewers back to that alien happy stranger-land where they belonged.

News of their mini property hot spot had got Val and Tony as worked up as the slickback boys at Giles, Benson & Haycock. Though Val suppressed her excitement Tony, despite his wife's hisses, did not, and never stopped fishing for details. It all helped Sally's allotment and holiday avoidance tactics no end. Sally only had to change the subject to the sale and Val & Tony were all ears.

The downside was she could almost physically feel the ledge of support she'd been clinging onto for so long being pulled from under her. Muffins, allotments and even, in her weakest moments, latching a tent annexe onto a Winnebago tour of Germany, became increasingly appealing by the day. She started doing the lottery and eyeing up the Get Rich Quick sections of the Waterstones self-help shelves.

The only up-side was that it seriously looked like she was going to be getting quite a bit more money than she thought. And she did need cheering up.

As she'd hoped, there'd been no awkwardness with Ramone after her rant. Ramone didn't know what a grudge was let alone how to hold one. Sally kept quiet about the house, knowing her grumbles about people competing to throw large sums of money at her as the kind of luck Ramone only wished she could magic up herself.

Ramone's nattering on and on about the musical was a welcome distraction.

'What isn't wrong with this show, Sal. The lyrics, the costumes, the timings, the sound levels, the duets are hell. There are major rewrites as we speak. We'll be into extra rehearsals soon.'

Sally made empathetic noises.

'Heck no, bring it on. Overtime honey! Rate and a half, double on Sundays.'

'But it'll all come together, right?' said Sally, wishing

she could turn disasters into positives so effortlessly. 'On the night?'

'I'm a chorus girl, Sal. In the big scheme I don't give a fuck but, you know what? It's going to be great on the night. We got a whole fucking mountain on the stage. A volcano, can you believe that? A volcano that blows off real fire and hot shit. The health and safety guys are freaking out but we'll get there. Shit, I'm not supposed to tell you that, don't tell any of those four walls of yours.'

'I might do that.'

'You OK?'

'Yes, why?'

'You're not, I can tell. Done anything on that list of mine yet or you still on the water and mascara?'

'I'm working on it.'

'Good. Sorry there's no time to meet, but you're coming to the opening night yes?'

'I wouldn't miss it for anything.'

'The ticket's on its way.'

Sally smiled. Ramone's attitude unfurled her like a flower.

She looked at the list again. Maybe she could splash out on some serious hair attention and partywear? And what about a holiday? What was a thousand here and there when property prices were involved?

Alone would be tough, though. Maybe she should rent a dreamy holiday house somewhere, to prove to herself there were others beside her own. The idea grew. A fantasy house. Fantastic enough to tempt Ami and maybe even Nick? Didn't they all deserve it?

Would it be so irresponsible to blow money on a

holiday? If one buyer fell through there'd be another. And another. Once she committed to spending, though, that would be it. She wouldn't be able to keep her house as well without going into debt. Debt she wouldn't be able to clear. But she was selling the house. It was happening.

Sally had never sold a house she didn't want to sell before. The removal men had never turned up a second too soon to take them away from the tenth floor ex-council tenement in Camberwell, or the basement in Earls Court or the raised ground floor in west Ken, even. Camberwell was fun and central but going out onto the estate after dark needed serious safety strategies. They thought they'd hit gold with the Earls Court basement, close to the tube and with a secluded, burglar-proof patio. They hadn't reckoned on the Mind The Gap underground station announcements booming through the garden and into the bedroom at all hours. They'd finally found peace in a pretty little Victorian flat with white pillars out front and lovely shutters only weeks before Sally discovered a baby was on the way.

The house knew. It had never been at such a pitch-polished best, like a dog that'd been clipped to within an inch of its skin. Hair grew back though. This felt like a breakdown. An ungraspable disintegration of the furry edges that no how-to book or any list could help with. Dismemberment crept quietly through the place like mould, slowly releasing an alkaline melancholy into every corner of every room, seeping into cupboards, drawers and shelves, the very walls.

The squeaky-clean smells of mint and lavender in Nick's bedroom felt all wrong. The airing cupboard had too many naked, wooden slats.

Ami's room was as spick and lifeless as an army barracks since she'd sorted and cleaned it to a whisker. There wasn't much joy in the visit. Ami didn't know how to not wear her feelings on her sleeve. Her palpable misery and superior bossyness about her own indecisions had been yet another extension of the whole bloody business.

'It's your choice when to move out mum, not theirs on when to move in. Let them fight it out between themselves and stall the winner,' she'd advised. 'It's a property deal. You hold all the cards. Make them wait.'

Nick's absence never felt as encompassing as Ami's. Whether it was the boy/girl thing, right or wrong, she didn't really expect it from him. He'd always been a Tweet away at any time since Dom had gone. Now she could hear him every week on his radio show.

The most difficult room to deal with was the poor, neglected north-facing back bedroom. Still known as The Office though it had been many years since they'd moved the desk and computer down to the warm, buzzy kitchen. Would it be a baby's room next? A gym? Or a bathroom? If the bathroom became a dressing room as that woman with the big amber jewellery and the man's voice planned, would they rip out the lotus and tulip tiles Dom had found in that Shepherd's Bush skip? Would she be allowed to make her claim on them now? Where would she put them? Where would she put anything?

Getting rid of the clutter was easy compared to treasure decisions. The back-bedroom seconds, the let's-keep-but-not-displays that hadn't made it into the main house had as much right to their own presence in their own hidden ways as the table and the kilim rugs down below.

She looked at the painting over the miniature fireplace. Framed in flimsy, lightweight wood sat a stiff profile of her mother in her 30s, all rippled hair, brown and green. She'd been banished there by Dom who'd mocked its amateurish thick paint and not quite straight pot in the foreground. How did she ever let him get away with that? At least her old mum would have pride of place next time round. Over the main fireplace she'd go. What the hell then did she do with the original Hendrix poster? Sell it or keep it stored God knows where for the kids' inheritance?

The thick, brown marble pillar outside the bathroom, another of Dom's skip finds, sat right on the keep/junk borders. Like the plinth in Trafalgar Square they'd never quite found the right thing to go on it. It became the random extra surface, for towels, scarves, homework and the smelly socks that had littered the floors of every home since they were married.

Even the fridge had had a personality transplant. There'd always been something so satisfyingly virtuous, life-changing even, about a defrosted, decluttered freezer but now as she reached for the ice for her cocktail hour drink, she ached for trays full to bursting with old loaves and forgotten Bogoffs that creaked in protest when you tried to slide them out.

She stopped the Satie and switched on the laptop. With mixed feelings of trepidation and pride, Sally sank into the big front room sofa with her G&T and Doritos, clicked through the web pages until she found Nick's show and hit Listen Again.

*Hi Nicky, how's it going?*

*Standard, Kirsty. Hi everyone, welcome to Saturday Night on Sunday Morning's Nicky Lightfoot Nights with a great show lined up for you.*

The sentence came out almost as one continuous speeded-up word, like a real DJ, but – Nicky?

*Kirsty: And how's Grace?*

*Nick: Grace? Who's she?*

*WHO WAS NICKY?*

*Nick: Ah…*

*Jingle: HISTOR EEEE, she's historee, jingle.*

*Nick: This is it Kirsty, I've met the one. Her name's Melinda, I'll give you the rundown. She's petite, right, petite and dark, verry dark with this silky brown hair that hangs down to her waist..*

*Kirsty: Out of ten?*

*Nick: Ten, man, ten plus.*

*Kirsty: The one?*

*Nick: There's a story behind it.*

*Kirsty: There's a story behind everything.*

*Nick: She's from Northside. I met her at Laker's Bar, you know, on the far side of the lake at Hawkley? She was with a group of mates…soon as I saw her I knew she was different from all the rest.*

*Kirsty: Why's that?*

*Kirsty, Kirsty, Kirsty, whoever you are, why are you encouraging him?*

*Nick: What works with one girl doesn't work with another. She's living in digs over the west of town, so she agreed to come out with me.*

One track later and Melinda was history. Back to

Northside and her old boyfriend.

*'I'll never forget her,' said Nick.*

'Oh for goodness SAKES, Nick!' Sally yelled at her computer screen.

*'It was like – intense! Until, [slushy music] that was, Wednesday night when, on my one regular night in, I nipped out to get some milk in...*

Real milk? Or was that a codeword?

*'..and clocked the fittest girl I've ever seen in my life. Don't believe me yeah? Any cynics out there, go and check her out if you don't believe me, Morrisons on the Wakeley Road, ten items or less, you won't regret it. I don't even know her name yet. But I will.*

Feeling slightly unsavoury, like she'd been peering into his diary, Sally allowed herself a stiff second drink. What was her child *doing with himself*?

## CHAPTER TWELVE

Sally moved fast, wriggling through the pavement crowds to the crush of the foyer that buzzed with the first night hum. If she stopped, crazy ideas would take over. He'd arrive, breathless from the tube, smiling through gritted teeth and desperate for a drink.

Chemically unable to relate to any stage that didn't have a drum-kit on it and roadies going 'one two' into the microphones, Dom had detested and loathed the theatre with all his heart. He'd never understood that curtain-up, governed by a bell and a disembodied voice that sliced right through your boozing time, wasn't a negotiable. He couldn't fathom the lack of support acts that you could take or leave, or preferably be rude about, before skipping out after one number back to the bar.

Sally found a miniature shelf for her G&T and grabbed her phone. Ami had promised to be on stand-by so that she didn't have to feel a complete Sally-no-mates.

They talked about Nick.

'It is all a joke, right?'

'No?'

'They don't really exist, these girls.'

'I know Nick's got an imagination mum, but you can't honestly believe he's making it all up.'

'He's making such a twat of himself.'

'He's not. That's the point. Amazing I know, but the

more he goes on the more he's getting away with it.'

'So...' Sally hesitated. Like any mother, she knew more than anybody else on the planet the appeal of her own son. His skinny physique had more to do with bone than brawn yet however distressing his unhealthy pallor, the combination of doey-innocent green eyes and evil crooked-toothed grin got her every time.

'Is this Nicky a different person – to Nick? Is that it?'

He was a hyper-prattler alright, but he'd never had the gab when it came to girls.

'You can hear it's an act.'

'An act of will? Or brought on by chemicals?'

'Don't fret. He's doing well now, for once. Have faith.'

'Do you think he'll make it to Greece.'

'You've booked?'

'Yes. All I've got to do now is tempt him there somehow. And you.'

'Have you paid?'

'Yes.'

'How?'

'Plastic. For the insurance cover you…'

'I know, I know. So, you're sure it's sorted with the winning bidder?'

'I told you, they're in Bahrain till October.'

'Dodgy.'

'They've paid their deposit and you know what? I don't really care. I've done my bit, the bank's happy, the villa's booked, now all I need is your dates.'

Huffy expiration of air. 'This minute?'

'Oh and there's the bell.'

The bar started emptying.

'All right, put me down for the middle week.'

'Why not the first? We could travel out together.'

Non-committal sigh. 'Is Nick going?'

'No.'

'Can Pete come as well?'

'Pete?'

'You know, the guy I've been seeing for…'

'I know – yes. Yes! Why not! If he can spare the time.'

'I know you'll grow to love him if you could get some time together.'

'If you two could get some time together it'd be a start.'

'If we came to Greece, we would, wouldn't we?'

'Yes – yes, bring him along. Call you in the interval?'

'Oh mu-um. But yeah, sure. Enjoy the show.'

By the time Sally reached the packed auditorium the lights had already dimmed. Everyone in her row stood up, announcing, 'Cue, lone woman,' to the rest of the audience. 'Look everyone, here's a lonely person going to that sad space for one!'

It was the opening night though, she could be a critic for all they knew, she thought as she settled into the darkness.

The curtain opened to a dazzle of yellow. A prairie desert, scattered with cacti merged into a mirage of distant lakes and mountains. Sally crossed her legs cosily.

Two of the larger cacti moved. Heads grew out of their tops, hands out of their branches. They sang a slow country and western ballad in sing-talking rhyming couplets which didn't quite rhyme, with rhythms that didn't quite match.

Sally shifted in her seat.

A mini-explosion of stifled, hysterics broke out a few rows behind her. More followed. Sally's skin crept with sweat. Teething troubles, they all have them, she said to herself, willing it to get better.

It didn't.

The staged jokes were met with shivers of forced, unnatural laughter. A helpless feeling of voyeurism overtook her embarrassment, like she'd camped out next to a motorway accident. An accident with her friend in it.

The first appearance of Ramone's chorus got the biggest laugh of the night. They looked like an outing to a Grayson Perry convention. Sally became convinced that the audience were all laughing at Ramone alone, all 6ft 1 of her, squeezed into a short, blue chequered dress and topped off by a blonde plaited wig.

When the curtain fell for the interval a smattering of applause plopped out of the astonished silence before the lights came up, killing it dead. Sally stood up with the rest of her row and followed them to the bar, listening.

'It's the script.'

'Kids played by grown-ups? What were they thinking!'

'Saves money but ruins the show.'

'No no no, that's supposed to be ironic.'

'Yeah but it's crap.'

'Did you hear the voices off stage?'

'Rival shows pay the technicians to sabotage, everybody knows that.'

'They needn't have bothered.'

In the second half the friends and relatives in the audience did everything but get up on stage and physically carry the cast through to the end.

It was exhausting.

In the middle of the second act, the mountain rose creakily out of the stage and finished everyone off. The whole auditorium, and some of the cast, laughed together.

Rehearsing her own lines, Sally made her way reluctantly round to the back of the theatre. A tiny old man sitting behind a desk surrounded by envelopes and hooks guided her to the chorus' Dressing Room.

She nervously navigated the warren of narrow, shabby, white-tiled corridors. What the hell on earth did she say now? The redolent reek of greasepaint was overshadowed by the rancid smell of false jollity coming from the dressing rooms.

'Darling, *you* were marvellous!'

Mmm that was a good one. Sally could hear Ramone before she saw her and followed the sound to a long, narrow room, crammed with Grayson Perrys in various states of undress. In the centre of it all was Ramone in her underwear, wig askance, cadging a cigarette from a cactus.

'So. Whaddaya think?' Ramone put her hands on her hips and beamed at her expectantly.

'You were fantastic Ramone, fantastic.'

'Yeah?' Ramone's grin widened.

'All of you, the chorus I mean,' Sally added, not meeting the eyes of the other singers. Ramone squeezed herself into a crimson net, lace and lycra dress. Then Sally had to wait. She stood about uncomfortably, looking at the floor.

'Come on, we're so out of here.'

'How long will the party go on for?' Sally asked as they waited to cross Shaftesbury Avenue.

'All night, honey, through to the first editions.'

'Where everybody waits up for the first newspaper reviews?'

Ramone stepped out into the slow-moving traffic, 'Showbiz all the way, I'm telling you this musical crack is so cool Sal! Shoulda done it years ago instead of backing up all those ego-ridden wasters. It's wild, a buzz.'

'You're not going to pay any attention to the crits are you?'

Ramone stopped abruptly and turned to her. 'What do you mean?'

A taxi hooted.

'I mean,' Sally said, dragging her by her arm, 'let's not get run over.' Though that might be an option, she thought.

They reached the pavement. Ramone pulled her arm away and glared down at her, incomprehension and fear clouding her eyes.

'Go on. Say it. Say what you're thinking for once in your life. You thought it was a crock of shit, didn't you?'

'All I'm saying is be ready for it. You don't know which way these critics are going to go. Even… – ever!'

'Even when it's good. That's what you were going to say. You think it's a pile of cack.' Ramone marched on ahead.

'I think there were places where it could have been

better,' Sally said catching up. 'But, like I said, you were great.'

'What's wrong with it?'

'Um, well, I think the leading lady's a bit of a mistake.'

'But that's Narina Ferina – she's a – she's…'

'She can't sing, Ramone. I'm sorry. But you – you sang better than I've heard you sing in a long time…'

'But you haven't heard me sing in a long time?' Ramone said suspiciously.

'You're better than I remember you,' Sally ploughed on. 'You've improved, maturity suits your voice. Like I said I thought you were brilliant, the best singer in the whole show…….'

'Really?'

'By a long way,' Sally said emphatically. 'I could hear you above the rest. Loud and clear!'

They turned into Coventry Street in awkward silence and stopped at the navy-blue carpeted steps of the Café de Paris.

'Good we're early,' said Ramone.

'Blimey,' said Sally, surveying the largely empty ballroom floor that looked like it had been decked out for a wedding.

'I told you the backers had dosh.'

They set off down the stairs and walked through the sea of round tables, empty but for the rows of cutlery, stiff white napkins and glassware gleaming beneath the chandeliers.

'I got something to show you. It's to do with your list,' Sally said when they'd found their nametags.

'List?'

'I got myself a villa,' Sally punched in the site which had almost burnt into the screen on her phone she'd viewed it so often.

Ramone squinted at the screen.

'I've hired it for three weeks.'

'On your own yeah?'

'Sort of. Ami's coming for a few days.'

'No tour groups?'

'No.'

'No fucking DOGS?'

'No.'

'Where is it?'

'Hydra. It's an island.'

'What, like Ibiza?'

'Ibiza for the real old hippies. The traffic-free, spiritual home of the affluent hippie. Where Leonard Cohen wrote all those songs.'

Ramone handed the phone back.

'Fancy it?'

'What are you saying?' Ramone said coldly, waving at some late arrivals. 'I gotta show to do.'

'For a weekend, you'd love it.'

'Weekends are our busiest time.'

'Call in sick for a couple of days. It's only the chorus.'

Ramone cackled, 'Yeah, only the chorus. I'm only the chorus, a chorus girl in a chorus wig.'

'Let me show you a good time for a change. It's so laid back this place, no cars, no roads, it's full of artists, you'd love it.'

'No cars? How the fuck are you supposed to move around!'

'Donkey.'

'Donkey, right.'

'Well, there are mules as well. And speedboats.'

'Now speedboats I can handle.'

'It's not remote. Loads of Athenians go at the weekend. Like Long Island, but more wild and alternative.'

'Have you been?'

'No.'

'Don't get your hopes up. Nothing's ever like you think it'll be. But you're going for what you want and you're doing it, Sal, good on you. You go.'

'I'm going.'

'Don't forget, it's your world now. You are looking out now. We've been the scenery now it's our turn to take what we want from what we see. And, hey, thanks for asking me. I appreciate it.'

'Think about it. A couple of days off sick, yeah?'

'OMG isn't that Sienna with Jacks and Frank? Looks like we got a real celebrity on our table. 'Hey, Jacks! Over here!' Ramone waved and surged off again, squealing hi's and 'how was that's?' as their table filled.

A few of them glanced at Sally, some straight through her. None looked twice. At first she didn't mind sitting there simply admiring the sheer, unrestrained life force in her friend as she camped it up with her new actor mates. This was Ramone. Living in the present, speeding into the future and enjoying the deviations along the way. Her determination not to feel self-conscious only made her feel more so. Ramone was as much a part of this arty, city hyperbole as she, Sally, could never be. As the evening dragged on she started to feel resentful.

It was all a load of old play-acting, she knew that. And the blood of the show didn't race through her veins. She was in a zero possibility situation. But still the snatches of sharp laughter, the happy happening people all around her hurt. A deep loathing of all the exaggerated greetings, double kissing, big hugging, silver service hard-edged noise of it all around her made her long for her fireside and home.

She looked down at her shoes, her new Tracey Neul shoes that had torched her credit card into meltdown. She remembered how great she'd felt when she'd left the house that evening, trotting down her street with her new short but still long hair swinging about her shoulders. She remembered the sound of her shoes clip clopping along the pavement as she hoped she'd bump into somebody she knew but hadn't. The feeling of the soft, sexy but functional Rigby and Peller bra and not so sexy, but even more functional, pants. They were strictly for her own consumption but did, as every magazine said they would, make her feel gorgeous to the core. All topped off by the Dress. The even more fantastic clingy but not clingy at all, red bias-cut Westwood that hadn't even been in the sale.

The next time Ramone passed by, Sally pulled her down to the empty chair next to her.

'Hey? You all right?'

'I know it's your night, Ramone, but despite all this I've been sitting here as invisible as, as,' she took a teaspoon from her coffee saucer and banged it hard against the table, 'this! You didn't notice my dress, my haircut and these shoes that together cost twice as much as as...'

'Wo wo wo,' Ramone leant back and tried to focus on Sally's new look.

'Don't worry about it. You know what, Ramone? I really don't care. You've helped me decide in fact. I'm going to fuck off to my island and let my legs grow hairy, wear nothing but baggy kaftans and flat as flat sandals and chill. I'm going to chill and read all those books I've never gotten round to reading and not give a toss if anybody notices me or speaks to me ever again. Now excuse me, I need the loo.'

Eyeballing the gawping girl across the table Sally gathered her things and marched off.

Oh bed and slippers, where are you?

'Hot chocolate, drinking chocolate, hot chocolate drinking chocolate,' the old ad slogan played in her mind along with a black and white vision of her running through the cold, wet lamp-lit night with her black and white husband and black and white children to their warm home and bed.

She was tempted to leave. If she slipped off home now before the dreaded papers arrived would Ramone even notice? So why stay? Nobody wanted to meet her, or talk to her and why should they? Why should she? She epitomised the opposite of cool, she was tried-too-hard-sad.

On the edge of life now. An outsider looking in.

She unpeeled her Magic Knickers, sat on the loo and breathed deep sighs of relief as her tummy took up its rightful shape again.

How long would the show last when all this died down? Days? Weeks? Losing it would hit Ramone hard, even with all her indestructibility. She'd be giving in on her dreams here and Ramone didn't do giving in easily.

What kind of a friend would she be if she scuttled off now pretending Ramone would ride this like she coped with everything thrown at her? It had happened with enough of Dom's artists. One day they were hyper high, the next they'd gone down faster than a leaky balloon, never to get up again many of them. Whatever happened she'd be there for her. Hell, the Greek house would be Ramone's sanctuary as well.

When she got back, the food had arrived. Right decision. Way too late to eat but at least it gave her something to do.

Ramone glanced over. Sally didn't care. What did it matter if the squint-eyed little turd in a silver waistcoat in the next seat ignored her? That was the natural order of things. They had Nothing In Common. She wouldn't care anymore if she went around looking like Worzel Gummidge. She wouldn't care if she didn't have to do this, or buy that, or go there, and she certainly wouldn't give a toss if she never heard the word 'celebrity' again.

She ate in silence trying not to begrudge the excitement in some of the young faces around her. To be in a musical, even a rubbish musical, was a big achievement. She'd been there and done all that herself. When she'd started out they'd had to fight off hundreds of other hopefuls without the help of a panel of sneery TV judges or organised auditions.

Ramone could sing all right, but she'd got through those difficult early days with sheer guts and personality. For Sally it had been trickier.

Sure, she had the skill that blew anybody she sang

with away. Backing up others was what she'd been born to do. She totally knew when to fulfil and enhance and when to hold back. She knew exactly how to get the best out of a lead vocalist without them even realising she was doing it. Nobody gave Ramone the breaks, she'd had to fight all the way for everything. Sally might have the sensitivity, but she didn't have half her friend's guts. You needed guts now more than ever.

What would have happened if, when her opportunity had come, she'd said No? If she hadn't slept with The Corelles' promoter and got out of the pub circuit, she'd never have met Dom. So there. It was the right thing to do. There'd been no moral dilemma. She'd been with lots of guys who didn't have to offer anything in return, not even a date. Casual sex had been for the girls as well as the boys and everybody was at it. Besides, she didn't like saying no. Yes was an easier word to say.

Dating was never her scene. Getting on with it after a few beers seemed more honest, cutting through the façade when she knew, and he knew, what he wanted. Nothing to feel guilty about, nothing to bury away. And if it was with a tour promoter staging the biggest acts on the planet, she'd have been nuts not to. Without Ramone's chutzpah she'd have stayed forever on the pub rock circuit, living at home, lying to her parents about what she got up to.

Her poor Victorian father, who'd had her late in life, wouldn't have begun to comprehend. She could understand his shock and horror now at her first boyfriend, The Hairy Carpet-man, turning up in all his silks and peace badge T-shirts. Till the day he died he thought she'd smarten up one day and join his beloved army. Their non-relationship was sad but her lies had been necessary and more about protection than deceit. It was called the Generation Gap and it had never been bigger.

With Dom there'd been real respect, the first she'd ever experienced with any man. He'd wanted to stay with her the next day, and the day after, and the day after that. Had stayed with her. Mostly.

At three in the morning a pile of newspapers was finally brought in on a big silver tray. Though the shit was about to hit the fan, Sally wanted to sob openly with relief. The party was over.

At first, everyone was so high, they barely noticed. But gradually a collective variation of Chinese whispers reached her ears.

'Exquisite awfulness.'

'Disastrously low on energy.'

'Is this the worst musical ever?'

Someone threw a broadsheet up into the air. Somebody else followed and soon the room snowed with torn up newsprint.

'They've got it in for musicals at the moment.'

'There's so many hidden agendas, everybody knows that.'

'Fuck it who cares,' Ramone yelled as she fired a motoring supplement dart across the room, 'I'm up there and I'm not coming down. Not this time, oh no no.'

Feeling a cheesy churning of responsibility and fear, Sally hovered. Mass, fake hysteria had taken over.

The cold light of day when it came would be arctic.

## CHAPTER THIRTEEN

Sally hurled herself against the ferry door. It moved a fraction before clunking back into her face. She pushed harder, slotting her heavy hiking boot into the gap followed by her suitcase. A third heave produced enough space for her to squeeze through and clamber out onto the deck.

Clutching her hair against the wind, she narrowed her eyes and surveyed the deck. Apart from a blue tarpaulin roof rattling noisily it was nothing like the orange Greek rust-buckets that had cruised her memory for all those years. There'd be no unrolling of the beach mats and strumming guitars on sun-warmed decks she'd fancifully imagined back in London. She shivered. Mistake number 1, she should have taken the faster, enclosed, Flying Dolphin. Sunshine would have been something.

There were only two other passengers out there: a dark-haired girl in a pale blue raincoat and gangly hiker in a bobble hat. The girl sat stiff and hunched on a fixed white plastic bench. She'd been in an argument and was waiting for somebody to come and find her, Sally decided. Pleased with her decision to come outside, she settled on a nearby bench. Better this than the hell-hole down below full of smoke, escalators and plasma advertising she thought, nodding at the girl who didn't nod back.

She wriggled her toes inside her boots and stretched her legs in front of her. Comfortable, woolly-clad toes now, happy unheeled, free to roam feet. Her khaki hiking shorts didn't exactly hang elegantly from the thigh and her knees were freezing. She eyed the girl's ice blue raincoat enviously.

Practical I don't care statement shorts felt like a bad choice. She became fascinated by the girl's raincoat. The over-sized gold buckles and broad collar meant it was either one of those designer looks that was so cheesy it was cool, or it really was dated, or it was a copy. Designer, George at ASDA or a Greek mother's hand-me-down, she'd never, ever know would she. She leant sideways to try and see the title of Bobble hat man's book, but he'd bent the cover too far back for her to see.

The skies were grey and overcast. Unseasonal for May her Weather App said, but not unheard of. Away from the port, the wind blew hard, spritzing sea mist into her face and whipping her hair up into a candy floss. She didn't care. Touche Éclat lip gloss would be her only make-up. There'd be no more mascara every day rubbish. No more morning clamp-ons with the eyelash curlers or squashing boobs into push up bras or trying too hard at after-show parties.

Athens rose in a shadowy outline through the yellowing mist. The further away they got from the shore, the closer, and smellier, the smog seemed to get.

Suddenly, blue raincoat girl disappeared beneath a fog of thick, black diesel billowing from the funnel. Sally grabbed her case and rushed to the open metal stairway.

At the bottom a single bench rested against the lower base of the funnel, facing to the side of the ship.

'It's better here. More shelter,' said Bobble Hat Man, sliding up the bench and leaving exactly half free.

German. Or maybe Dutch, she speculated, gulping in lungfuls of fresh air.

'You've done this before?' she enquired chattily.

'Many times.'

Sally opened her mouth to continue the conversation, but he'd already returned to his paperback.

Don't get huffy, get used to it, she told herself, taking a travel-tissue from her designated shorts tissue pocket and wiping her side of the bench. He has no interest in trading traveller's tips with you, but this is not an insult.

Decide. Do. If you wanted to speak to him again you speak to him. He was enjoying his book. Nothing to do with her. Nothing to do with how she looked or didn't look. Even if it was, *it didn't matter.*

'Land!' she squealed three and a half hours later. It felt like they'd been at sea for months.

He gave her an indifferent look like they'd reached another stop on the tube before returning to his book.

Suit yourself she thought, swapping her reading glasses for her prescription Chanel sunglasses. The sea polarised to a deep purple.

She moved over to the rail and leant on it, cruise-style, feeling ruggedly exotic all of a sudden. Why? Why were sunglasses so high on the flattery scale when reading glasses were so very the other way?

She watched her Greek island slowly grow out of the sea – steep, green gullies gave way to broad patches of scrubland clustered with dots of yellow. The low-key chug of the ferry felt too matter of fact for the beauty of it all sliding towards her.

'So,' came a Teutonic voice from behind.

Sally turned.

'How long are you staying?' he asked, packing his book into his rucksack.

She replied abruptly, irritated that he should decide when to call the shots. He felt like speaking to her, a stranger, and therefore he spoke. In that case why hadn't it worked for her earlier? Had she given up too soon? If she'd persisted would they have fallen into a conversation like this two hours earlier?

'You have friends there?' he asked.

'Family,' she nodded. 'Coming to join me. How long will you stay?'

'Six, maybe seven if my money lasts – days for me, sadly.'

'I hope this weather cheers up.' Bland, but keep it up, keep it going.

'Raining means the sun will follow. When the sun comes after rain on a Greek island, it will be better than you have ever known.'

'That's what they say about Wales. It's so green. Far greener than I imagined,' she turned and looked up at the cliffs. The smell of damp earth, goat and donkey manure mingled with the salt wind. 'An island with food and wine and bathrooms and rocky bays but no cars, no roads, no whiney mopeds, it seems too good to be true.'

For a moment she thought he'd chosen to stop speaking again but instead he got up and leant over the rail next to her. 'Now wait. Here it comes,' he pointed to an unprepossessing, craggy outcrop.

The ship swerved to the left and suddenly they were in a lagoon beneath a steep crescent of houses, like they'd taken centre stage in a Greek amphitheatre.

The deck quickly filled with the passengers from below. Squashed up against the railings, Sally scanned the tumble of white and grey stone houses with their tiny windows and blue wooden shutters. Which one had her name on it? The clouds were so low the highest houses looked more like ghosts looming out of the mist than solid bricks and mortar.

At the dock, men with urgent looks on their faces unfurled ropes and great, clunking chains. The only calm was the 'taxi rank', donkeys and mules standing lethargically in line, their heads drooping, and eyes dulled with resignation to the life they'd been dished.

Sally turned to say something empathetic about the donkeys, but Bobble Hat had gone, evaporated into the crush without as much as a goodbye.

She spotted him at the bottom of the gangplank where fond reunions were breaking out all over the place. He'd found another souwestere'd outward bound type and they were hugging and slapping each other on the back; they'd go for a beer now, she thought wistfully. She spotted the girl in the blue raincoat – smiling finally as a serious-looking man-friend relieved her of her over-sized chequered shopping bag.

The cold, clammy feeling Sally had been suppressing since she'd double locked her front door at 6am that morning surfaced with stark clarity. There was nobody to share this with, not even an automaton in a bobble hat. And what with the weather? She took a deep, shuddery breath and gripped the railings tighter, wishing they didn't have to arrive, wishing the boat could chug on and on.

She reached for her phone. After comfort-clicking through the internet pictures of the villa, she double-checked the name of the bar where she'd find the key and her donkey porter.

Donkey porter. It had sounded fun in hyperspace. She scanned the row of harbour shops and restaurants for the Marinha. 'The only bar with no name', her Greekseek Villas instructions told her helpfully. 'Before the monastery, beyond donkey corner.' She could see lots of donkeys but they weren't on a corner and none of the buildings looked anything like a monastery.

Cats skulked beside the port wall and a group of boys hovered, watching the new arrivals like the latest catch of fish. She thought of Nick. After unpacking she'd get his latest show on the laptop and listen with a celebratory glass of retsina before braving it on her own to a restaurant. Ramone's list was wrong on that one. Sometimes cheap, local wine was exactly what was needed.

Spotting a cluster of tables at the end of a terrace of souvenir and gold shops, she strode purposefully along the harbour, her suitcase bumping along behind her.

Sally stood at the empty counter. Nothing happened.

She took out her phone for comfort and test texted Ami. It worked. She'd got Nick's number up when the waiter appeared. He ran two delicate manicured hands up through his spiky, gelled hair, placed them carefully on the counter and observed her without expression.

'Ah, at last I've got some service here,' Sally said to

the ringtone. 'Gotta go. No, everything's fine, listen, I'll call you later.'

After proving her identity, she was handed a key and shown to her donkey.

The Villa Lobos stood on the crest of a narrow, steep track where the houses stopped and the shrub began. The walls were more grey than pink and without the tumbling purple flowers, the black balcony railings looked bare and bleak.

Inside the small, dark brown hallway, the damp mustiness of her childhood bedroom hit her in the face.

Leaving her suitcase, she climbed the steep, stone stairs ahead of her.

A wall of narrow, red sofas and a heavily carved dark brown coffee table faced a row of floor to ceiling windows rattling in the wind. She knew about the sneaky tricks of wide angle lenses, but, thinking this was a hall they'd dragged bits of furniture into, she looked around for the non-existent living room.

On the coffee table was a large, moulded glass ashtray and a fat, padded maroon book with Welcome embossed in flaked gold on the cover.

She picked up the book and sat down, but jumped up again and lifted the woollen throw. Stone. Stone sofas. Great, Sally. You've landed yourself the only Flintstones house in the whole of Greece.

A door at the side led to the bedroom with the stained-glass window she'd so loved in the online brochure. She felt the air cool as she walked in. The mustard-yellow and purple light glowing dimly on the white marble tiles couldn't have been more spookily different from the summery Matisse-like reflections in the photos. The bed was small too, but at least still a double, and hopefully not made of stone.

Following the Welcome Book's instructions, she switched the air con system to reverse. It leapt into thundering and growling life, competing for all it was worth with the wind. After a rush of cold, a lukewarm breeze was as good as it got. Sally perched on the concrete sofa and put her head in her hands. She'd got through all the jitters of travelling alone without bothering anybody, not even herself. She let the plug out on the self-pity and allowed the deepest sense of abandonment she'd felt since Dom had gone take over.

She shook rather than cried. A stiff, cold, bone-chilling shake.

This is what happened when you tried.

This is how it felt to be alone for the rest of your life. She reached for her phone like it was a drug.

'Ami! I thought I'd check my mobile reception, did you get my text?'

'Mum! You OK?'

'Well, I've arrived.'

'Can't hear you. You'll have to speak up. What's that noise? Sounds like you're in a fairground.'

'It's the heating.'

'In Greece?'

'It's raining and the villa's freezing.'

'What?'

'I feel like I'm sitting in a fridge.'

'Oh mum.'

'Like the soggy carrot, squashed at the bottom in the vegetable drawer.'

'What about that view?'

'I suppose it's out there somewhere. Hang on, I'm going over to have a look now.'

Sally pulled aside an edge of nylon curtain wired close to the windows, top and bottom. Rain fell steadily onto a wide expanse of red concrete tiles and overturned pots. Against a side wall a transparent plastic sheet, wrinkled into puddles, covered a table and folded chairs.

'Can't see anything.'

'Oh mum.'

Be strong, keep smiling. Be strong, keep smiling.

'There's nothing that can't be sorted, I'm going back down to the harbour to have something to eat and get the heating fixed. By the time you get here the sun'll be out I promise.'

'Ah – can I, there's something I needed to talk to you about there.'

'You are still coming?' Joke, it was a joke.

'Yes, it's that Pete…'

'Can't make it?' Sally asked trying to keep the hope out of her tone.

'We might be a couple of days late that's all.'

'A couple of days?' Dismay, open, undisguisable dismay.

'We're coming by train now you see...'

'Whatever for?'

'Pete won't fly.'

'He flies all the time!'

'Yes, but he's refusing.'

'Feeding the world's poor, healing the sick, that's what he does!'

'But this is a holiday, mum. His carbon footprint is

way over the top as it is – and mine come to that.'

Keep strong, keep smiling.

'We *are* coming, mum, it'll take a little longer that's all.'

'So, I – oh never mind – well, thanks for letting me know sooner rather than later.'

Sally clicked her phone off. It fell out of her hand and dropped hard onto the table. That's for Pete. Oxfam bloody Pete.

Back at the Marinha Bar she slammed the keys on the counter and demanded to speak to the owner.

'He's not here,' said the spiky-haired barman.

'Well get him.'

'He's in America,'

'Call him in America.'

'South America.'

'Call him in South America,' Sally said calmly.

'I don't have the number.'

'You are his agent,' Sally pointed out. 'You have his number.'

They locked eyes.

'I have email.'

'Email him.'

'Is better for you to do that.'

'No no no, you do that. Now.'

'He speaks English, you speak English, my job is to hand over the keys.'

'And manage the place, yes?'

He shrugged.

'I'll take that as a yes. All right, listen, what I want right now is a heater OK?'

'Wait here please.'

Sally waited. And waited.

'Where is it then?' she said when he eventually reappeared, empty handed.

One more shirty, waitery glance did it.

'It's a fairly simple request I think. I require a fire. A wall fire, a storage fire, a little electric bar fire, I need heat. NOW! And you will arrange it for me. Now. Or I will stand here and keep on shouting at you for the next three weeks. Oh kay? I also need a hot water bottle.'

'A bottle and hot water, OK, sit, please,' he made to leave.

Sally grabbed him, 'Not a bottle, a, a, a hot water bottle, you know, a rubbery flat thing you put hot water into.'

'A rubber bottle?'

'Forget it. Fire. I. need. a. fire.'

'Like I said to you, it has the heating the villa. The air conditioner, it is simple, you put it on to the red button, then you...'

'I am not stupid. Do I *look* stupid? Do You think I Haven't tried that? It's not *enough*! It is not hot, it is lukewarm, but above and beyond its lukewarmness it is NOISY, VERY noisy, even NOISIER than I am being here, shall I show you? It goes BRRRRRRRRR, BRRRRRRR, RATTLE RATTLE, BRRRRRRRRRRRRRRR...'

Flapping her arms up and down, more in imitation of a crashing bi-plane than a dodgy air con system, Sally rattled out of the cafe, past the few moustachio'd old men now fully distracted from their domino game, and back again.

The barman looked terrified.

'OK OK, calm down *please*,' he said, putting his hands up in the air. 'I find you fire.'

Sally stopped and looked at him. 'Two fires. One for the bedroom, the lower bedroom mind you, the master bedroom is unsleepable in, and one for the scraggy little living room, Oh Kay, and now and I am going to stay here because I want to see them leaving on the back of a donkey, I am not leaving this harbour until I see with my own...'

'Please now please, lady, please, you are disturbing my custome...'

'Your customers,' Sally turned, noticing her audience for the first time 'Oh oh OH! And am I...'

'Please, take a seat, have a drink, I will do something now.'

'You'd better do that.'

Holding one arm in the air in half shelter, half surrender, he backed away.

Sally chose the white plastic table closest to the Calorgas convector, pulled back a white plastic chair and sat down. She put an arm protectively on the heater and nursed its warmth, plotting its kidnap if he didn't produce something similar.

The men went back to their chatter, about her she didn't doubt, but what did she care. She'd never see them again, except for the next three, long, cold washout weeks.

A boy came towards her with a cup of Greek coffee and a glass of local brandy. He left them on the furthest edge of her table before retreating fast. This small act of thoughtfulness after all the indifference brought a sudden rush of tears to her eyes. Holding them in for all she was worth, with a shaking hand she drank her coffee back in one.

One of the old men got up to leave, taking a wide berth as he passed her table. Tough shit old man, she thought, reaching for her glass. The Metaxa burned and soothed. Phrrrrrrr, even children's shoe shops had never got her that annoyed. Another Metaxa would be good now. Sit here and simmer, or go to another bar and come back? Who knows, she thought as she stood up, she might bump into someone she knew out there. A friendly face! How well that would go down right now.

She strolled up and down a few times, making sure the Marinha knew she was still out there, looking in all the restaurants, hoping she might spot her Dutch friend.

The girl in the blue coat would have done.

'Hellooogh, remember meee? Nodding woman on ferry? Can I buy you a drink? You don't speak English? Never mind, we can nod friendlily at each other. We can make signs!'

# CHAPTER FOURTEEN

The email to South America was never sent. With the Calor heaters installed and Radio 4 gurgling away on the laptop, the Villa Lobos started to feel like home. The lower bedroom was small and dark, but Sally slept like she hadn't for years. It was the sleep of victory. For the first time in a long time she'd won.

The lounge really wasn't large, but it had a table and comfortable chairs big enough for one. The cupboards were full of chunky, creamy bowls and enormous multicoloured South American serving bowls. But staying in and eating alone all the time wasn't her intention. Ready for the next challenge, she had to crack the village.

The next evening, Sally approached the Marinha Bar for the fourth time. Counting down from ten to zero, she forced her body into a right turn until she stood uneasily next to the bar. The sudden warmth brought her cold rising to the surface. Out of her raw right nostril, a watery dribble trickled towards her upper lip. Sally put her head to one side and reached in her bag for a tissue. The block in her left nostril fell down soothingly into her right, leaving the left one red and sore.

All the confidence gained by her achievements evaporated. Dom used to talk about failure stench. Too much bad luck, he reckoned, and people could smell it.

Now she had her own version of it, lonely stench. But it wouldn't get the better of her she determined. Stiffening with resolve she put on her best half-smiling demeanour, gazing generally into the distance. Feeling brave, she cast an un-needy, but nevertheless sociable, 'I'm looking for a friend, actually,' gaze around the bar.

She scanned the faces: everybody was with somebody else. Old men, shopkeepers, donkeymen, no chance; the artists and the drifters, all looking so much like they belonged. She recognised the old hippy woman from the ferry terminal gold shop. A possibility. English or American? Too scruffy to be American. Shame. The English never spoke to each other. If she were American she wouldn't be having this conversation with herself, she'd already be down and in there.

Outside, a Sea Dolphin charged in off the horizon like it had a mind of its own. The widows were in position at the gangplank and the harbour boys were gathering over by their wall, smoking, talking, laughing together, waiting to see what girls the sea would throw up for them this time. She thought about Bobble Hat Man. What if she went back to Athens and came back again? Made another entry? She could get talking to some more people on the way back.

She tried the slow look round again. This was the locals' bar, there must be somebody she could talk to. Glancing eyes, pitying stares, quick look-aways? Her imagination or indifference? All she could be certain of was that everybody had a life to live except her.

At foot level, hungry feline eyes touted for food, but even the cats ran away if she tried to stroke them. An old man growled something in Greek and gestured at her with his hand.

'Sorry for being here,' she snapped.

'You're blocking the game,' an American voice drawled from the back of the tables.

'Oh, *sorry!*' She leapt to one side.

She pretended to study the TV perched on a shelf behind the till. She hated football, but she recognised a good break when it presented itself. She had focus.

'Take a seat, you'll be served.' She turned and searched the tables. The American voice belonged to a weary, wiry little man with a full seafaring type beard and lazy blue eyes.

Sally prickled, 'If I sit down, I'll never get served.'

'Try it why don't you and see.'

Everything about him from the casual cheesecloth trousers striped with thin blue lines and draw string waist, to the way he sat in a sideways slouch, made him look like he belonged as solidly as she certainly didn't.

'I think I might be banned.'

Stretch it out. Stretch it out. This was almost a conversation. A conversation with a person who wasn't on the end of a phone.

But it went nowhere. The football reached half time.

She watched a skinny, pale Japanese boy drift about, gazing into space, white iPod wires dangling from his ears. He looked even more lost than she felt.

The scruffy jewellery shop woman glanced up. Sally caught a glint of recognition. Say something! Now. Quick, before the moment passed. But something about the woman held her back. Either her long, unkempt hair with the top half lying close to her head, the bottom half frizzing out, or the bulky jewellery that jangled about a cream arm-covering shawl, or the combination perhaps, made her look like more of a liability than anything. Sally could imagine the conversation already. Children/grandchildren even, whether sunblock F factors meant anything and if Jonathan Franzen was worth the read or not, winding, as always, back to the weather and what they missed from home. But what if she was thinking exactly the same about her? What an idiot she was. Of course appearances mattered. Even so, the rude American with the friendly voice would be a better bet. One of the affluent hippy types this island seemed to specialise in she thought staking out an empty chair close to him.

She took confident possession of her seat making a display of arrival that couldn't be missed. Before sitting down, she reached over and held out her hand in an unignorable gesture, 'Sally Lightfoot. Pleased to meet you.'

Holding her gaze, he took her hand. A light, fey, reticent shake.

That's all? She sat down and pretended to do something important with her phone. The waiter with the spikey hair appeared with a tray of cokes and beers. He came towards her but went straight past in a way that made her seethe inside all over again. The Times Sudoku called to her from her bag, but she wouldn't give in yet.

The American leant back to let a girl pass through.

'So,' he said, 'how are you finding the Villa Lobos?'

'How did you know?'

'You're on a small island now,' he smiled a twinkly smile.

Sally grinned back. God bless America! Americans spoke to everybody. Why hadn't she gone to America? America was full of people who talked and smiled.

'In that case, you'll know all about how cold and damp and uninhabitable it is,' she said, her eyes falling greedily on his table filled with beer and brandy and little green dishes of olives and nuts.

'But Spikey got you sorted with the heaters now eh?'

'If people are renting for top dollar they need to get their basics sorted.'

'The houses here are built to keep the heat out, not the rain. 'Hey Spikey,' he called the waiter back. 'Aren't you forgetting the lady here?'

'The same,' she said without smiling, pointing at his table.

'No need to be polite round here. Everybody feels the same about this shit weather.'

Everybody! A glow of acceptance washed over her, followed by the tiniest but still registrable all the same, rush of happiness.

'Most folk end up liking that place you're in. A lot.'

'I do. It has character.'

'You were lucky to get it. Views are rare and that's got one of the best. The same folks been block booking for years, it's only because one of them…'

'Stop,' Sally held up her hand. 'I'd rather not know.'

'Sure,' he shrugged and turned back to his friends.

The length of the silence grew dangerous. She searched for a question, something, anything.

'Er, can I ask you, what's the best beach round here?'

He turned his head back but stayed facing away from her. 'Beach?'

'Yes.'

'No beaches around here.'

'I know.'

'If you want a beach you need to travel, boat's best. Ask Spikey, he'll set you up.'

'A boat with holes in if he's got anything to do with it.'

The Japanese boy sat down at her table, making her jump. He leant over as if to speak to her but instead took her half-full beer bottle.

'Hey,' Sally made a lunge for it.

The American turned and put his arm on hers.

The boy carefully poured a little beer into the empty ash tray, got up and moved to jewellery shop woman, engaged in conversation with an old man in a creamy, crumpled suit and matching Panama. The boy took off the man's hat and put it on the floor. The man didn't flinch but chuckled benignly at him.

'Got a fixation with anything not fixed down,' said the American.

'Poor guy.'

'Bah, crazy's not such a bad way to be.'

'It's good to see he's so tolerated.'

'Expected and welcomed. Flakes are a symbol of good luck to the Greeks.'

Spikey brought her beer. 'And my olives?'

'You didn't ask for olives?'

'I said the same.'

'The same drink, this is the same drink. The same drink, if you want the same food you say the same drink the same food.'

The American slid his bowl towards her. 'Here, you

154

can finish them.'
    And he left.

## CHAPTER FIFTEEN

Sally knew something was up before she'd opened her eyes. The church bell that woke her every morning clanged away as usual, but its pitch had gone up by at least half an octave. She pulled the blankets closer, but her thoughts were ticking. What was going on? Had the church moved closer in the middle of the night? Had some Bacchanalian bell-swapping ritual been going on in the hours of darkness?

It wasn't only the church. The rooster sounded different, like the farm had slipped down the hill. She lay still and waited for the donkeys to pass by on their way to their taxi ranks. Sure enough, the hooves were sharper against the cobbles. Their bells, too, sounded higher. Every tinkle had a static in it, holding its own in the air for a noticeable fraction longer than yesterday.

She threw off the covers and sat up. A line of light ran across the top of the basement window. She pulled the curtain back. The sun hit her retinas so sharply she felt a sting as they contracted.

'Well, well,' she said to herself, pulling on her Demis Roussos kaftan and rushing up the stairs. She wandered through the villa in a daze. Even the mangy old multicoloured sofa throws, were warm to the touch. She knelt down and undid the catches of the terrace doors. Instead of fighting back they swung lazily open on their springs with only the tiniest of squeaks. She went outside and looked down over the mosaic of rooftops falling away to the harbour. Instead of dropping dangerously down to the sea, the cliffs and crags pointed rapturously up to the sky. Even the lumpy bits of green in the plant pots against the wall were sprouting fresh leaves and fat, shining buds.

The gentlest breeze caressed her skin as she stared in awe out to sea. A chain of islands had appeared like they'd risen up overnight. Fishing boats dashed busily in and out of the port, gashing white streaks into the sheet of blue. It reminded her of one of those French Fauve painting with the lines drawn round the edges in bold, black felt tip.

She quickly dressed in her walking gear. Before leaving she took off her wedding ring and slipped it into Dom's photo-frame.

The goats had come down from the hills and nibbled furiously at the grass. She climbed and scrambled up to her rock, looked out to sea and held up her hand. The breeze blew softly around her naked wedding ring finger. She opened her mouth and screamed as hard as she could. The wind deleted the screams as they left her, but the sound hadn't gone. It had been picked up and carried away, back to that place where the wind, where everything, began and everything ended. That's where he was.

Back down in the heat of the villa, she slipped on her wedding ring again.

'Sorry Dom, only testing.'

He grinned back at her.

'All right. All right, Dom. I can give you the frozen

157

look too, you know.'

Down in the harbour, the floating market did a swift trade. Even the surly harbour boys looked happy, laughing and joking with each other. The black widows were out in force with not a sign of a ferry in sight.

She settled into her seat in the Marinha Bar. Panama hat man said something.

'Excuse me?'

'I said, is it any wonder the Greeks celebrate spring?'

'This isn't spring, it's summer.'

'Please yourself,' he sniffed and returned to his cigarette and newspaper.

Spikey brought a small glass of Ouzo with her coffee. After she'd confirmed with him that this unheard-of gesture hadn't been a mistake and it really was a gift, she felt emboldened.

'Spikey, can you fix a boat for me?'

'Now?'

'Tomorrow.'

'What time?'

'10?'

And so the next morning at 10, Sally found herself sitting in a speedboat, clutching her bag tight to her chest watching Hydra get further and further away.

'Not out to sea! To a beach!' she yelled.

'Yes yes,' said the boatman.

'Why are we going away from Hydra?'

'Yes yes,' said the boatman.

'I want a beach!'

'Yes yes.'

'So why are we going out to sea?'

'Yes yes yes.'

'No no,' she gestured wildly pointing back to the island. He gestured wildly back at her with a torrent of incomprehensible Greek.

The boat bounced over the swelling waves with dark, ominous thuds.

'Where are we GOING? PLEASE turn this boat around NOW and take me to a BEACH. A local local local local fucking local BEACH.'

She grabbed the steering wheel.

The boatman swore at her in Greek and pushed her roughly away.

Whimpering silently, she felt in her bag for her mobile. The island had disappeared altogether now. Was this kidnap? Rape? Don't be ridiculous, who'd want to rape her? Robbery then? Or murder? Best to check in with someone now, before they got too far away from land.

'Yes yes,' the boatman said, pointing.

A strip of land appeared ahead of them in the distance. 'Yes yes.' A broad, toothless grin appeared in the folds of his face.

'Where are we?'

'Yes yes,' he pointed.

'But where is it?'

He shrugged.

'All right, yes yes,' Sally stood up and leant forward into the windshield, double-checking she wasn't hallucinating. It looked like a rather good beach as it happened. Sand, gentle sloping hills behind, deserted. The boat slowed to a putter. The sun felt like heaven, the water the most crystalline turquoise she'd ever seen outside a holiday ad.

Feeling the postcards she'd so far been unable to write forming in her head, Sally checked her bag. Thank God she'd remembered her snorkel, and her picnic and her wine. She felt like hugging the boatman now. How could she have ever thought this toothless old fisherman was a kidnapper? What would he want with her anyhow! She hated her own mistrust sometimes.

The boatman looked at his watch. She held up three fingers.

'Three. Three hours. OK? No. No.' Remembering Greek timing, she corrected herself. 'Make it two 2. Two hours. Dua hora.' That way he'd be 3, 3 and a half hours.

He returned her V sign, spun the boat round like an aquatic Jenson Button and sped out to sea.

Sally stood at the water's edge and watched the boat shrink to a dot. The warm sea nudged at her toes.

'Cheeky old git,' she hoisted her beach bag on one shoulder and turned to stagger up the beach.

'Shit!' Her wet heels skidded off her flip-flops, pinching the plastic into her big toe. She bent down and took them off.

'Fuck!' she jumped in the air to get her feet off the burning hot sand.

Balancing on the wet flip flops, she pulled her towel out, threw it in a lump on the ground and stood on it to gain her bearings.

Now she was on it, the beach felt quite small, and enclosed, surrounded by gorse-covered cliffs. The sand was grey and grainy, the sort you sank into rather than the shell-scattered sandpit sort.

She chucked her bags down and looked around.

'Welcome Sally fucking Crusoe.'

Was this a peninsula off the mainland? Or another island? The only sound was the high-pitched drone of cicadas and the rhythmic lap, lap rippling of the millpond sea.

The sound of loneliness.

Distant cars might have been nice. Donkeys? Goats? Birds? A ten-lane motorway over the hill, there perhaps? With a service station and loos with two types of towels. Or a beach bar with chequered tablecloths and a kitchen clattering with lunch preparations.

Fresh fish. Ice cold coke from the bottle. Fat, crunchy chips and meze dips.

She emptied the contents of her beach bag onto the sand. Sun-cream, water, already looking very precious, wine, not so, her lunch and her book. The Salman Rushdie she'd get through if it killed her.

'Note to self, Sally, note to self. Don't pick arguments with men in charge of boats that drop you in the middle of nowhere.'

She felt in her handbag for the hard little brick of mobile, pausing a moment before clicking on a number, Ami's number as it happened, at the top of the list.

'No signal.'

That evil little barman back at the Marinha. Of course – this was all his doing. Right down to the free ouzo. Oldest trick. Gain her trust. Tell the boatman, his dad probably, to bring her out to sea and dump her.

No no. Now keep cool Sally. It could all be a misunderstanding. But could he have thought she'd meant 2 days, not 2 hours? What was hour in Greek? Why didn't she speak Greek? She was despicable. All her own fault. Everything was her own fault.

She flopped back on the sand and stared up at the sky.

'Calm down, calm down. This is supposed to be a happy thing. He'll be back. You've only been here ten minutes. What are you going to do? Panic for the next couple of hours or enjoy it? So stop anticipating the worst all the time.

Look at where you are. It's mind-blowing. So, you hate being alone. So, this feels like all the loneliness you've been suffering made concrete. That's good. Treat it like one of Ami's corporate outings. You are facing your fear. You must be alone, and you must trust the boatman to return and collect you like he said he would. You must not think the worst of people you don't even know.

You're like an old woman. Grumbling about the cold one minute the heat the next. So, bake yourself in the sun and frolic in that lovely cool water and act like you're enjoying yourself.'

Being forced to contemplate her own body in a bikini-out-of-the-question swimming costume did nothing to improve her mood. Discarding the pointless swimsuit altogether, she set to with the Factor 60, dug a hillock of backrest out of the sand, opened Salman Rushdie and closed it again.

Not knowing if she was on the mainland or another island bothered her. She couldn't get rid of the image of Spikey and the old boatman raising a glass to each other. 'Chin chin old man,' Spikey was saying. 'No problemos pal,' he responded with a broad, toothless grin and they both cackle merrily at a job well done.

She looked along the shoreline for bones. She looked

behind her at the hills again. They were climbable. Climbing? In saggy flip flops? In this heat?

Never again. She'd never do this stupid sort of thing on her own ever again. If she ever got back. If she ever got off this island. Or land or whatever. The anger boiled up again. Why hadn't he taken her to a Hydra beach!

She thought of the harbour. The cosy, circular harbour with all its shops and restaurants and tourists, sensible tourists, and boats and food. The fridge in the villa. Her laptop. Why hadn't she settled for that? She'd turn to sunburnt skin and bone and… STOP it Sally. DO something. Go for a swim. Eat. Read.'

She opened her book and closed it.

Salman bloody Rushdie.

Out at sea, a trickle of boats sailed by. If only one would turn in her direction. Stop it. What did you ask the barman for? A quiet beach. What have you got? A quiet beach.

When in doubt, Sally – eat. Yes. Eat. Good idea. A big hunk of cheese, a loaf of bread, tomatoes and salt. Should she make it last? Or go for it?

If the worst came to the worst, she could always swim out to the boats. Yes, eat! And, more importantly, drink!

Like most picnics, its success was mixed. The wine too warm, the cheese too melty, but the tomatoes were sweeter than strawberries and the alcohol went straight to her head. She grabbed her snorkel on and ran into the curling waves, stark naked, arms outstretched, screaming at the top of her voice. She swam a few strokes, dropped the snorkel down around her neck and trod water, gently waving her arms and kicking her legs.

163

She stretched out on her back. The sea felt cool on her head as her hair went under. The water took it. She lay flat, floating free, looking up into white-blue sky. The rain and the wind and the cold were so distant she couldn't begin to imagine them. As, one day soon, she wouldn't be able to imagine being alone any more. Ami would be coming, and she'd remember these last hours of solitariness. No, life wasn't bad. Life wasn't bad at all.

She rinsed her snorkel, clamped the mask over her face and with a gentle mermaid-like flicker of her ankles, pushed herself out to sea. The sound of her own breathing magnified as she moved into the parallel world that had been beneath her all along.

Sunlight rippled on the sand below, seaweed and rock grass swayed in the currents. A school of tiny silvery fish swam past. Below, a large grey fish with a powdery blue spot on its cheek hovered near the rocks. But between her and the rocks was a swarm of transparent globules. Glutinous umbrella shapes, tentacles trailing, drifting, pumping themselves forward in little jet-like spurts. She looked to her right, more pumping jelly. To her left, pump pump, translucent, gooey, pump.

Her breathing quickened, she bit hard on her tube and slow, slow, slow motion slowly took her face out of the water. Flickering her feet as gently as she could, she turned for shore.

Ow!

How did the beach get all the way over there?

Don't panic.

She kicked out and swam like the clappers for land.

It wasn't getting any nearer. She felt another sting on

164

her leg. Don't think about stinging think about swimming. You're getting away from them.

Don't, whatever you do, stop.

One arm over, other arm over, do it.

Eventually she reached the shallows. The sand sucked her feet down thickening her footsteps as if in a dream. She hopped up the burning sand and fell onto her towel in a shuddering collapse, sheltering her face with arms, covered in sharp, red, streaks of sting.

## CHAPTER SIXTEEN

'Next time, piss on yourself.'

'There isn't going to be a next time. Ouch.'

'Hold still there.'

'Where are we?' Sally looked over the narrow café balcony down to a gloomy patch of walled-in scrub somewhere high above the harbour.

'This is The Main Bar, my friend,' said the twinkly bearded American from the other bar whose name was Barry. 'The Hub, otherwise known as The Moonlight Bar…'

'I thought the Marinha was the centre of everything,' said Sally, picking up the menu.

'We're the yin to the Marinha's yang. The back passage...'

'Where all the shite comes out,' came a smoky, theatrical voice from behind her. 'That smell is vile.'

'Be glad, Charles, it's ammonia in a bottle not my wee.'

An immaculate, tall Englishman laid her table with cutlery and long tall glasses of iced water.

'Found her down in the port,' said Barry. 'Legs slashed to pieces, hollering at poor old Horas the boatman.'

'I was desperate for a doctor or a pharmacist.'

'And you got the passing barman,' said Barry. 'That's how life works around here.'

Afternoon tea definitely wasn't what she'd come to Greece for, but she was mightily pleased to see buttered toast, tea and biscuits on offer.

Charles returned minutes later with her order.

'That smell is disgusting,' he said, tilting his nose.

'Sorry,' said Sally.

Ignoring her, he set a tray down and began laying the table: white china cups and saucers, linen napkins, buttered toast fingers and a saucer of sliced oranges, each presented with fussy flicks of the wrist.

The anger implied by the precision of this unasked-for hospitality made Sally feel instantly grubby. The sheer, sleek pinky cleanliness of Charles' Daz white shirt and khaki shorts was intimidating. Shorts very like her own, she noted. Except his military-sharp creases stood to attention against cool, smooth, lotioned skin that made her think of scented baths, Penhaligon's candles and white fluffy robes, whilst hers, Jackson Pollocked with sea-salt against sting-slashed thighs, were very much the saggy, soggy distant relative.

Sally dipped her gnarled toes out of sight but changed her mind. They had a right to exist as any other part of her. Apologising for herself wouldn't get her anywhere any more than suffering quietly. If she'd not screamed and shouted when she got off that boat where would she be now? At the villa. Recovering after staggering all the way up that hill with her wet shorts scraping against her stings, trying to resist putting in yet another needy call to Ami at work or to Val, busy hurtling down some German autobahn somewhere.

Charles noticed her legs.

'Nasty,' he said, avoiding eye contact.

Sally silently agreed. Hairy legs was a step too far, even though in her wildest nightmares she couldn't have envisaged this scenario. No matter what, disposable razors were going into the shopping basket first thing tomorrow.

'It could have been worse,' she said, wincing at the thought of razor slicing across sting. 'I thought they were a whole load of condoms at first.'

'Sex and shopping, always on the mind eh,' said Barry.

'It's the way they move spooks me. Pump pump, ugh.'

'There, that should do it,' Barry stood up and screwed the lid on the ammonia bottle.

'Really, I should be thankful to them – swim back out and shake their tentacles one by one, at least they led me to you.'

'Bah, you'd've found us soon enough,' said Barry.

'The right ones always do,' said Charles.

Sally took the packet of McVities biscuits, inserted a knife in between the top two biscuits and sliced the top off in one slick sweep.

Over tea she learnt that, though Barry owned the bar, it was run by Charles. That they were a couple who'd been together forever. That they had a good word and a bad word to say for everybody and that they wanted to know more about her than she wanted to tell.

Realising everything she said was being noted to be mulled and discussed between them later, Sally spoke carefully, running through her family, the studio, her singing, smattered with a light dusting of name-dropping of some of the people she'd sang with. When she reached Dom's accident she didn't even pause for breath to think about it.

'And he's in the States now, working on an album. I'm doing my own thing for a few weeks.' Her voice faded to nothing. The silence felt like it was going on forever. Why'd she done that? But it was out now, she couldn't take it back.

Paranoia took hold. The look boring into her from those twinkly little eyes made her feel totally transparent. This man knew. Barry knew everything.

'You know what?' he said eventually.

Sally raised an eyebrow, one hundred percent expecting him to break the news to her that her husband was dead, that he'd died on a skiing weekend in Austria which her neighbour Tony, currently somewhere in Germany...

'You got a lot of suspicion in you.'

She took the top biscuit out of the lid and placed it delicately on her plate. 'I'm not used to such kindness from strangers.'

'That's what I'm sayin. You think the speedboat taxi's gonna dump you and abandon you, you think we're stitching you up in some way.'

'I didn't say that! When did I say that?'

'If you keep on thinking it you'll bring it on. It'll all come down on top of you.'

'Ha, it's done that already.'

'Always does, sooner or later.'

The moment had passed, and she breathed again.

'Quite right, keep on your guard Sal,' said Charles. 'Everybody's business is everybody's business in this place. When you leave a room, everybody talks about you. Remember that and you'll be fine.'

Charles loaded the tray with a pronounced finality to

his cluttering, like she'd failed a test.

'I can't thank you enough,' she bent for her bag. 'It's time I paid what I owe and go and get myself cleaned up.'

'Oh no no,' they chorused. 'After teatime,' said Charles. 'Comes cocktail hour,' said Barry.

'But I'm a mess!'

'Well go home and change then.'

Sally thought a moment. 'Yes – yes, all right I will.'

She returned to find the bar was buzzing in a small, dark, low key kind of way. Soft American country blues purred and most of the dozen or so Formica tables, lit only by citronella tealights, were occupied. The flames threw shadows onto the peeling white plaster walls, filling the air with the sweet, lemony smell of mosquito repellent.

'I had my perfect Greek bar so worked out, too,' Sally said, perching on a high bar stool next to Barry. 'A few simple chequered tables. Van Gogh chairs. A quiet beach with tiny, rippling waves.'

'How do we match up?'

'Better than perfect. I think I've gone off beaches for life.'

She watched Charles put out the glasses with his busy, fussy flicks and unscrew the wine. Another tick from the list if ever there was one, she thought. Big double ticks even. This is more than talking to strangers, this is making friends with the locals. Holiday friends maybe, but still.

The feeling of unease wouldn't quite go away. The Tweedledee and Tweedledum act. The sheer, open inquisitiveness of them both. About her for some reason. Why would two gay guys be interested in her other than for drumming up business in a bar that was, by the look of it, doing well enough already?

It took a few glasses of the cool, resiny wine to relegate her mistrust to the prissy, saggy peg bag of her middle-aged mind where it belonged. Through the evening conversations grew to natural, casual crescendos before dribbling out to nothing, if they ever started at all. She'd carry on enjoying this. How long was it since she'd met new people, made new friends? Talked about herself like this?

'I recognise this track, what is it?'

'Allmans,' said Barry.

Sally grunted approvingly, 'Makes a change from Leonard bloody Cohen. I know, I know, he's a genius,' she added quickly, seeing the expressions on their faces. 'But hearing that – dark, rich voice – over and over all over the island ruins it. Like too much Christmas cake.'

'Shhu- uuhhh,' Barry and Charles hissed in unison.

The whole bar stopped talking. Even the music missed a beat. Barry had lifted a hand and was grinning widely over her shoulder and tinkling his fingers.

'What?' Sally twisted round in her stool and followed his eyeline.

A pair of large, dark, almost black, watchful eyes were fixed steadily on her.

And that was it.

One moment he hadn't existed in her life.

The next, there he was.

His dark hair fell in loose shaggy curls. The kind of curls that gave the illusion of long hair though it fell short of his neckline. He wore jeans and a loose, soft beige checked shirt, open at the neck.

'This is Sally!' she heard Barry's voice next to her.

'Hi,' she said faintly.

'Sal here's a singer like you,' Barry said.

'A backing singer,' Sally corrected.

An eyebrow lifted. The penetrating look intensified.

'I do – I do the do wa wahs, you know, the bits in brackets.'

A serious half-smile. 'I do know, yes,' he said with a soft, low voice. 'I know all about those brackets.' He glanced over at the two girls at his table.

They both giggled as if he'd made a hilarious joke. Sally didn't blame them, but she hated them all the same. Who were they?

'She's toured with Queen,' said Barry proudly. 'And Bowie,' Charles added from behind the bar.

Take that, teenyboppers, she thought, pleased to see that the unashamed name-dropping had stirred his interest.

'Married to a big producer,' said Barry.

Damn! She fingered her wedding ring and formed some words and, somehow, got them out there, 'Do you sing – solo or –?'

'Sally, darling,' Charles interrupted. 'Don't you know you're speaking to Leonard Cohen?'

Sally nearly fell off her stool.

No way. But in a way – yes, those eyes. But no. Not unless this bar really was a time warp portal. This guy wasn't grey and in his 70s, even sexy-Canadian-Jewish 70s. More her age for starters, or late 40s at a pinch.

Swallowing hard, she turned to Barry for an explanation. His round blue eyes twinkled with devilment.

'Loro's the resident tribute act, darling,' said Charles filling her glass. 'Packs the Harbour Bar three times a week.'

'Aaaaah–!' she slapped her thigh hard. 'Haa – eyeuuch!' Right on a sting.

She gritted her teeth. Is that why she was there. The entertainment. The new fall girl for the locals to giggle at?

Sumo, the Japanese boy she'd seen at the Marinha, came over and held Barry's hand whilst he talked into his ear. She turned back to say something to Loro, but the moment had gone. In that quick glance she took in the expressions of the two girls looking adoringly at him as he hunched over the table towards them. Which one was his? Or had he not decided yet? Stop these idiotic thoughts Sally Lightfoot. You are not in your 20s like those, go on, admit it, gorgeous creatures.

She turned resignedly back to her drink. Just Looking! She muttered to herself bitterly. Looking.

'I beg your pardon?'

'Nothing, Charles. Nothing.'

*She* was nothing. Gorgeous clothes, gorgeous food, gorgeous men: Not For You. Appreciate from Afar. Get Used To It.

Sumo moved a vase of flowers from one table to another.

'He's in his own game of chess,' said Charles.

'Flower chess. There could be worse things to fill your time.'

Alert to the table behind her, she tried to carry on as normal, fighting with all her might the strangely compelling urge to turn around and check him out one more time.

Moments later, she sensed a stirring in the air. Her heart sank. They were leaving. The rest of the night stretched ahead, cold, meaningless and empty without him.

Instead her stomach took on a life of its own, leaping into an Olympic series of back-flips. He was standing next to her. *Right* beside her shoulder. And here's Charles darting up to serve him. He's staying! Leaning forwards to cover her sprawling thighs, she took a sneaky sideways look. Dark whiskery features through and through – more Greek than Jewish. Dur, as Ami would say.

Quite slender, elfin almost. Not her type at all. Her pretty lead guitarist phase faded as soon as she met Dom. Johnny Depp had never done anything for her. Jewish men had always fascinated her though. Maybe because Dom had been such a big, straightforward what you see is what you get, Aussie, bloke bloke. Was that why the Dustin Hoffman, Sasha Baron Cohen, David Schwimmer types so intrigued? Dom's sense of fun, she imagined, rubbing up against that brooding intellectual intelligence.

It had never been lust, or even fantasy, more of an impassive acknowledgement – an oh he's attractive, as if attraction were something that didn't belong to her any more. In the thinking woman's crumpet league, Leonard Cohen had always been up there. The eternal sighing man who belonged to nobody but himself, the lover who would love and leave but might well write a song distilling your parting moment that was so poignant you'd never regret parting for an instant.

Woops stop gawping, say something, quick.

'You had me there for a moment. Though you don't really look like him at all,' she said clumsily when he'd finished ordering, hoping to God the whoosh in her nose didn't mean she was blushing.

'As every singer knows, it's the voice that matters,' he said to her, putting one hand on the bar.

Large hands, she noted, hairy arms, plectrum nails.

'Have you ever done Cat Stevens?'

'Excuse me?' He was keeping direct eye contact now, American style, but there was a distance in those eyes, a vulnerability that even pride and intelligence couldn't hide. She recognised it well. The last weapon that drew the final resistors in.

'You look more like him. Early, I mean, you know, *Tea For The Tillerman*, *Harold and Maude* music? About a boy dating a really *really* old woman...' you're babbling Sally, stop the babbling right now. She looked for Charles, but, finished with his serving, he'd gone.

'And you sing – where exactly?'

'The Harbour Bar.'

'So, you are Greek?'

'Er, yes. You?'

'Oh, English.'

He did his serious half smile again, 'I mean where do you sing now?'

Shy. He's shy!

'I don't. Any more.'

'Oh.'

He looked sad for her. 'Here on the sarongs?'

'What songs?'

'You're not selling sarongs? In Barry's shop?'

'Oh, I see. No – no, I'm on holiday.'

He moved to go, but changed his mind. Closer now, even closer, leaning forward. Fuck! Touching her shoulder! Like a first sip of good wine, he smelled how he looked. Cinnamon and resin, high and bittersweet, like cherry and cool, smooth powdery sugar almonds.

He bent towards her. Every bone in her body turned to so much mush she thought she'd melt right through her stool. 'The cruise ships are due,' he said into her ear. Sally melted a little more. His breath was musky. Nice musky, like creosote and dirt after summer rain.

'Be careful,' he continued. 'Barry will have you out there, pimping his sarongs at the harbour.'

And with that, he left.

Oh my God! Oh my GOD! She never said Oh my God. Not even in her thoughts. There it was. She might as well admit it. She'd had to hold herself back then. Every instinct in her had been telling her to pounce, to wrap herself inside the husky, rough warmth of him. If she Could, she Would. Like a shot. No longer would it be for lack of want if Ramone's wididity challenge wasn't fulfilled. Stop these thoughts, Sally, before you make a total idiot of yourself. Out of Your League, 'girl', times a hundred. Thousand. Hundred-thousand.

A corner of her eye and at least one ear stayed keenly trained on the activity behind her. The girls' laughter said it all. They were the blessed ones. Swedish, she guessed. That pleased her. They'd all met that night, and the girls were now playing each other off for him. Competing. Two there was better than one. A chosen one hogging him to herself. Sally clung to the bit of him

176

she'd had, the depth of the look, the knowingness, the shared smile, the voice in her ear. 'The cruise ships are due,' hadn't exactly been 'I want to ravish your imperfect body with my perfect mind,' but it was a start.

'So what's this about the sarong shop?' Sally asked Charles the next time he was near.

'Barry's shop you mean? Oh, Balinese sarongs and Italian ice cream, funny old combo but works well.'

'And I had Barry down as an old hippie.'

'Oh, he is. Summers here and winters in Bali. Gets all of us doing his work for him.'

'That's not hippie, that's smart.'

She struggled to keep her voice at a level. Her stomach had sprung into action again, tweening and leaping up to her throat. There'd been a sound of movement behind. He could be next to her again at any second. But no. There was too much scraping of chair against tile going on. The girls were up too, the three of them were leaving. Together. A threesome. It was going to be a threesome.

'See you later girls,' he said as they passed.

Sally took a last look at the shoulder-tickling dark curls and the baggy rear of his jeans as he followed his friends out of the door and into the night.

She felt bereft. It wasn't right. He should have felt the same about her. He should have dropped those two girls and stayed with her long into the night.

'Nice arse hmm?' said Charles, wiping a glass.

'Strange kind of life, pretending to be somebody you're not,' said Sally.

'Suits him down to the ground,' said Barry.

'Flowers to be picked,' said Charles.

'Nothing wrong with pickin' the flowers,' said Barry. 'Take em in the moment and enjoy eh.'

'Don't let my daughter hear you say that,' said Sally.

'Was I being gender specific?'

'Girls can pick flowers too,' Charles qualified.

'But not old women,' said Sally.

'Here,' said Charles kindly. 'Put your mind to this.'

He passed her his crossword. Sally felt sick to the stomach. He'd completely missed the joke and taken it for reality.

# CHAPTER SEVENTEEN

Sally tucked her head in tight and rested her cheek on Dom's chest.

'Let us off this thing. Let us. Off. Now!' She felt the vibrations of his screams through his ribs.

Every time the car hurtled towards the ground the drop lengthened, catapulting them higher at every rise. On the cusp of a peak, a violent jolt threw them out of their seats and up into the air. Sally fell to the ground like a stone, pitching right into the arms of Loro, squashing him steamroller flat like a cartoon.

'Shit.'

She curled under the sheet and squeezed her eyes tight, feeling as guilty as if she'd already shagged him there and then in the middle of the bar.

Damn you!

What's the point of trying to sleep herself back inside that one? She flung back the sheet and rolled with a thud onto the soft flokati rug. How dare you, how dare you invade our precious dream time. It's all we've got left. Clutching the bedside table, she clambered up, looking to Dom's photo for his smiling affirmation. She made the bed quickly, punching the pillows hard before rearranging them side by side. Taking the sheet, she lifted it high and shook it so hard it crackled like thunder, dissipating any leftovers of dream back into the ether.

My husband is dead.

Say it Sally. Tell yourself again.

My husband is dead.

Why hadn't she *said* it?

She quickly threw on her kaftan and, after double-checking for keys, slipped on her sandals and went outside. Pausing on the doorstep, she turned, unlocked the door and went back to her bedroom.

My husband is dead.

In one, quick furtive movement she slipped off her rings and placed them slowly and reverentially in front of Dom's photo before rushing back outside.

My husband is dead.

With a stomp that bore no relation to the intended power walk, she turned left and climbed the narrow high-walled dirt track that led to the farm.

Deep down she knew that man was even more remote and inaccessible than the voice of Bob Flowerdew. He might as well *be* Leonard bloody Cohen. A crush to be crushed. Except she hadn't had she. She'd been back to the bar every night since and not a peep. Still holed up with Rat's Teeth and her mate obviously, loving each others' beautiful bodies up for the last three nights in a row.

Head down, she turned left through a zig zag of donkey tracks between the high pine trees leading away from the farm across the hills.

Her only consolation was that she'd been warned about bizarre romantic aspirations in the *Four Stages of Grief* chapter of *How to Win As A Widow*. Right alongside the searching for your husband in crowds and the vivid dreams in Stage 2. Her timing was a bit out that's all. Or was it more to do with death books being as confusing as parenting and baby books when it came to scheduling the changes? Stage 1, numb disbelief, had been allocated 'anything from days to weeks'. Stage 2 had kicked in all right ('6 months') but whilst Stage 1 was still going strong and there were still no signs of Stage 3, less anger and more organisation, ('1 year'). The final stage, some form of acceptance ('after 1 year'), didn't stand a chance. Acceptance! Accept what? When she still expected him to leap out from behind a door, giggling behind his hand. 'Boo! Ha ha, had you there!'

'My husband is *dead*.' she screamed.

The breeze turned to a wind as she climbed, serenely pushing her from behind through rocky, cropped grass hillocks grazed by goats.

'My husband is dead,' she yelled at the wild flowers, goat and sheep droppings.

At the top she paused and looked out to sea.

The only sounds above her breath were the wind flapping her dress and the goats' frantic nibbling of the grass still lush from the rain.

The delicate pink clouds marching down to the horizon promised another perfect, sunny day. She stepped up onto a rock, held her left hand up high and spread her naked, ringless fingers wide to the wind. Her hair blew all over her face obscuring her hand. For a fleeting moment she felt him close. No, she didn't. She was going crazy.

'What rot!' she screamed into the wind.

She reached in her pocket for her phone. 'Are you sure

you want to delete this number?' The phone asked.

Her finger hovered. She had to do it. Paying his mobile bill so she could hear his voicemail really was insane.

OK, she clicked. It felt worse than taking the rings off. Diamonds may be forever but all the time his voice in her handbag had been nothing more than a click away from deletion.

Back at the villa she slipped the two rings back on her finger.

'Only testing,' she said, kissing his photo.

Most widows kept them on forever – didn't they? Until they met somebody new. How did that work?

## CHAPTER EIGHTEEN

'Is he hiding?' Sally carefully examined the last few passengers stepping off the Sea Dolphin gangplank. 'Or fallen overboard?' she added hopefully, squinting in the sunlight and looking out to sea.

'He's coming on later.' Ami dropped her suitcase at the bottom of the gangplank, wiped the sweat off her brow and hugged Sally with her cool, public hug.

'Later when? Why didn't you tell me?'

'Tomorrow. Probably.' Ami held up her camera phone.

'Oh!'

'Thought you'd be happy.'

'I only said oh.'

'In that way.'

'In what way!' Sally said in her half-laughing way. 'Come on, let's get into the shade.' She tucked her newspaper under one arm, picked up Ami's case and flip flopped through the heat towards the taxi rank.

Ami, seemingly oblivious to the breakout of winks and nudges from the harbour boys' corner of the jetty, darted around taking pictures of the gold and silver shops. Who could blame them, eh, Sally said to an imaginary Dom, wishing he, too, could see her now with her freshly cropped hair and little white strapless sundress lifting high up her thighs as she clicked.

Sally remembered her own slip back into struggle and

toil that morning as she prepared to meet the elusive Pete. The agonising attempts at shaving across the fading, but still active, stings on her legs. The endless debate she'd had with herself about whether to pull out, or not pull out all the nice stops for somebody she'd disliked from a distance for so long. The repeated switchings of the city Westwood dress to shorts grunge to kaftan and back again. All to make an impression on Pete, who wasn't even here, on Ami's behalf, who'd never notice or care anyway. What a result, though. It'd be the two of them and, despite her curtness, Ami's mood swing pointed at high.

'Is he coming overland?'

'Plane,' Ami said in a dur way.

Sally stopped in her tracks. 'What about his carbon footprint!'

'He flies all the time for work,' Ami said impassively.

'Ami! All I've been getting from you for weeks are second-hand lectures on the evils of flight. You are here two days later than planned because of it! Because Pete says this, Pete says that. I've been telling myself for days that I'd like him, that we were going to meet and get on and, and...'

'You were expecting to dislike him on sight?'

'Why didn't you simply tell me he'd be coming on later?'

'I didn't *know* until the last minute – I kept hoping that... he'd...'

Oh, that hope for things to turn out right. That expectation that all would be well in the end. Sally knew it so well. Used to know so well.

'I'm sorry Ami. What are we like, arguing about Pete

already? When I meet him tomorrow I'm sure I'll fall for him as you have. Come on, we're going to have a fantastic, quiet supper on our terrace tonight, the two of us.'

'Pete's going to so love this,' said Ami watching her bag being loaded onto the donkey. 'It's all so – sustainable. Do you think I should send a caption with this saying hint hint as well or is that too pushy?'

Sally looked at the gold shop on Ami's phone screen without comment.

'Do we ride them as well or what?'

'Walking's easier.'

The text-photo commentary to Pete continued as they followed their donkey up through the warren of alleys to the villa.

Ami ran onto the terrace. 'Oh my *God* this view's amazing. So romantic mum! Oh wow.'

Sally took Ami's bag into the upper bedroom. Now warmed into a sensuous, musky place with air that mingled with the scents of sea, herbs and pine coming in through the open window.

Ami joined her. 'But this has to be your room, mum.' They stood together looking at the bed. The stained glass threw streaks of purple light over the white sheets and down onto the white-tiled floor.

'Though it does look inviting.'

'It needed a good airing, but it's fine now.'

'You don't have to move for us.'

'I'm at home in the single downstairs. I want you to be comfortable. I want you and Pete to be comfortable. I'll leave you to unpack.'

He'd better be worth it that's all, she thought, closing

the door behind her.

That night they sat out on the terrace. With the background sighs of the sea and the clutter of the harbour night below, they caught up on their news and listened to Nick's latest show.

*Kirsty: Hi Nicky, how's it going?*

*Nick: Man what a busy week. Hi everyone, Nicky Lightfoot here with more peng sounds for you.*

'Nicky!' Sally rolled her eyes.

'I know,' Ami smirked.

*Kirsty: And how's the nameless one?*

*Jingle: Nameless one, who's she, who is she?*

*Nick: Ah…*

*Jingle: SHE'S STILL THE ONE FOR ME.*

*Kirsty: Nicky! Is it love?*

*Nick: There's a story behind it.*

*Kirsty: There's a story behind everything.*

'His voice has changed,' said Sally. 'What does it mean?'

'Why should it mean anything?'

'He sounds less hyper. Why's he's not naming this new girl like all the others?'

Ami laughed. 'Listen to you believing it all. That's his trick, mum. It's not real! It's not really happening! Any of it!'

'How do you know?'

'This is Nick, remember. Nick who can't pull a ring-can without making a mess of it.'

'Sounds like Nicky's having more success.'

'Oh mum.'

'What time's Pete getting here tomorrow?'

'I'm not sure yet. You will come down with me to

meet him, won't you?'

'Sure,' Sally nursed her glass of wine, wishing it didn't all have to change so quickly. That it could be them for a few days longer.

'I'd get really lost in all those alleys.'

'It's impossible to get lost here. You keep on going downhill till you get to the sea.'

'We could have lunch at that neat bar you were talking about.'

'We could, except...' Sally hesitated. 'Except... I've, there's one thing I have to tell you before we go there.'

'What's that then?'

Nobody there knows dad's dead.'

'Why ever should they?'

'They don't know I'm a widow.'

'What are you talking about?'

'I mean I've been saying – I simply wanted to be normal, OK? So, I said dad was in the States, working on an album.'

Ami went quiet.

'I didn't want people to feel sorry for me. It's what I've come to get away from.'

No response.

'You can blame those women down at the harbour. Did you notice them? The widows. I didn't want to be associated with, you know, old women in black. I know that sounds terrible, but I didn't want anybody to start feeling sorry for me. To have that look in their eye, to never know if – oh… it's hard to explain, but I've said it now.'

'Who?'

'Who what?'

'Who is it you're telling dad's not dead?'

'There's no reason to blow it into something it isn't. There's no reason why his name should come up, I'm saying in case, that's all.'

'Who?'

'Nobody important. Look, it's only a couple of people, the bar owners in fact. They're a gay couple, they're lovely but they're hideous gossips. They tell everybody everything, so we have to assume that everybody knows. Not that anybody's interested. All I'm asking is that you don't put me on the spot, should his name crop up, which, as I say, there's no reason for it to do anyhow.'

'You're asking me to lie,' Ami said coldly. 'I'm going to have to ask Pete to lie. It's not going to be a brilliant first impression is it. "This is my mum, before we go out we'll all have to get on the same page and here's what you can say and what you can't say, in case, she's been fibbing, see, about my dead dad.'

'That's it with you isn't it, it's all back to Pete. Everything goes back to Pete, why didn't I realise that before? I agree it's a stupid thing I said in the moment. I'll even tell them if it comes up if it stresses you out so, but as I said it probably won't. It's a silly little thing that's all. You don't have to bother Pete with it.'

'I tell Pete everything.'

'Tell him and we won't go to the bar.'

'Hold off. You're saying you found this totally real place but now we can't...'

'Ami! If you want to go, we'll go. Say what you like to Pete. I don't care.'

'I want to see it. Christ, you've been going on about it

so much.'

'We'll go for breakfast. Before Pete gets here and you can decide. You'll probably think it's a dump anyway, but they do very good toast.'

# CHAPTER NINETEEN

The Moonlight Bar had become a habit. In the mornings Charles served his toast with Radio 4 burbling in the background. Cosy English voices coming from a studio in central London made it feel a very long way away and dangerously close. A reminder of the confusion of Sally's own real life back home getting closer and closer.

In the evenings she sat up on the back balcony, reading and drinking ice coffees, talking to Charles until cocktail hour when the fairy lights came on and the citronella mosquito candles came out, glowing in red globules of glass on every table. The door to Barry's hut would open and up the iron stairs he'd come, sucking at a cigarette, closely followed by Morrissey, his heavily panting dog, and the wine, the cheesy Doritos and the backgammon would come out.

But the morning she took Ami, everything had changed.

The pit of Barry's short, tattooed, arm released a faint, straw-like smell as his hand moved across the Formica surface, wiping their table that didn't need wiping.

Ami screwed her face up and leant back into her seat.

A loud warble came from the bar. 'I carry the sun in a golden cup, the moon in a silken purse.'

Great, thought Sally. Instead of Charles' cosy morning

tea, toast and Radio 4 they get Barry, Lady Gaga and poetry sound effects.

'Yeats' birthday,' Barry explained apologetically to Ami. 'Big day for Graves.'

Sally recognised the old man in the crumpled cream suit from the Marinha. White earpieces dangled from his battered panama hat.

'Don't know how loud he's talking, plugged into that thing.'

'Hot enough for you?' he said, indicating the single beam of sunlight lasering through the window.

Ami fiddled with her phone.

'The Peloponnese block the sea winds. We're the hottest of the Greek islands in many ways.'

'Call him!' Sally said to Ami. 'Find out what's going on. Have a conversation,'

'He's on *vibrate*.'

'I bet he is.'

'He's in a meeting.'

Ami's thumbs sprang into life, moving in rapid stabs across the keyboard.

'What's he say?'

'It's Simon.'

Barry stopped mid-wipe and looked to Sally.

'Ami's boss,' Sally clarified.

They exchanged a look and Sally hated herself. Why did she mind so much that he was there instead of tall, neat Charles? Because hairy little hippies with tattoos and beards weren't Ami's thing? So what! This place was hers. Still, at least it would be simple enough to stay away after this. Pete wouldn't need any debriefing. She'd repossess it. Come down on her own and leave the lovers together in their own space.

Ami's mobile flashed again.

'Ah this is him.'

'It had better be,' Sally said, staring anxiously at Ami staring at the screen. The efficient businesswoman of moments before turned back into a little girl. As Ami's face fell so did Sally's. She couldn't not surrender to Ami's moods, rising up like a bubble in the mud only to pop flat again into a floundering squelch of gloom.

Ami's face lit up again. Sally stayed doubtful.

The ones who messed you around and kept you guessing were always the ones you wanted.

'No, listen to this. He's hoping to get away tonight.'

'Hoping?'

'He'll fly into Athens tomorrow. There's a ten-minute window for me to call before he goes back to the meeting.'

'Phone calls out the back,' Barry said sternly, jerking his thumb towards the balcony.

'Fine,' Ami said pointedly. 'So much more disturbing than iPods and poetry recitals.'

'Why didn't the little shit call her in the first place?' said Barry. 'Does she jump to what the hell he says?'

'He's got this power over her. Yet she's always had to control everything. Everything. She used to throw her toys out of her pram before she even had a pram.'

Barry put his cloth down and took Ami's seat. 'Love's a different country when you're young.'

'Do you think so?'

'I'll tell you one thing, it gets harder with time, remembering what it was like. Why we wanted to possess each other so much.'

'This guy's been messing her about for years, though. It's such a waste. She could be having a ball, have the pick of whoever she wanted.'

'Maybe she don't really like being in control. Maybe that's what kicks her off about him.'

'At least she's cheering up a bit now she knows she doesn't have to hang out with me for the rest of the week.'

'There you go again putting yourself down. She thought she'd been stood up and she hasn't. That's pretty powerful energy.'

'I wish some of it would come my way.'

'Maybe it did,' Barry chuckled, looking at the door.

Sally felt the familiar whomp and her whole world changed.

Barry got up to follow him to the bar. After managing a level 'Hi,' in response to his brief acknowledging glance, she casually swivelled sideways into corner of eye vision. She'd never get a part but at least she could watch and appreciate the view.

His presence in the room changed it completely. A force field whipped up that was so strong she could almost touch it. Lady Gaga's lyrics were full of meaning. The black and white Sutherland Brothers and Quiver poster of a shipwreck tacked to the wall opposite full of omens. It had become a different place, like time and distance had telescoped itself inside the long narrow room.

He half-perched on the stool next to Graves and touched him lightly on the back. Sally registered the warmth and kindness, the focussed attention, even on Graves. The armour of charm. Nothing wrong with that.

The shape of his shoulder-blades, visible through his beige and white checked shirt, fascinated her. Each one of his curls fell into its neatly unkempt place, touching the top of the collar here and there.

Thanks to Barry, she was a stranger sitting there who knew more about him than he could have imagined.

He had that easy-going, life's a gas aura of never having to try too hard for anything. Uninvolved and unevolved, he got as much attention, as much of anything as he wanted, at any time. For him new adventures were everywhere, ready to be plucked, tasted and spat away when love threatened to get too personal.

Sally was a bit disappointed to discover he was one of the original affluent hippies. Another artist, in quotes, who didn't have to prove himself to survive. His parents, a wealthy Athenian businessman and an American artist, met on the island long before Cohen's time. He'd grown up in the States but came back to look after their property interests.

When Ami bounced back in, all smiles, he was hunched over the bar talking to Barry. By the time she reached her seat his stool had swivelled 180 degrees and without a second's hesitation he was up and coming towards them, holding his little white Greek coffee cup out in front of him.

'How's it going?' he said, slipping onto the bench next to Sally like she was his oldest friend in the world. The weight of him next to her made Sally's seat rise up slightly. She should have been furious but instead she felt ridiculously honoured, clumsy and breathless all at the same time.

She introduced Loro to Ami in the same way that she'd been introduced.

'...and Loro's Leonard Cohen.'

Ami's receptive, open countenance crumpled into a reproachful, questioning frown.

'I'm not the main man and I don't pretend to be,' Loro said with a smile that boomed in the wake of Ami's radiance. That Ami's primordial glow was because she'd been speaking to Pete and was nothing whatsoever to do with him would never occur to him, Sally thought happily as she clunkily moved the conversation along.

'The scene is really big in the UK as I'm sure you know. There's a club that puts on nothing else and a festival as well, like Glastonbury but all tribute acts.'

'I'm no tribute act. I sing a few old songs in a few old bars that's all.'

'It's big business.'

'Music and business are words that don't belong together.'

'A lot of people manage to survive on it. Like me, for instance.'

'It's not the destination that's important, it's the journey,' he said, slipping a cigarette into the side of his mouth and lighting it.

'Very good, but that's Dylan's line.'

He didn't flinch but took another long drag of his cigarette. Ami stared pop-eyed in disgust at the smoke wisping into her face.

'We're so used to smoking being banned now,' Sally blundered on, worried he'd get up and leave.

'It's good for business, Barry knows that.'

'He's a smart operator.'

'A businessman who's scared of numbers,' he leant forwards and lowered his voice. 'He ran away from the States because of it. You know, many people come to this island to get away from something. That is his.'

'Charles does all that side?' Sally said glancing nervously at the bar, worried that Barry's beady eye, let alone beady ear would pick up on them.

'He has no choice. Barry had a breakdown – thought numbers were taking over our souls. Too much acid or mushrooms maybe, but there you go.'

Ami rolled her eyes. 'Talk about hippies and loonies.'

'Splits his time between two special islands,' Loro said to Sally taking his eyes off Ami for the first time. 'His passport gets him in and out of Greece and Bali, for the rest there's Charles, or other friends to help him. He always finds people to help him. That's his way.'

'Like the sarong sellers?'

'Yes.'

'He has no credit cards?'

'Don't get him going on plastic passwords.'

'Or me,' said Ami. 'But he must have a bank account?'

Sally swallowed. It was uncanny. He couldn't have picked a better subject than money to draw Ami in.

'Charles does all of that.'

'How many have I got?' said Ami. 'My house, my phones, bank, national health, PIN number, hole in the wall number.'

Don't think about it thing too much. It's crazy but catching.'

'Those are only the ones you remember,' said Sally.

'He thinks we'll be having bar-codes micro-chipped

into our bodies before long,' said Loro.

'Or our ages tagged on our ears, like cows,' said Sally. 'Our pin numbers hidden in our pants.'

Why'd she said that? *Why*!

'It's a true illness,' Loro continued without reacting. 'The good thing is his instinct. If he trusts you, he trusts you. That's it. It's up to you how you do things from there.'

'But why run businesses if you're like that?' said Ami.

'To live where he wants to live?'

'I'll drink to that,' said Sally.

'He's achieved more than many.'

'Thanks to Charles' hard work,' said Sally.

'It works for both of them,' Loro said, half-smiling at Ami.

Ami half-smiled back. Sally felt sick. She'd been left dangling in the empty space between two smiles that had nothing to do with her.

'So!' she pipped up like a dowager granny pouring tea all over the cake. 'What time's Pete getting here tomorrow Ami?'

## CHAPTER TWENTY

Sally stood on her rock high above the harbour and sang a sustained top G. When all the old, stale, bitter air was out of her she crumpled down to the spiky grass and stones.

'I meant it, and I meant it,' she repeated to herself, picking up pebbles and putting them down again. 'I asked Ami to leave and I meant it.'

After Pete finally confessed he wasn't going to make it and, almost in the same breath, suggested Ami return early to stay with his parents instead, Sally had leapt at it. An opportunity not to be missed, she'd plugged on. Ami would be so much happier in cool, leafy Shropshire with her man. She wouldn't miss her no, not when she was like this. And she'd meant it.

Had she tried, or had she tried? Before the few perfect, sunny days had turned chemical she'd done her best. They'd been to the beach on the other side of the island with the bar and martini loungers (too crowded), the chic boutiques (too Eurotrash), the jewellery shops (too expensive) and art galleries (as with all art galleries in Ami's eyes, Emperor's new clothes), so came the invisible Pete. If Sally breathed a word against him. If she dared suggest the increasingly obvious fact that he'd never had any squeak of an intention of ever showing up, she was piously slapped down with the important work of charity defence.

Sally took a swig of her water. It was already warm and tasted of plastic. Soon there'd be no breeze at all, even that high up. Down in the harbour the sun would have boiled the air into an almost un-inhaleable furnace that felt like it could scorch lungs to a cinder.

They'd given up on the costly, crowded air-con restaurants and taken to sitting beside the fridge or in the shower, venturing out at night to the terrace or down to the Moonlight Bar. At least she had company there other than Ami crooning into her phone, moaning about the heat. Some company, too.

Since Ami's arrival he'd been every which way she'd turned. Reeled right in by her stunning, sulky daughter. He was always alone and waiting, like a cat at dinnertime, ready to join them as if it was his automatic, undeniable right. An up-front arrogance only a few men could turn into the charming kind of cheek that got welcomed more times than it was ever rejected.

Staring out at the limpid sheet of sea, she questioned her motives one more time.

How much of her wanting Ami gone was to do with Pete and how much to do with Loro?

Her denials came thick, fast and, worryingly, way too vociferously. She was old enough to recognise that denial was the first sign that there had to be something going on to be denied in the first place.

Apart from not wanting to put up a moment longer than she had to with Ami's misery, two simple facts stacked in her favour. She'd seen him first and Ami wasn't in the remotest bit interested. This, of course, had only made him try all the harder so he was around them all the time. Waiting. Watching out for them. What became increasingly obvious as time had gone on was how much more in common they had between them. So, the pattern had become evenings spent talking to each other about everything under the sun whilst he stole long, longing glimpses at Ami who stared forlornly at her phone waiting for the next message from Pete. It was insane.

So, no. There wasn't any encroachment or tacky stealing of daughter's limelight. In her full, outside looking in mode, she'd been getting to appreciate the proximity of such masculine perfection. If, as it so happened to be the case, he was doing exactly the same but with her sulky, sculpturally divine but untouchable daughter, so be it.

She noticed an unusual shape on the horizon, a white rectangle that looked way too big for a boat. Shading her eyes with her hands, she squinted hard. It was a Barbican-sized block of flats by the look of it, doubling in size by the minute.

'Yeeoooowh,' she shouted into the tepid breeze and raced down the hill to the path below. At the track to the villa she hesitated for a moment before rushing on downwards. No time to get her bag, get changed or haul Ami out of bed. Barry had told her the first SeaGreek Line docking of the season couldn't be missed. The whole island turned out to greet it.

The harbour buzzed and The Marinha was standing room only. Bumped off their regular pitch by the frenzy, the black widows stayed well back in the shade. Spikey and the woman from the rip-off purple tablecloth restaurant were squabbling like geese over their ice cream cabinet pitches at the donkey stands. The hairy harbourmaster waded amongst it all, soothing tempers, waving his arms and bringing order to the chaos wherever he went.

Sally squeezed through the boat and donkeymen until she found Barry.

'Don't you love it?' he greeted her with a wistful, benign smirk she hadn't seen before. 'The sweet exchange of supply and demand. Everybody on that ship itching to buy and everybody here ready and waiting to sell. Beautiful.'

'You're such a money man at heart, Barry.'

'Needs is. Finding the easy way's the trick.' Barry dropped his carpetbag from his shoulder took out a sarong, folded it into a bag and gave it to her. 'Here.'

'Here what!'

'See how many you can shift.'

'Me?'

'You don't do nothing. They sell themselves.'

Sally fingered the soft rayon mustards, pale blues and dusty pinks.

'Only Balinese sarongs on the islands.'

'But...'

Doggedly avoiding her eye, Barry looked at the sky and sniffed noisily. 'I love the smell of dry cleaning fluid in the morning.'

Sally looked up at the line of coiffed and blow dried, white and pastel crimplened passengers, standing at the white railings. Below them the fishermen thumped octopuses against their dinghy hulls as if on cue from a Disney director.

The frenzy grew as the ship spewed its catch onto the

harbour. In the mood now, Sally hoisted the heavy piece of fabric onto her shoulder and turned towards the crowds. Barry grabbed her arm. 'Wait. Hold back a little, let the keen ones go in first. They're always a bit bewildered when they hit the land, give 'em the space to say 'no' a few times. I'm taking the first alleyway up there, you take the second, that's where they'll be ready to go for it.'

Sally broke free. Forgetting the heat, she hurried towards the ship.

'Sarongs! Sarongs! Balinese sarongs,' she yelled. 'Who wants one?'

'Here,' a round woman in a taut white two-piece and white plastic rainbow-rimmed sunglasses made straight for her, dragging her shuffling grey husband behind her.

Alarmed, Sally turned and ran.

'Hey, you!' the man called.

'I'll be back in a minute!' Sally called back. 'Barry? Barry where are you!'

Running was difficult. At each step her knees felt like they were going to buckle down with the weight. The bag thumped uncomfortably against her back.

She'd got half way up the first alleyway before she had to stop and catch her breath. The plastic sunglasses woman was gaining ground.

'Where are you, you little...? Ah – no no no, wait a minute, I think I know.' Zig zagging past the woman, she raced back to the sea and there he was, in the Marinha bar, leaning back in a harbourside chair, smoking a roll-up, a fresh cup of coffee in front of him.

'Barry – I don't have my bag with me. I have no money, no change at all and what the hell do we charge?'

'Ak, numbers,' he drawled, 'don't talk to me about numbers.'

'This is no time for your stupid phobias, TELL me!'

'Work it out.'

The white plastic sunglasses were marching determinedly towards her.

'How *much* or I'll thump you?'

'How much?' said the woman.

'Ten dollars?' she said, smiling sweetly at the husband.

'*Each?*' said the husband.

'Hey that's good!' said the wife.

Shit. Sally glanced angrily at Barry.

'Three for twenty-five.'

'We'll take six.'

'Barry, I sold six!'

'The first sale fuels the next, that's the buzz,' Barry chuckled over his coffee. 'Like pickin magic mushrooms, you find one, you find more, and more.'

The liner threw its shadow over the little harbour like a cliff. The cruise passengers evaporated as quickly as they'd appeared, ferried off on excursions.

Spikey brought them coffee and water.

'And some wine,' said Barry.

'Good wine,' said Sally, 'A bottle. Put it on my slate,' she picked her sticky t-shirt away from her skin. 'I'm shattered. It's like breathing custard in this heat.'

'That's hard work for you.'

'And I thought I was hopeless at selling.'

'Here we go, don't catch his eye or the rest of our bottle is history.' Graves was in, earphones off, looking around with startled, watery blue eyes.

'Where's that chirpy girl of yours?' Barry said conversationally.

'Packing her bags, I hope.'

'Now you don't mean that.'

'I do.'

'She got the call?'

'He's not coming.'

'Oh boy.'

'She's leaving early, going to meet his parents.'

'No? That's mean.'

'I really don't mind.'

Pete wasn't to blame. The mess was her fault for trying to work up a family holiday that couldn't be.

'I guess when you're in love, being together's the only thing that makes sense in the world.'

Sally sighed.

'Seen Loro about today?' Barry asked.

'No.'

'Me neither.'

'He'll be sad when she's gone.'

'For a minute or two,' Barry chuckled.

'You think?'

'The lure of unavailability that's all that's going on there.'

'Powerful,' Sally sighed inside.

Sumo wandered by. They both automatically reached for the bottle and their glasses.

'Where's Charles?'

'Back at the bar.'

'Couldn't he have locked up for a bit to come and see the action? Everybody's down here after all.'

'That's why. Hates crowds. Don't care to be close to water either. Hills is his place.'

'Does he move to Bali in the winter as well?'

'Who'd run the bar? Like I said, he hates water.'

'Don't you – miss him?'

'He's always here, why should I miss him?'

Sally tipped forward of her chair and kissed him on his hairy cheek.

'Hey, what's going on?'

'I know exactly what you're saying, I think that calls for more wine, Spikey!'

'You waiting for someone?' said Barry.

'No?'

'Sure?'

'Is it that obvious?'

Silence.

'Oh alright then. He must get it all the time I know but there's no tax on dreaming. Not yet anyhow. Has he ever been married?'

'He fell heavy in love once, won't give his heart away again. Stayed true to hisself, got to give him that. You know what they say. Once a harbour boy always a harbour boy. They grow up all right, keeping the chase in their hearts. Got it made those kids. Quick love, love that comes and love that goes, handed to 'em day after day. Talking of which, I better be going.'

'I should too.'

'What's should about it?'

'I left in a bit of a huff this morning. I thought she might have called me by now. Maybe she's texted.' Sally reached instinctively to the ground for her bag. 'Damn, I don't have it do I. Oh well. That explains that.'

'My tab – see it as wages.'

'If employment could always be that simple.'

'That's my point. It can. You coming up the hill?'

'I think I'll stay here awhile.'

She sat in a wooze, sobering up through the afternoon with coffee and water on her earnings tab, feeling as settled as if she'd lived there forever, watching the passers-by.

Watching out for one particular passer-by.

What the hell had happened to him anyway?

Without compromising himself in any way whatsoever, he knew he had more to offer than Ami reckoned on. This was, Sally decided, a corner of blind arrogance she hadn't considered before. Self-belief worked. It was downright inspiring. Even allowing for the circumstances of his natural beauty, something she could perhaps learn from. Barry was right. Ami's indifference and barely disguised disgust was what made him keep trying. His persistence upping the ante of Ami's negativity even higher. She'd be glad to get away.

As The Moonlight was a dingy little overheated cupboard that might as well be on the back streets of Balham in Ami's eyes, Loro was cheesy, arrogant, second-hand, precious, pious, hairy and old. And she let him know it. But did he give up? Did he know he didn't stand a chance. Did he hell.

She watched the last dregs of the cruise passengers trickling back to their ship as it prepared to leave port. She imagined their evening ahead. Cooling showers, freshly laundered gowns and iced cocktails waiting for them in the Captain's Lounge. She remembered the ease of her conversation with Bobble Hat Man. The attractions of cruising multiplied: bathrooms on tap, permanent sea breezes, the scenery sliding along all by itself in front of you. Removed from reality, yes, but maybe that's the point she'd been missing. Sailing round in circles with the world outside turned into nothing more threatening than a revolving theme park. No wonder so many widows ended up there.

She watched the liner slide back out to sea, imagining it was the island that was moving rather than the ship. Staying in one spot was turning out to be a mixed blessing. But at least she was meeting the locals.

As if he'd heard her thoughts, Spikey appeared with a coffee and Metaxa she hadn't ordered and stood beside her chair. Together they watched the ship fading away into a dot in the pearly evening light.

Sally thought about all of the people who'd been swarming about the harbour inside that tiny speck. Their souvenirs stored away. A piece of gold, a sarong, a rotten orange sunset painting, sipping their sundowners being taken to the next place to load up with more goodies. No need to turn, no need to look back.

Her own black widows were back in position ready for the evening ferry. Did they ever get on and go? Did they go on package tours? Had they ever hankered after a Norwegian Fjord or an English wood? Had any of them ever been on a punt, gliding through Oxford's shaded rivers, shopped in Boots, eaten in an Indian, smelled blackcurrant bushes in a suburban garden or seen a daffodil?

Through the brandy wooze, she thought about home.

The blackbird who always sang in her front garden after rain. The garden that, come October would no longer be hers.

Finding a smaller place to buy hadn't worked out as yet. Small didn't have to mean ugly, but when it came to cottages in her price range, there was nothing she could put up with. Renting and storing till she found somewhere further out that didn't have a windowless bathroom or a north-facing garden was her latest idea.

Spikey clucked.

Sally looked up, 'What's up?'

'This is what make me angry,' he said. 'Always they sail at the evening time. Keeping all the customers inside for themselves. They don't like it they eat here. Bastards. Still, another one comes tomorrow, and the day after two, three. Maybe they stay. One day a ship will stay for supper and I will retire for the rest of the sum…' he looked up sharply.

'I suppose you think this is funny,' Ami stood scowling.

'Sit down and have a coffee,' Sally said trying not to slur.

'Coffee,' said Spikey backing off. 'I bring it now.'

Ami sat down. 'Where have you been?'

'Selling sarongs.'

'I was so worried about you. I've been horrible, I've been mean, I'm sorry, mum, let's forget about Pete. I promise, swear I won't mention him again. I was being such a selfish bitch. I figured we'd stay down tonight and eat something here.'

'But I'm a mess.'

'You're on holiday mum, look around, everyone's in

shorts and t-shirts.'

'But I'm hot and sweaty and...'

'Go up and shower, I'll wait here.'

'Did you lock up?'

'Yeeees!'

'The front windows?'

'More than you ever do, but yes, I did. What's that out there?' Ami pointed to an outcrop of rock.

'Looks like a bar.'

'Let's give it a try.'

## CHAPTER TWENTY-ONE

The bar was little more than a roof twisted with vines jutting out on the sea wall, but their chairs were pulled out with the exaggerated courtesy that went with an expensive menu.

A light, comfortable breeze came in off the sea. In a dark unlit corner by the back-kitchen swing door Sally noticed a guitar, propped up precariously against a stool. Her insides bounced. He was there. Standing with his back to them, sipping beer at the tiny counter where the waiters took their orders.

'Someone's Ami radar working well tonight,' she said casually. 'Look who's here and playing by the look of it.'

'So, at last we get to hear what he's been boasting about,' said Ami cynically taking a menu from the waiter.

Soon after they'd ordered, he moved, without any sign of noticing them, towards the makeshift stage. He fiddled with his amplifier, perched on his stool and hunched over a nylon-strung guitar that looked way too small for his big, red-knuckled hands.

A lonely, echoing growl of *Ain't No Cure For Love*, floated over them and out to sea. He sang close to the microphone, still and tense. A gentle but powerful voice without a trace of arrogance. His sincerity was touching. Sincere sincerity, Sally wondered, or part of the act?

Sally risked putting her glasses on to get a better look.

His shirt was too tight across the chest. The high-waister serge trousers and black leather slip-ons, creepily out of fashion but oh, all the more heart-meltingly endearing because of it.

'He should be centre stage,' said Ami. 'Not tucked away in the corner like that.'

'There isn't a stage.'

'Well there should be.'

From Ami praise indeed.

He sang *Bird on a Wire* gazing up to the stars with a pained, twisted expression on his face. Logically she knew this was unbelievably camp and he'd be sneered out of a Camden pub night in minutes but there, in that setting and with that music it didn't matter. Short romances and long affairs full of sun-splashed rooms and all the goodbyes still to come. The song held so much past in him she forgot about the cheesy shoes.

What is it about a man with a guitar round his neck? Why didn't Ami get it?

Maybe charity workers were the lead guitarists of the day. Maybe it was more to do with freedom than all that do-gooding? Out in the world doing their own thing their own way. The men who feared getting tied down were always the ones you wanted to get the most. The girls that ran the ones they wanted to catch.

After an upbeat *Sisters of Mercy*, and something she'd never heard before, the simple acoustic guitar sound of the five opening notes of *Suzanne* repeated and stopped all the restaurant chatter dead.

Again, the humility towards the song shone through. It felt like he was telling a real story, letting the audience into a secret.

Crackles and thumps came from the microphone as he took his guitar off, picked up his beer from the bar and joined a couple beside the entrance. But moments later he backed away from them, turned and zig zagged pointedly through the tables towards them.

He knew they'd been there all along.

'How did you like it?'

Sally bobbed her head up and down.

'Thank you,' he grinned at Ami and pulled up a chair.

'Sort of like the original but original at the same time,' said Sally. 'I mean there are so many cover versions, gazillions of them, but I heard a definite authenticity in there. And in this setting...! *Suzanne* was amazing.'

'Sing it with me and I'll do it again.'

'What?'

'The song needs backing vocals.'

'No no, I'm not singing at the moment.'

'Go on mum.'

'I'm a mess!'

'You look beautiful.'

Did he say that, or had she imagined it? She remembered the hillside that morning, the top G, she remembered Ramone's list – if you feel like doing something do it. She did feel like it, but what if... *No what if's*... do it, *do it*... Ramone would be up there like a shot. She looked at the set, she'd be at the back of the dark corner...

'Take that as a yes,' said Ami.

'Good,' he patted her shoulder affectionately and

spoke in her ear. 'Nothing to worry about, it's all low key here, laid back yes? I'll give you a sign, after *I'm Your Man*, OK?'

'After *I'm Your Man*...' Sally nodded, trying not to mind as he lifted his hand away.

He touched everybody's shoulder affectionately, Sally reminded herself, he was a touchy person and spoke in all sorts of people's ears.

'I must get back to work. But it was a good lunch, no?' he touched Ami's arm.

A volt shot through Sally.

'See you later.'

Later? What was going on here?

A term of expression, she decided, like, after the set, he'd be coming back. This was Greece, there was no kicking out time. That'd be it.

'So!' she said calmly and as non-accusingly as she could. 'You had lunch. You knew he was playing here all along.'

'I looked for you in the Moonlight. We ended up eating, yes, and he told me. It was a surprise for you, mum. I knew you were dying to see him play but didn't want to make it a drag for me. But you know what, it's great! Not normally my kind of thing as you know...'

Later?

She couldn't bear to ask. It would be childish to ask. Childish, churlish, rude, prying, but out it came.

'Later? What did that mean? He said see you later. Is he coming back with us or what?'

'Oh no he meant tomorrow. He told me about this beach and I thought, you know mum...'

'But you're leaving tomorrow!'

'There were no flights!'

'But...'

'That's what I'm telling Pete anyhow. I'm going to make him wait a bit longer for me, rack up the jealousy.'

'I see.'

'It was you who kept on saying Pete needed to know I'm not waiting for him to call all the time. That nothing gets a guy going like the threat of a rival. When Loro suggested we check out this bay I thought, you know what, yes. It's an ideal set up mum, I'd be crazy not to, after the way Pete's messed me around.'

'So, it's to make Pete jealous?'

'One date.'

'Dates around here move pretty fast. What bay is it?'

'How should I know? We'll find out tomorrow.'

'We?'

'You're coming as well.'

'No way.'

'It's my last day, I can't leave you.'

'I won't be wanted, Ami.'

'I want you. You can take some shots of us together, on my phone, that might work.'

'No way, oh oh what have I let myself in for,' she heard the familiar refrains of *I'm Your Man*. 'I can't do this, Ami. I'm not going up.'

'You have to. I'll film it on my phone and tag you on Facebook. You said it's the perfect setting. Go on. He's impressed us, now you go and knock him out.'

The thought of Ramone seeing it on Facebook got Sally to her feet.

She slipped onto the stage behind him. They exchanged a special sacred look. Like all stages everywhere, it held an atmosphere that she knew so well. It might only be the corner of a tiny bar in the middle of the sea, but Shea Stadium couldn't have given her a bigger high.

Looking up into the clear, night sky, she waited for the familiar chords to come. When they did, she found the note and went for it. He sang to the audience, but she knew he felt her presence behind him and right through him. She knew all about the humble stillness in him now. It was a lie, but the perfect lie. He was a ladies' man and music was the main mistress.

He gripped the microphone and clenched his fist, stooping forwards and bending his knees as he dug the feel of the sounds out with every bone in his body. She watched, listened and, note by note, adapted, blending her soft, restrained strength with his husky rhythms, welding herself to his voice until they were one.

## CHAPTER TWENTY-TWO

The cathedral bell took a deep breath and rattled the air. A brooding claustrophobic silence hung in the heat between each beat, echoing the tolls back at themselves from the hills above.

The heatwave gripped, trapping what air there was into a pool of heat, making movement difficult. Mornings and evenings were the only time people could operate and nobody moved more than they had to. Every breath out was laboured, every breath in felt like it was the same air but dustier, thicker, hotter. The sea was as still as a lake.

Sally sat in the Marinha watching Ami's hydrofoil speed into the distance. The hot tears that had threatened all morning appeared. All the progress she'd made as an independent woman of the world dissolved back into the simple longing of motherhood.

Alerted by Loro's interest, Pete had bombarded Ami with texts and calls through the evening and into the night. She must leave immediately. With convincing restraint, Sally agreed. Ami's game at making him jealous by spending the day with Loro could backfire. If not with Pete, (or, from the sound of it, his parents) then with Loro. Or, not least, but in heftily unspoken brackets, herself.

'Don't be hard on yourself.' Barry flip flopped slowly

round their table to his seat. 'She's goin' where she wants to be.'

'After all Pete put us through she still jumps at his every request.'

'You said yourself it's for the best?'

'It is, but he still annoys me.'

'Maybe it's not all about Pete,' Barry said impassively.

'What's that supposed to mean?'

'Like, maybe it was more about missing her dad.'

Sally took several slow sips of her drink, letting the granules of the sweet Greek coffee linger like fudge at the back of her tongue.

'No, but with respect, Barry. Bollocks.'

Sally chewed over this new worry. Throughout Ami's stay, in between the Pete, Pete, Pete, Loro, Pete discussions, Dom hadn't been mentioned once. There should have been something, an acknowledgement. Shared fond memories at the very least.

'What do you mean?' she exclaimed, suddenly realising Barry's implication. 'You said missing. How do you know she's missing her dad?'

'Don't all girls miss their dads?'

Sally looked at Barry long and hard. 'You know my husband's dead, don't you?'

'This island's full of folk who've lost things, their way. People. Especially in car accidents.'

'How do you know *that*?'

'See it all the time here.'

'Most people think he had a skiing accident. He was walking with his skis on his shoulders, like everybody does. He forgot which side of the road the traffic went, stepped out to let some people go past. And…'

Barry did a soft whistle. 'Good manners. What a way to go.'

'I lied to you. I'm sorry. I didn't want people...'

'No explanations now. Whatever gets you through is what you need.'

'Getting through would be progress.'

'It'll happen. In time.'

'How are you supposed to move into the future, Barry, when you know you won't ever be in a place where you can turn a corner in your life and BAM! You know, like you see someone, or something, that gets you really fired up about life again. Maybe it's a person, you are really attracted to them and you think hey I'm really attracted to that person. Let's go see if they're attracted to me too. Because I can't do that anymore and it pisses me off.'

'What's stopping you!'

'I'm old, Barry. Too old.'

'Only your mind.'

'Too old. Too fat.'

Barry shrugged. 'You think like that, then those are the vibes you're giving out there.'

'No, Barry. Fact. She was meant to be seeing Loro today, to make Pete jealous. Did that news reach you yet?'

'Oh boy oh boy, really!'

'I encouraged her at first but now I'm glad she's gone and feeling guilty as sin because it was me who was jealous because I've got this silly stupid crush on him even though I know I'm past it. There, I've said it. Now you know everything.'

'Now that I had kinda guessed already.'

'I'm not the first I'm kinda guessing?'

'What can I say? He's one of them guys…'

'Brings a different girl through your bar every week eh?'

'A serial loner who's never alone for long.'

'And gets away with it.'

'Ain't faithful to no one that one, not even himself.'

'He'll be mad when he finds Ami's stood him up.'

'Bah no.'

'You don't think so?'

'Occupational hazard with all the coming and going around here,' Barry chuckled. 'He'll get over it.'

'They were supposed to be meeting here at noon. She hasn't told him yet.'

'When's she planning on doing that?'

'When she's safely away in Athens.'

'There's your answer.'

'What answer?'

'You turn up instead.'

'Oh sure.'

'Explain what happened.'

'And?'

'Take it from there!'

'Don't be ridiculous. I'm too old, Barry. Way too old for him.'

'You're not!'

'You don't think?'

'Never say I'm too old for him, say he's too young for me.'

'He's not!' Sally shrieked. 'that's the craziness of it. Can't you see that – we're the same age near enough.'

'So, you got even more going for you then. And

besides, he's an old tart, ain't that fussy because of it.'

'Thanks.'

'You analyse too much that's your problem.'

'There's something so – I don't know – trapped about him.'

'That's an island thing.'

'Musicians don't normally have it, there's always a freedom about them. If they're any good.'

'See? Listen to you now. You're understanding him where he don't even understand himself. Turn up. Think up something to say and say it. That's all you do. Give him an opening line.'

'He's surrounded by opening lines!'

'Today you know he's free. Listen, I seen you together. You don't attract people, Sally, till you're ready to attract them. You two get on! He's always talking to you more than your girl.'

'Talking yes, looking, elsewhere.'

'Men aren't so complicated. Sal, you know that. The one switch. On. Off. Call Ami, tell her you've seen him about, so she don't have to call him, a little white lie is all it takes, then you go for it.'

'No way!'

'Sometimes you got to go for the things you want, Sal.'

'But I'll be rejected!'

'Don't let that thought get a look in.'

'It's not a thought. It's what would happen. It'd finish me off for years. For a lifetime.'

'So – be finished. Then start again. A lifetime can go by in a flash. You pick yourself up and you move on.'

'Men don't like women offering themselves up to

them. They like to pick out what they're after and fight for it.'

'But remember they'll also fuck anything in sight, most of em, given a chance.'

'Thanks.'

'It's what you want ain't it? Listen, you're not a kid, a teenager where everything, all your happiness or all your misery is depending on whether something happens or not. If you really want something strong you gotta put your hand up and ask for it.'

'And ruin the rest of my holiday.'

'Your choice. None of this what's in his head shit. You're a grown woman. You got a human right to ask for what you want.'

'Asking doesn't mean you'll get. Especially in this situation.'

'Concentrate on what you want. Think about your son. How many women does he go after? He don't get every one every time. Nobody does.'

'If his show's anything to go by, he does. He's making a career of it!'

'It's like football. He scores, he misses. He wins he's happy, he loses he's miserable. But sometimes he gets results. What's the worst that can happen?'

'It's not going to happen.'

'If you don't say something. I will.'

'You will not.'

'Wanna bet?'

Sally glared at him.

'Something's brewing up already I know it.'

'What do you mean?'

'The singing last night was a little magical – no?'

'How did you know about that!'

'Think up something. Not a direct line, something ambiguous. Take it from there.'

Sally stood up.

'You be back down here now,' he called to her as she left.

Back at the villa Sally put Dom's old swing band tracks on iTunes to add to the confusion. Jazz always made her feel like she wanted to be somewhere else. If she went she'd regret it, but if she didn't go she'd regret it even more.

She opened and closed drawers, picked her mobile up and put it down, tried clothes on and took them off again, scowling long and hard in between outfits at the spongy nakedness even her best Rigby and Peller couldn't disguise. On the other hand, she thought, doing a twirl, a tan did help. Despite the sags she had a glow about her, a buzz she could feel inside. The idea that she could choose to go and meet him in an hour or so….

She texted the lie to Ami and dug out her beach bag. What the hell was she doing? Setting herself up to gatecrash an afternoon splatted next to him on a beach surrounded by lithe, semi-naked young things. Presumptuous insanity. But what the hell, she was on holiday. She tipped the bag upside down on the bed, even though her heart was presuming way, way more.

How would she get through his disappointment when he discovered Ami wasn't there? Even if, in a scenario of madness, it could all go her way for the asking? What sort of a line was she supposed to think up?

Should she do a Ramone and come out with it, 'hey, fancy a shag?'

An image of Loro bursting into horrified laughter presented itself. Or, worse, staring at her in stupefied silence.

She couldn't do it. Suggestion was the only way. Letting it all unfold casually. As *if*!

She picked up her phone but put it down again. She could hear Ramone's scoffs without having to call.

'One more tick on the list, Sal. You'll be on the way to being a living, breathing creature of the world again instead of a woolly old bat heading for the bingo halls and garden centres of life.'

All right, she thought, pulling out her Caribbean Jeannie McQueeny kaftan, the only piece of clothing she possessed that could be seen as either casual, smart or both. She'd go down and explain about Ami. An explanation with no expectations and take it from there.

Take, take. She had to stop giving all the time and start taking.

## CHAPTER TWENTY-THREE

The Marinha was empty. Suspiciously empty.

Convinced that the regulars were all crouched down behind the bar, elbowing each other and cramming their fists in their mouths, Sally tip toed through the unoccupied tables to check.

'Hello!' she called out to the deserted kitchen, 'Anybody serving round here? No, obviously not.' She sat at an outside table. The heat was nuclear. She could feel the hot plastic chair through the thin silk of her dress.

She had to be visible. If he didn't like what he saw he'd have plenty of time to adjust the drop of disappointment on his face. He could make up a really good, convincing, face-saving excuse in his head as he approached whilst she could gauge his body language and prepare for the worst.

When he did appear, she could do nothing but quietly admire the mirage of casual, coolness coming her way. The cool, faded jeans and thin, white T-shirt revealing enough of his taut thighs and dark hairy arms screamed undiscovered sex God and didn't he know it and yelled to her at full decibel volume – NO CHANCE! Absolutely NO WAY chance! All ideas of propositioning him became ludicrous, insane, speculation with a gossipy old queen. He was a player and had every reason to be as much as she didn't.

Her welcoming, desperately unapologetic smile stiffened. He wasn't turning on his heel and running away at the sight of her. Maybe the kaftan was overdressed. She should have worn shorts and t-shirt.

'Hi,' he said, looking around for Spikey. She allowed herself a tiny stare, bathing in the presence of him. The shadowy chin, the proud, almost beaked nose, the big, still, mesmerizing eyes.

He'd shown no surprise at Ami's absence. Barry was right, no-shows were an occupational hazard. But his other predictions were way off.

'I hope you're not too disappointed,' she qualified, her thighs now sliding about in a puddle of squelchy, silky sweat.

'It's a little hot for the bay anyway,' he looked behind him and then out to sea.

'This sun burns right through to the other side of your skin. Can I get you a drink?' PleasesitdownpleasesitDOWNwillyou.

'Not here.'

'Er…'

'It's cooler inside.'

'Yes Good! Good idea. Can't stay out for too long anyway, she said, following him to a table in the shade. 'I expect you've got things to be getting on with.'

Why the hell did she say *that*? Where did that idiotic, self-effacing habit of saying exactly the opposite of what she wanted *come* from?

'You people, you do everything to be somewhere hot then you love to complain about it.'

'You started it. But I do think it'll be Scotland next

year for me. This is insane. Like living inside a furnace.'

'It's because the buildings are around us in a circle. They take in the heat, even the sea breeze, trapping us all inside the inferno.'

'Look, I'm really sorry Ami had to rush off so quickly.'

'Ah there he is, Spikey!' he called.

When they'd settled with their drinks, the awkwardness evaporated and that feeling that she knew him so well returned.

Time passed quickly.

There was something so strangely elusive, so there and not there about him. When he was there it was like he'd been with her forever. But whenever he left, it felt like he'd been gone forever and she felt lost all over again.

She couldn't let it happen that's all. She didn't want him to leave without her. She couldn't give him the chance to say no.

Well, if that's what you want you've got to say something. NOW. Those that don't ask don't get.

'There's so little air down here. Where we need to be right now is up in the hills. The breeze on my terrace at the Villa Lobos is a Godsend to me.' *Godsend? Where did that come from?*

'The view is good, no?'

'Do you have a terrace yourself?'

'I do.'

'That's what's so good about having a space so high up. You must get it on yours as well. The cool breeze I mean…'

'I do.'

226

'I wouldn't mind seeing that view of yours sometime.'

There. The words were out. Hanging motionless in the air like a fetid fart.

'Very like yours, along the hill to the East,' he said, with a little smiling shake of the head. Condescending? But he talked on like he hadn't noticed. The more she hinted the more she battled with herself. She had a list to complete, she was in for the game now and wasn't going to let herself lose.

Shit, fuck and damn, her hopes sank as, in one quick movement, he drained the dregs of his coffee and stood, picking up his keys.

His body shaded her.

She felt sick. Should she, could she bear to say it again?

'Let's go.'

'Sorry?'

'Let's go. Like you said, it's too hot here.'

'Yes, yes, it is isn't it.' She stood up.

Before she'd gathered her bag, Spikey was there, collecting his money, clearing the table. She caught his eye as she followed Loro out, the puddle from the plastic chair dribbling down the back of her legs.

This, she thought, almost shaking with a little interior giggle, would be straight back to Barry within seconds.

They turned off the harbour front by the monastery and set off through the dark, hot lanes.

They carried on chatting so easily that she forgot what exactly was happening, or wasn't happening, until he said something about it being too hot to do anything except lie around for the rest of the day.

Sally felt light, giggly and amazed but still she didn't

trust herself.

Wasn't everything sounding like it had double meaning? To be safe she pretended she didn't hear him so she'd get a replay that she could analyse.

'I said,' he repeated. 'There are some songs you hear and you are with them from the first note, like when you meet special people, you're with them. It's like something deep inside has touched you.'

'I do know that feeling!'

They crossed a shady square covered in crunchy pine needles and cut through a smaller, darker alley.

'So, what music makes you tingle?' he asked.

'Oh um, Aretha, Ella Fitzgerald…'

'Not the universal, no Neil Young, Van Morrison, something more – individual to you.'

'Quirky, you mean?'

'Different? Something I don't know.'

'Obscure,' Sally thought. 'Well, lately it's been a bit weird, like Iron Maiden and Bob Flowerdew.'

'Bob Flowerdew? Good name. I'll have to look that one up.'

'He's not on iTunes.' Sally had a horrible thought.

He looked at her with pleased puzzlement, 'Oh?'

'It's a voice.'

She'd been deluding herself. She was all supposition here where none was meant at all. His villa and hers were in the same direction.

'Like a mantra. It's a man on the radio. Wise organic man, caring.'

'You are listening to the radio, not music.'

'I only listen to music I can't stand. Dischord suits me at the moment. That's why I haven't been singing.'

'You sang with me.'

'That was a one off.'

'I'm flattered.'

'You should be.'

They were reaching the turn-off for her villa.

When she turned left, he would turn right. Go home make himself a drink, lie around for the rest of the day, play his guitar, none the wiser that he'd ever been propositioned so preposterous was the idea.

'Why listen to music you hate?'

'Memories. Too many memories. Songs are like smells, hardwired to the past. Like when I'm back home, wherever that will be, one day I'll listen to Cohen and I'll think of this island and all the people I met here, Barry, Charles, Sumo, Spikey, Graves – you.'

'Everything dissolves into memory in the end.'

'This won't be easy to forget,' she looked at him pointedly, ' – any of it.'

They were a few steps away. Now or never. Now. It would be now. She would turn to the right with him, even if he wasn't expecting it. If that was the case, he'd have to get rid of her, that's all.

'Oh, I know another one I love – The Shipping Forecast, it's a radio weather forecast...'

'Radio again.'

'It's still music.'

'A weather forecast?'

A few steps to go. Keep in pace, keep natural, whatever you do keep talking.

'I'll show you. It goes, Viking, North Utsire, Forties, Cromarty, Dogger, Fisher, German Bight, Humber, Thames...'

Two steps to go.

'Biscay, Fastnet, Lunday, Trafalgar, Wight... Hebrides, Shannon, Irish Sea,' oh hell, keep, keep, keep it going, 'Viking, North Forties, German Humber.'

He made to slow down.

'I can't wait to compare your view to mine,' she said, taking a large step right with him.

She waited for the 'No! Go away, go home with you.'

But instead he speeded up and said, 'It's this way.'

They turned into a narrow, dusty pathway and stopped in front of a heavy, broad brown door cut into the whitewashed wall.

She followed him into a small, cool kitchen with dark, wood-panelled walls and a noisy, humming fridge.

'Come, I'll show you the terrace.'

She gathered the silk of her long kaftan as he bounced out of sight up a precarious open-slatted staircase. Sun fell through a skylight onto a pine table with a candlestick, a small mirror and a large church bell on it.

There were two acoustic guitars on one wall and on another a frieze with sailing ships. It was furnished simply with a white rocking chair, a white rocking horse, a couch with an old blanket on it and, next to a white wall with very high windows, a white piano.

'Oh wow, I didn't expect this!' she said stepping outside onto a terrace as fully-furnished as the room behind them was empty space.

'Have a seat. I'll get us a drink.'

She looked around. It was as if she'd stumbled into the final sequence of an old Grand Designs.

Fresh dilemma. Which seat? She fancied the English-style garden swing chair covered in flowery, sun-baked chintz but knew the upright next to the marble table scattered with multicoloured worry-beads would be more diplomatic.

Standing was easiest, she decided, and went to the edge of the wall to look down at the rooftops and the sea beyond.

'I see what you mean,' she said when he returned, keeping her eyes fixed on the panorama spread out below. 'Our views are similar aren't they, but so different. You must almost be the same level as me, as the streets go, but it feels much higher. You can see so much more of the harbour.'

She could hear him chuckling and turned. 'What?' she laughed. 'What's so funny?'

'I thought you meant the way we see things.'

Sally laughed nervously. He's seeing double meanings as well! Good sign or what?

'But you're right, we are more to the west here.'

'I love it.'

'You haven't seen the best.'

She avoided all eye contact.

'Oh, look, a guitar!' she said, going over to an acoustic Martin that was worth, she knew, all of several thousand pounds leaning casually against the wall. 'This is some guitar. Can I hear it?'

'Later,' he said, laying glasses on the little table in front of the swing chair and uncorking the bottle.

Oh em Gee! she thought, taking a snapshot of the moment to savour for later when she was back at home in darkest Strawberry Hill with the washing machine buzzing away and nothing to look forward to on a cold winter's evening but *I'm A Celebrity Get Me Out Of*

*Here.*

'White wine, lovely!'

She sat down carefully next to him on the swing chair, leaving a polite gap between them. She mustn't have more than one glass. Leaning back in that thing with a loud grunt would be all too easily done after a glass or two.

'Why don't you use that guitar on stage?'

'The nylon strung is part of the act. That one's for my own music.'

'You never sing your own songs?'

'Leonard Cohen is my living. See there,' he leant forward making the chair swing and pointed down towards a cluster of roofs. 'There. That's his house.'

'When was he last here?' Sally said keeping her balance.

He shrugged.

'Are there, like, pilgrimages?'

'Sure. A big one in June every two years.'

'And you make a killing, right?'

'Oh yes.'

'Do you know him?'

'A little. Not much. Like anybody knows anybody.'

Oh don't! Sally fanned her face, 'Does he know about you? Does he come and see you when he's here?'

'His songs have been recorded by thousands. I am simply one more.'

'But you're here. Where people treat him like a God.'

'He is a God. Kohens are Hebrew priests who come directly from Moses' brother Aaron. Like all the greatest people, he knows the worth of those who back him. Backing singers, the spiritual female presence with him on the stage, balances it out…'

'Please, sing something of yours now. I'd really love to hear what you do.'

She jumped off the chair, grabbed the neck of the guitar and handed it to him.

He looked at his hands finger picking a melody of opening chords, then looked up at her and sang

*Songs of love*
*And songs of hate*
*And songs that sing and cry*
*Songs that break…*

Sally concentrated on the floor and tried to listened closely but her mind kept wandering. How could she though, how could she, yet on the other hand how couldn't she.

How, having got this far, was she going to leave with a bye bye thanks for the drink wave of the hand. Who cares anyway, that's what Ramone would say. Nothing ventured. She was old enough to accept rejection on the nose, Barry would say. She'd felt that way for so long anyway. This was about what she wanted. And, sitting there looking at him, so near but so far, she did want.

But if she did launch herself at him he could totally freak. So, nothing physical, no. Having got so far, she must now keep on the side of safe. Concentrate, concentrate on the music now. His voice still had the Cohen gravel in it, but he had a wide range. Far from perfect, but with a soul of its own.

*And songs that fly*
*Songs that break your heart in two*
*Some songs never lie.*

His steady, dark eyes furrowed into depths of distance

and concentration. He was, on really close, critical inspection – apart from the perfect thighs – really looking quite paunchy on that swing. She liked finding another flaw in him. Wasn't that the way it worked? Once the flush of instant attraction took hold, it was the imperfections that grabbed at the heart and finished the job.

*A song is why*
*My soul's beneath*
*You don't love me any more*
*No words.*

Their eyes locked in a charge of recognition. She caught the doubt in him. The knife-edge belonged to them both. Fear hiding behind lust? Or lust hiding behind fear? Or both?

'Very good. If that song was produced it could come out so strong.'

'That's all there is now. Producers mixing for singers and their songs to feed into their machines. If you write a song and get a co-writing credit you are unusual.'

'But producers do so much of the work!' Sally protested. 'Remember who you're talking to here!'

'Ah, your husband, yes. I'm not complaining but it isn't something that interests me. They all make the speeds so set. So rigid. Fast of 3, 4 maybe 5 and that's all it is. Music by numbers.'

'Is that song down on a file or CD?'

'Yes.'

But, she must wait. He was the man. There'd be a sign. She must wait. Not leap no. But what if no sign came?

'Chorus again – now sing it with me.'

*A song is why*

*My soul's beneath*
*You don't love me any more*
*No words.*

He looked up at her, 'I love this when you sing with me.'

She recognised the dark loneliness in his eyes. No words all right.

'Thank you. It's good to be appreciated.'

'You have it,' he said. 'You find the feel of the lead, get the range in a second and harmonise in a delicate way. Such a purity of instinct and skill – the work of the angels.'

DAMN. It was her voice he loved. That was all.

'I'm proud of what I've done. The front line was never for me. Leads need their own depths and style to carry it off.'

'Integrity! But you have it. You are true with yourself when you are singing with me.'

'Thanks. It does work well with us, as a pair.' Oh NO! Did she say that? 'But you've got a great song there. And I think you know it. I know you know it. So why not do your own music as well?'

'I'm too lazy.'

'There's more to it than that.'

'Why run after something that's so far from perfection, when I can make his songs well enough and have a good life from it. I have music, girls, the sea and sun – everything I need.'

Sally heard denial in his voice. There was something so missing. Something big.

They talked until the sun went down and the stars came out. But now it was dark, and she really was in danger of outstaying her welcome. Maybe there was an unspoken dating rule she didn't know about. Whoever made the opening suggestion should continue with the follow-through pounce. Logical. But no way could she be so presumptuous. At the same time, she couldn't simply get up and leave.

She had to. Had had had to.

When he next leant forward to pick up his glass she carefully sloped sideways, so their shoulders were touching. 'If you put that song on CD my son might play it on his show.'

'It's in the computer.'

'He has this kind of dating show, where he talks about his serial dating. Every week it's a different girl. It's funny though. He never talked about his girlfriends at home. He was so secretive. Ami was always falling in and out of love and bringing boys back and kicking them out. Nick? Never! Kept his love life to himself. He's a shy boy broadcasting his love life to the world.'

NOW WHAT? He. Hadn't. Moved. An. Inch.

She moved a fraction closer.

'That's the show,' she blabbed on. 'Every week you think this one has to be the same girl as the week before. But it never is. No one thinks it'll last.'

'He loves until the next time.'

'Isn't that what you do? With the girls that come here?' Bold. But she wanted him to understand that she knew he'll be off with the next girl anyhow and she would be, huh, so cool about it.

So can we, yes? Her eyes were locked onto his. Now! She laid her left hand out on her left knee, a fingernail's width from his own right hand on his right thigh. They both looked down. She slid her hand a fraction higher. Closer to those thighs. One movement, one more slight movement and... time stopped. Breathing stopped. He moved. Away from her and up.

What the hell? He was standing!

'This has been too nice but if you excuse me, I do have a few things to do tonight.'

'Sure!' she leapt up. I must be getting on as well. Lots to do when you're on holiday you know!

Outside in the lane, she paused for breath, swaying. She felt physically sick. And angry. The prick teaser, or whatever the reverse of that was.

'Pop a paper bag over your head if you feel like crying. Never fails.'

Val's bossy tones popped into her mind.

Already the image of his hand, lying there next to hers cold. That chilling silence. The thoughts that had raced through that silence. He didn't. That was the truth of it. Overriding everything that had gone before.

He could have.

She'd given him every opportunity.

And he didn't.

He didn't see her in that way.

Simple as that.

She'd been right all along.

# CHAPTER TWENTY-FOUR

Mature Sally could take it for what it had been. Lust. A crush. Through his rejection she'd come to terms with herself. She had to come to terms with herself.

Alone was good. Alone was fine. She wasn't stumped by any crazy relationship crisis any more than he was. Huh! She was a grown woman.

But as soon as she was outside her villa all sense evaporated. Silly Sally might bump into him. Every word, gesture, glance, look and touch they'd shared was taken apart, analysed and reassessed. The words that had been said. The words unsaid but heard loud and clear by her heart. The bemused tenderness, the smiles, the modesty. For all his surface arrogance, the quiet modesty beneath.

The longer she didn't see him, the more time she spent on preparing herself for when she might.

Every time she left the villa she rehearsed the right amount of friendliness, with a bit of supercool on the side – not superbitch smarm. An ordinary style another day, another person on the planet. Whatever. She wouldn't winge, or crack up and burst into uncontrollable tears if he was with a girl.

Normal wasn't normal any more. Every corner she turned, a buzz of excitement preceded her. At any moment he could be there, walking towards her.

Standing in a bar. Coming out of a shop.

Legit bumping into wasn't stalking. She kept her surprise 'hey! how's it going?' ready. But as her final days on the island came and went, she'd worn her flip flops to the ground pacing around every corner, into every shop and every bar on the island in a circuit of insane frenzy.

When he wasn't even at his weekly gig at the Sea Bar she became convinced it was all about her. He was hiding.

Every time she was about to step inside the Moonlight she felt dangerously alive. The idea that he could simply stride in at any time was better than being on a beach or alone at the villa.

The heat continued its grip and conversations were lazy like it was too hot to think of new things to say.

'What's it like here in the winter?'

'Quiet.' Charles put out a plate of oranges and biscuits.

'Is it dead, or do other things take over. Do the goats come down to the harbour? I imagine strange goings on.'

'It has its own patterns, yes. Elemental, yes – some people prefer it.'

'Does Loro still do his sets in the winter?'

'He stays in Athens.'

'Does he?'

'He has a little apartment I think.'

Ah so that's where he'd gone?

'So, the island boy persona is a game, for when he feels like it.'

'Coming and going, we all do it. This place thrives on it, how it survives. Always has been.'

Knowing everybody's else's business before they knew it themselves half the time wasn't, she knew, a phenomenon restricted to Hydra. It happened in all small communities, especially gossipy Greek ones, but the sensation of a network of invisible tentacles spookily going about their business became increasingly strong and strange. Liz, the jewellery shop woman and the other hippies told her it was the ley lines. Charles put it down to the lack of motorised transport, Graves the old poet to the island's many-headed Hydra namesake working behind the scenes. Barry said the passion for politics and gossip in all its forms was simply the definition of being Greek.

Barry was suspiciously quiet about her disastrous failure. He'd asked how it had gone without his usual prying curiosity, clearly knowing the answer before she gave it and commenting with little more than a shrug. He Knew.

The hours marched relentlessly forward. Sally's moment of departure like everything seemed to speed up and slow down at the same time. One moment she'd be flopping back into the ubiquitous inertia of the heatwave, the next she'd panic and snap back into phoning, texting and looking up websites for flights, boats and taxis. Checking and double checking herself, not trusting her sweaty old mind not to make a crashing mistake somewhere along the way.

She could bear it no longer and, on the night before her last day, confessed to Barry and Charles about her failure and frustration at the lack of closure.

'Forget about it,' said Barry.

'I've tried but I can't.'

'We're all going stir crazy now,' said Barry. 'Happens every year. All of us breathing in the same air we breathed out yesterday filled with other people's minds and all their numbers.'

'Yes, well it's driving me nuts.'

'Lovers are selfish,' sighed Charles lovingly unfolding the backgammon board.

'Yes, but they weren't,' said Barry.

'That's the point!' said Sally.

'All over before it started eh?' said Charles.

'Don't take it personally,' Barry said, shaking his head. 'Scared of emotion, that guy.'

'But I am taking it personally.'

'We're all other people at different times. Look at you. A singer here, a wife there. All roles we're actin out.'

'Is that why he's never bothered making it on his own?' said Sally. 'Is that why he's locked into this impersonation business.'

Barry shrugged his shoulders. 'Who's to know who's the dreamer or the dreaming?'

No way would she pursue him any further. Or go out of her way to see him.

## CHAPTER TWENTY-FIVE

Sally waited next to a short row of steps cut into a wall. The straps of her bag, heavy with stake-out rations of water and fruit, dug into her shoulder.

Half an hour later she spotted him, ambling up the hill in that relaxed self-possessed way of his that made solitariness look enviable. Enviable in the way highly desirable men so often managed.

She darted up the steps and flattened herself behind a bougainvillea bush. Her heart thumped in a racing, counterpoint off-beat to the steady flip and flop of his black Havaianas getting closer and closer. She flattened herself into the wall until the stones dug into her back.

He reached his door. Through the petals, Sally watched him digging into his front jeans pocket for his keys. For a happy moment, she got a good, concentrated, uninterrupted look at the curve of faded denim against thigh before the door opened, closed and he was gone.

Five minutes later she splashed her neck and throat with water, crossed the alley, rapped hard on the door and waited.

And waited.

A pair of builder's donkeys clopped past weighed down by towers of dusty white sacks of cement. They were followed by a group of tourists, all chattering together on their way down to the sea. The innocent, happy holiday laughter and the ringing silence that followed fed her paranoia, turning negative thoughts to fact by the second.

Here was the proof. He'd been avoiding her for days and now he was hiding from her as well. She held her ear to the door. With no warning of approach, metal scraped against metal right next to her ear. She leapt backwards. A bolt was pulled and there he was, holding the door wide open for her like he'd been standing right behind it, waiting.

He didn't look annoyed, pleased or even surprised.

Sally squealed a greeting in high octave surprise, like she'd only been passing, feeling as ambiguous as his unreadable expression implied.

Occupational hazard she thought haughtily as she stepped out of the blazing heat into his cool, dark kitchen. Probably gets scorned women knocking on his door all the time.

'I hope you don't mind me popping by, it's just that I haven't seen you around lately,' she said breezily, hearing, with horror, Val's accusatory tone she often got if she ever dared skip a muffin morning. 'I'm leaving tomorrow and ... and, I wondered if I could take a copy of that song with me?'

'Song?'

'The one, you know, that you played to me,' she said sulkily in a scorned woman tone that came out all on its own. She might as well have added ON your balcony, AT sunset with wine AND ALL THE SIGNALS before you REJECTED me. Ruining my confidence forever and banishing me to a life of woolly, cardigany celibacy.

'Look,' she took her bag off her shoulder and let it drop heavily onto the white-tiled floor beside the stairs. 'I have a contacts book Simon Cowell would kill for. You might as well make something of it.'

He stared fixedly at her bag as if she'd announced she was moving in.

'You don't have to do anything.'

No response.

'There's no need for you to travel London or anything like that.'

The fridge hummed noisily.

Slowly shaking his head, he finally looked up.

'To be blunt, Loro, I think you really have something,' Sally persisted. 'Star quality if you like. You have the charisma to make young girls fall for you and bags of old bones like me – well – um and a brilliant song. No hooks. Honest.'

'Thank you but enough people hear me here I think.'

'But there could be so many more! Think of it as your pension if nothing else. All this – tribute act work is fine for now but think ten, twenty years' time. What then?'

'I don't think about tomorrow any more than I think about yesterday.'

'I'm not offering this blind, Loro. I'm not some kind of – starstruck nut putting it up on the internet and waiting for millions of hits. I can cut through all that social networking chancing.'

'Who you know is not my business. Here, right here, this is enough.'

'Churning out Leonard Cohen songs ad infinitum ad infinitum?'

'They're special songs.'

'But you're special! Why be a shadow of someone else?'

'You people all you think of is to make cash cash cash.'

'That isn't what I meant at all!' Sally said, horrified. 'This is about you. No, not even you. The song!'

'You know as well as I do what it's all about...'

'That song is alive. It's a living thing! It deserves a life of its own.'

'The music becomes the smallest part of it. You have to be on the radio, the TV. It's an industry. Websites, blogs, movies, toys and all that is for to pay your tax bill! It's not worth it, Sally. None of it.'

'But you're too good, way too good to be a clone. That song is so, so special, Loro.'

'It's here, always here,' he put a big, hairy hand on his chest and spread his arm dramatically wide in a way only a Mediterranean man could get away with. 'Out there it lasts – how long? You tell me. 3 months?'

'Um a bit less than that, but there's the spin-offs, covers, car ads, and comebacks don't forget the come backs.'

'Spin offs,' he spat. 'I live for music, it doesn't make its living off me. Real music is the truth. That means it is in now. Always. There, gone.'

'Like all the girls you mean.'

He rubbed the back of his neck with the palm of his hand and looked at her with a pained, sleepy expression. 'Like everything.'

Sally noticed the stain of sweat on his T-shirt. Resisting the magnetic pull that made her want to fling herself into his arms and breathe in that liquoricy musky smell of him, she picked up her bag and hoiked it huffily onto her shoulder.

'I don't need it, Sally,' he moved with her towards the door. 'But thank you for thinking of me. It's sweet.'

'Sweet!' she turned on him. 'You know something? There was me, arguing on your behalf but now – now I realise what Ami said about you is so true.'

His eyes narrowed in readiness, like he'd heard it all before.

'You're a coward. You always have to leave the girls before they leave you don't you. Here it's so safe for you isn't it. Because everybody leaves.'

'You know nothing about me.'

'Huh! Enough, I think…'

'Thank you for coming but I don't need your judgement or your help right now.'

'Fine! See if I care.' She turned away but turned back again. 'I'm talking as a fan, that's all, nothing more. One day you've got to stop your, your – stupid act and let your own music sing.'

His face reddened, 'Stupid!'

'Sorry, I didn't mean, you know what I'm saying and you know it too. That song...'

'It's got a very good life. But thank you,' he said stiffly, patting her on the small of the back.

The voltage from his touch ran right through her body.

'I mean in a bigger way,' she said flatly. Inside the force field now, she struggled to keep breathing. She gave in and threw herself towards him but, at the same time, forced herself backwards, ending with an arm awkwardly lifted to his shoulders as if she was about to lead him away behind her like a donkey. Thinking fast, she gathered herself, stood on her toes and pecked him on the cheek. 'I'm sorry. I'll get out of your way now.'

But for all her actions and words, hope's irrational takeover of her senses never faltered. She made for the door, insanely waiting to hear him protest, beg, plead, indicate, hint, that she stayed a while.

'So long, Sally. Have a good journey home.'

Her heart dropped. She flung open the door and stepped outside into the furnace of the mid-day sun. The door was about to close behind her. There was nothing left to lose.

'Look,' she said, 'there is one thing before I go, can I ask you one straight question?'

'Sure,' he said dubiously.

'When we were on the terrace, I know I invited myself, but – why did you hold back on me? For future reference, you know. Life flows for you in a beautiful way I can see that, I'm another passer-by, but for me well – you see my courage has all gone now, I know I'm not some saffy kid looking for holiday romance, but, well, we seemed to get on so, well – well!'

'We did!' he agreed readily.

'So why – '

He touched his finger lightly over her lip, 'I'm a Greek man Sally.'

'Don't I know it! But half Greek, no?'

'That Barry tells you everything,' he said a little more warmly, raising the devil of hope again. 'Yes we know beauty more than other men. We love to love, maybe too many of us have secret lovers if we are married, or many lovers if we are not, but as much as we love the women, we Greeks love the gossip. We can't stop ourselves talking even if we wanted to, it's why Barry is so at home here. News travels fast, we have our rules to live by this as well. Don't look so sad, you see what I'm saying, no?'

Sweat trickled down the back of her neck, 'No!'

'I like you, you know that.'

Her throat dried. She struggled to get the words out, 'I like you, um as well! I think you know that too.' She looked up at him, giving him one last option for a kiss but saw only a sad distant look, waiting for her to leave.

'So why did you reject me?' she blurted.

He looked down to her hips.

'Your husband may be far away.'

Sally concurred.

The lost little boy oozed out of the sad, black pools of his concerned stare. Fat hips. That's what had stopped him, she thought miserably.

'But from England, even America, planes are very quick these days.'

He looked back down again. Sally followed his gaze. He wasn't looking at her hips at all but at left hand. At the third finger of her left hand.

'But!'

'No buts. Never, never any buts. In Greece if honour among men is lost the whole world is lost. Small islands have no fences.'

'But he's…' Her words faded away. The desire to kick that little gossipy tyke of a Barry right where it hurt dissolved into an inner glow of peace and equilibrium. 'That's true. Honour is important. I respect your respect. Bye now and good luck.'

Knowing his eyes were still on her, she strolled away

triumphantly down the hill, keeping her pace relaxed and easy-going. But as soon as she turned the corner she punched her fist in the air.

'Yessssss!'

Not noticing the heat, she bounded up the lane to her villa, grinning broadly at the simplicity of it.

Short of materialising in front of her and punching Loro in the face, Dom couldn't have been more present. When she pictured Dom in one of his belligerent, indignant, furious, hopping mad strops, she had to stop, throw back her head and laugh out loud. From the shade of an open window, a black widow stared at her as if she were mad. Sally beamed right at her and carried on smiling inside like she hadn't smiled inside for well over a year, secure in the knowledge that Dom's love for her was more solid than anything the world in front of her nose could throw up.

The ground that had dropped from beneath her feet so long ago felt like it had lodged itself squarely back into place.

Love really didn't die. He'd been with her all along.

## CHAPTER TWENTY-SIX

Humming quietly, Sally replaced the ugly South American crucifixes and ornaments she'd hidden away with as much love as if she were arranging her new home.

Of course she was still Dom's wife! She wiped the dust off a pointless miniature beer barrel. Like she'd always be Ami and Nick's mum.

Forever really was for ever.

As she disentangled her little piles of possessions room by room, humming quietly to herself, the alien feeling of contentment continued to grow.

When she was settled into wherever she'd be and it had been cold and raining for weeks on end she'd miss all of this. The to-ing and fro-ing, tides in and out. Riding the tides, that was the trick, catch a wave and ride it, effortlessly. Hydra was good for holidays, but give her the soft wisterias, blossoms, lilacs, brown rivers and damp, green grass over the relentless burn of the sun and the bright, still orchards any day.

Waterstones, she thought piling up the paperbacks to give to the bookshop on her way down to the ferry. The Sunday Times. Tea, crumpets and the telly – property shows, dating shows, trashy reality shows. Cool, leafy streets. Rain. Autumn! Bonfires. Cheese and pickle sandwiches and rainstorms. Rustling riverside trees and

Marks and Spencers Food Hall. Winter! Dave at the greengrocer's. Wind. French wine. Sandy's smoked salmon. Val. Filling Ramone in on her near-miss adventures. Moving to the perfect cottage. There was no better place for her than genteel suburbia, and no finer man to have married than Dom.

Life without Dom was still difficult to accept a lot of the time, but there had been whole chunks of time there, even a couple of moments when she had woken up in the morning and her first thought hadn't been where was he.

That evening Sally gave the Moonlight a miss in favour of an early night. She hated goodbyes, especially multiple ones, and the last thing she wanted now was to bump into Loro and lose all her hard-won dignity. Barry and Charles were used to it. They were almost Greek she told herself, the way their 'friends' arrived and left all over the place. Maybe she'd pop in for breakfast if she had time, she thought, knowing she really, really wouldn't.

When the sun had lost its force and the molten violets, lilacs and greys streaked in the promise of evening she took a simple supper of bread, olives, tzatziki and wine out for her last night under the real moonlight and fired up the laptop.

Not much had changed on propertyfinder.com but when she widened the search from a five-mile radius of Strawberry Hill to fifteen, a terrace with a big, airy bathroom and open fires minutes from M&S Food popped up followed by a detached 1750s cottage with wobbly whitewashed walls, tiny sash windows and thatch eyebrows with a garden that looked like it should be in wildest Devon rather than a 25 minute drive from Bushwood Avenue. If only she could move the fireplaces and M&S from the first house, but then the cottage wasn't that far out. Off the beaten track but only minutes from the station. She could keep up with Val and the neighbours at a safe distance. Even allowing for estate-agent-speak, trains to Waterloo, over the bridge from Ramone's flat, took 30 minutes – less than Strawberry Hill. Oh yes, get in.

She wanted that garden. Not as a retreat from the world but as her world. A place of wisteria, lilac and blossom in the spring, of sweet peas, nicotiana and roses in the summer. She'd put in a garden swing seat like Loro's and a marble round table. Not for big, hang out parties. She'd have small cosy dinners out there with incense and tea lights in jars hanging from that apple tree. There'd be good wine and good friends. She'd cook for friends again and there'd be a spare bedroom for Ami & Pete, or Nick & whoever, and Val and Tony, and Ramone. Even Barry and Charles, why not?

She thought about this. The image of them anywhere but Greece was even more bizarre than the idea of Loro off the island. Like Metaxa, they wouldn't travel well. Some people and things only worked in their own place, maybe because they had a place. So no, they could stay here. There'd be the occasional weekend away for her, and sometimes a week here on Hydra, right here on her terrace why not.

Resisting the urge to offer the full price there and then, she emailed a query to the agent, checked CheepyGreeky Airlines was still in business, emailed her schedule to Ami, poured another glass of wine and clicked through to Listen Again on Nick's new show.

*Evening, evening, happy Saturday night. Nicky Lightfoot here with Saturday Night, Sunday Morning.*

*Kirsty: Hi Nicky, how's it going?*

*Man what a busy week. Hi everyone, Nicky Lightfoot here with some more great music for you.*

*And how's it going with the Rihanna lookalike?*

*Nick: We're doing something a little different this week, Kirsty, I got a little announcement to make.*

'Oh no,' Sally popped an olive in her mouth. She hated people who announced they had an announcement and left a gap. Without leaving a gap was bad enough. Why didn't they simply come out with it? She sat through two back to back Panic at the Disco tracks before he built up to it all again.

*Kirsty: Come on Nicky, out with it.*

*Nick: This is it Kirsty, this will be my last show.*

*Kirsty: No! You can't go!*

'You tell him, Kirsty! You're getting settled and sounding so good and normal. She rolled her eyes and sighed the 'huh-our-kids-eh' sigh she used to share with Dom.

*Nick: But there's a story behind it.*

*Kirsty: There's a story behind everything.*

*Dramatic silence.*

*Nick: I been dating a while now, met some pretty girls, funny girls, sexy girls, bare beautiful girls. I said I got the best job in radio because there are so many girls out there, but here's my last dedication and I'm playin this for one girl only, my real special woman.*

*A giggle from Kirsty.*

'Not the music again!' Sally shouted at the laptop. She

hit fast-forward on the digital counter.

Was it the Rhianna Girl from last week, or had there been someone real behind it all? Kirsty. Was it Kirsty? She sounded all right. Too old, too like a sensible weather reading lady. Why don't you tell me anything, Nick, Why?

What could she have done to have made him turn out any differently?

It had never been easy for Nick. Dom had been a force of nature whilst she'd been bending backwards, sideways and every other way holding the whole bloody lot together. Their life together had been a success but a success she'd worked her guts out for. She was so busy keeping the show on the road right down to watching what Dom ate, how much he drank. If Dom was happy everyone else was happy, that's how it had been. When he sank into one of his moods, the house was black for days.

Singing had been her lifeline. The rock and roll lifestyle was nothing but embarrassing to Ami and her natural aloofness kept her sane. But Nick swam right in there and tried to play along.

If Dom wasn't fretting about money he kept his head down, working hard, not noticing Nick as much as he should have. The bands loved him, but joked too much sometimes at his attempts to be one of them. When a project was on it wasn't allowed to fail. When things had got really important was when Nick got sent away.

Who wouldn't turn to drugs? Why hadn't she realised emotional support was so much more important than independence?

*My woman of the day, of the year, my woman forever,*

*is Sally. My mum. Hello mum! This one's for you, from the coolest man on the planet, Leonard Cohen.*

Oh Nick! Sweet darling Nick. Her delight was short-lived, replaced by suspicion.

So! Ami and Nick were talking. But about her. What, exactly, had Ami told him? How much had Ami known about her stupid crush? Was this Nick and Ami's way of telling her it was all right for her to move on to another man?

She tried to concentrate on the dark whispery voice of the real Leonard Cohen singing *Hey, That's No Way To Say Goodbye* but it was no good. She thought of Loro, who, this minute, was moments away down at the bar. Should she go down and say a civilised goodbye?

*'If you don't mind me saying, you were an embarrassment to her, Sal. With that bloke, you and your guitarist fetish.'*

'Hmm, well you stopped anything happening there didn't you.'

*'Why's Nick leaving the show? He sounded so sorted there. Off the drugs, enjoying himself.'*

'I'll call him in a minute.'

*'Had to be too good to be true didn't it, had to be.'*

'At least Ami's future's shaping up, you're pleased about that aren't you?'

*'Pete?'* Dom said with the despair he'd always used whenever his name came up, but Sally detected a new resignation in his voice.

'You're happy for her aren't you?'

*'Yeah, Pete's not so bad, made my peace there. Her future's as steady as it can be these days. Charities aren't going to stop employing people, especially when*

*he's so experienced.'*

'She's got a good job of her own!'

*'Yes but when kids come along...'*

'Our grandkids you mean? Our grandkids!'

*'Maybe a bit more walking on the wild side wouldn't have done her harm though, Sal.'*

Was she mad spending her last night alone?

*'Oi you!'*

'What?'

*'Get those filthy thoughts out of your head, woman.'*

Sally lay back and looked up at the stars. There. She was feeling guilty now about upsetting Dom with her thoughts. How people ever had affairs she never knew. How had he... no. Don't go there. All marriages went through difficult times. Patches, they were called. It had been a patch. That's all.

What else had Ami guessed?

*'Ami's got her secrets too.'*

'So you do know what I'm thinking?' she said to the sky.

*'Maybe she set you up with that bloke.'*

'You reckon?'

*'Get it out of your system. She didn't fancy him did she. Way too old for her taste.'*

'And she had Pete.'

*'And you got me. I'm your man and don't you forget it.'*

'I won't. Dom. DOM! Don't go!'

She climbed into bed with her laptop, Tweeted Nick to give her a call and Google-earthed Shepperton. Swooping in and out until she found the cottage and set to examining the neighbours' gardens.

# CHAPTER TWENTY-SEVEN

Sally got up early and ate her final yoghurt and fresh fig breakfast on the terrace, etching the curve of the bay into her memory. In only a few hours she'd be through that horizon and out of the heat into the land of rain, soft rustling leaves and freshly mown summer lawns.

She was ready for it. Ready to go back to where she belonged. Not as an unhappy dieter clinging to her dying girldom, but as a rounded, middle-aged woman with a so-what middle.

She was fine about that and everything was well. She studied the ant-sized boats and tiny buildings no bigger than a thumbnail hiding the labyrinths of life.

The stillness of distance blew her away. Beneath it somewhere all the shopkeepers and artists, potters, tourists and old Greek locals were loving, fighting, laughing, dozing. Nutty Sumo, gossipy Barry, pristine Charles, Liz the hippy, Graves the old poet, the hairy harbourmaster, the hungry cats, the skanky dogs and the poor old hardworking, resigned donkeys. The spunky harbour boys, the fishermen bashing their squid, the kidnapping, toothless boatman and Spikey with his surprising bursts of friendliness. The cooks, the tourists – the black widows. So dignified in their graceful acceptance and sturdy inner power. No stressing on step machines or snipping off spot hairs for them.

And Him. Was he down there too? Or in his villa across the hill?

She took the last bag of rubbish out, sucking her teeth into a squeak for the cats skulking around the bins. For the first time, one of them came almost within touching distance.

'Typical,' she thought, closing the door on them for the last time.

Though she was looking forward to getting out of the heat, she'd miss the villa. Her villa. Still, they all had it coming sooner or later, she thought setting to with a last-minute tidy-round. Did they know it all ended like this for everybody?

Maybe not? This was, after all, a place of coming and going that had no farewells.

Feeling fidgety, she counted the cutlery, fluffed up the cushions and checked her travel documents yet again.

After putting Iron Maiden on at full blast, she set to ironing her travelling clothes. Not much longer she told herself.

She was bringing the villa's ancient steam iron down hard on her khaki shorts when Nick finally returned her call.

'What's this about giving up the show?' The iron hissed as she returned it to its stand.

'What's that noise, are you all right?'

'It's the iron.'

'Oh, so you listened? I thought you were still in Greece?'

'There is internet here.'

'Sick! How did it sound?'

'Great. But what happened, what's going on?'

'Nothing's going on.'

Sally glared at the ceiling, 'With the show?'

'All cool.'

'You said it was your last one.'

'Oh right that, I got a new gig.'

'Where!'

'I'm on the shortlist for the Power CNB night flight show. How sick is that?'

'Shortlist?'

'Down to me and another guy.'

'So you haven't, exactly, got it yet?'

'If I hadn't would I be talking about it on air?'

Yes, was the short answer to that. 'What's wrong with the show you've got? It was all going so well.'

'I'm quitting while I'm ahead.'

'Why!'

'Because that's what you do, mum. You got to keep with the speed. If you're not ahead you're dead.'

'You're so right,' Sally smiled, glad she'd resisted going down to the bar and ruining her elegant farewell with Loro.

'Muum?'

'What?'

'What with me coming to London and all?'

'London?'

'Power's a London station mum.'

'And?'

'And I was thinking like I could move back in.'

Sally balked. 'With me?'

'Yeah!'

Nick at home again? Friends, music, smelly socks, washing, meals. Big shoes in the hall. Wet towels on the bathroom floor. Doors slamming. Girlfriends. Laughter. Hugs.

'In our house?'

'Um yeah?'

'But the house is sold, Nick. you know that.'

'Yeah but they're mucking you about right?'

'A bit.'

'Tell them you're not selling after all.'

'I can't do that!'

'Why not? It's not like you're turfing them onto the street, they'll buy somewhere else.'

'That's not the point.'

'Your life's more important than theirs.'

'You mean your life. No, sorry that's not fair but neither is gazumping. I've had enough bad karma lately without adding to my quota.'

'I'll give you rent and everything. You can forget about moving.'

Sally let the idea float for a moment.

'Good plan yeah?' Nick jumped in as if her pause had decided it.

'No! You're asking me to get rid of a buyer for a job you haven't even got yet. I'm sorry, Nick, but there's no way. Your room's there as long as I am but if the sale goes it goes. Now I've really got to get on. I'm leaving in a few hours and I'm still packing here.'

'But...'

'Let me find out what's going on with the buyers. Oh bugger there's the bell, the cleaner's arrived early. Listen, I'll call you, Tweet you soon as I'm home I promise.'

'Kay...'

She clicked the phone off. With the sound of 'Kay' ringing in her ears she turned the music up.

'Oh Nick Nick NICK!'

It got her every time. The I'm disappointed with you mummy 'Kay.' Like he was six years old again. Did your kids ever stop being your responsibility?

'Poor Nick' had been a refrain all through his childhood.

Even if she was the gazumping sort, no way could she keep the house on such a tentative basis. There were too many things that could and probably would go wrong especially where Nick was concerned. There'd been no emails in from her selling agent since she'd been away. The buyers weren't pushing to complete which suited her fine. She'd childishly half been hoping the situation would go on forever and she could carry on in her home safe in the knowledge that money was on its way but not quite yet. But that was before Farthing Cottage. She couldn't afford to lose her buyers now. That was for the best. Wasn't it? Oh Dom! What am I doing? This is all your fault. Or am I as much to blame as you?

The bell rang again. Sally frowned at her watch. The cleaner was way early.

In the push and the pull of it all, maybe this is the time Nick needs me more than ever? Isn't this my chance to feed him up and make sure he's off the spiral?

Silence.

Dom's voice was nowhere in her head. Instead the cloying, chilling fear of being swamped by her own mother's neediness engulfed her. Supposing something happened to him down the line because she'd turned him away? She'd never, ever get over that.

The song ended.

The ringing was now one, angry and persistent note.

'All RIGHT!' she balanced the iron on its stand and went downstairs.

Holiday over, she thought grumpily. The outside world and all its problems squarely on top again. Feeling the same self-righteous anger she'd felt with Spikey on her first day on the island, she smoothed her hair down and opened the door.

Dark accusing eyes bored into her, 'So, you are here?'

She was given such a start she instantly jumped to the conclusion that Loro's family must have some stake in the villa and he'd come to do the cleaning.

'Where were you?' he demanded.

'What do you mean?'

'Where were you?' he raised his voice.

She recognised the restlessness in him. Whatever had compelled her to pound the alleyways looking for him – he had it too. She wanted to fling the door open and get him upstairs. But this was a dance. She wasn't throwing her cards away so easily again.

'When?' she said innocently.

'Last night!' his voice went higher.

'Here, where else?'

'It was your last night!' he squealed indignantly.

'I know!' Was this happening? After all that fruitless stalking that had taken up days of her holiday, here he was on her doorstep saying he'd been looking for her? 'But we didn't make any...'

'But you're always there! Every night you are there!'

The cheek of him! Sally continued with her calm, blank stare, doing a quick mental check on what he was seeing. Not bad for caught off-guard. The best she'd looked for ages even. Fresh and showered and her tan set off by her white kaftan which covered everything nicely, though she was still naked underneath. Oh heck, it wasn't see-through was it?

'Anyway, you weren't so...' He held his hand out sheepishly. 'Here you are.'

'Oh,' she smiled. So that was it. He'd decided he wanted to be a star after all. 'Thanks.'

She took the CD case and turned it over. 'Nice photo!' she murmured, hugging herself inside at the thought of showing Ramone what she'd nearly pulled. 'I'll see what I can do with it.'

He swallowed and looked at her expectantly. 'I missed you.'

'You want to come in a moment?' she said, feeling strangely Nicole Kidmanish.

He shrugged, looked away and looked back. 'Sure.'

'Hey! This is really good artwork. Very professional,' she said looking at the cover as they went up the stairs. 'Hang on a minute.' She stopped in her tracks.

'Ooof.' He crashed into the back of her.

'But this is a release!' she said.

'I know that.'

'But?'

She felt a hand slip around her waist and spin her round to face him.

'That feels nice,' she breathed, barely able to speak.

'Are you going to offer me a drink?' he rested his knuckles lightly on one cheek. 'And I'll tell you all about it.'

'I have to be out of here at noon.'

263

'Noon Greek time,' he said following her out onto the terrace.

The mid-morning sun beat down but a welcome soft sea breeze rippled pleasingly through her kaftan. Feeling like Kate Winslet now, she put his CD on her laptop and poured them shots of Metaxa from the owner's cabinet.

After chinking glasses she stood well back. Sally's body was in orbit, every nerve tingling with expectation. There'd been more than contact but she wasn't going to give herself the slightest chance of reading this wrong a second time.  At the same time the cosy feeling inside told her, with no deceptions or fantasies or lies to herself, that – yeuupp, it was only a matter of time now.

They stood side by side at the railings, self-consciously studying the view. 'Where did this breeze come from? Does this mean it's the end of the heatwave? Look, even the heat haze has gone from the horizon! What timing is that, as I'm leaving!' Kate Winslet had deserted her. She was waffling on in a cod Shakespearean way unable to stop until he reminded her that she was supposed to be listening to his song.

She stopped talking and looked to the ground in an amateur dramatic pose of concentration, recognising the song but only just. Annoyingly, the backing vocals were brilliant. Completely professional and as good, if not better, than her own. Her imagination ran away with her into pictures of countless other singers passing through the island. One by one joining him on stage and, later, to that terrace and his bed.

'Really well produced,' she said, going to the table and

picking up the cover again.

'And the song?' He stayed where he was.

'You know I love the song. And, as I said, I'll give it to some people I know...'

'That's not why I came, Sally.'

'It's what I want to do, for you, like I said, no strings.'

'And like I said...'

'No no, I want to.'

'Listen to me. The song was already a hit, Sally, it's had its life. A big one.'

Sally blanched. 'It can't have done.'

'It was in the charts for nine weeks.'

'No no, I'd have heard it.'

'The Billboard charts.'

'What?' Sally half sank to the floor. She picked up the cover again. 'In America?'

'It reached number two.'

'Number two?' Sally took out the sleeve and pretended to read. Without her glasses she couldn't make out any of it but recognised the record company logo. 'Barry didn't tell me that!'

'You know he hates the numbers. And even Barry knows to keep his mouth closed with the tourists about some things.'

Sally smarted, illogically annoyed at the label. 'No wonder!'

'No wonder what?'

'Oh, nothing.' She wasn't going to feed his ego any more morsels but that did explain the magical Keith Richards-like untouchable bombshell feel about him.

'You're teasing me now,' he said moving towards her.

'It didn't all come from the spirit of Leonard Cohen's

songs that's all.'

He took a lock of her hair and tucked it behind her ear, 'How did you think I live like I do, singing in a bar a few nights a week?'

'Inheriting your parents' house must help but, but that doesn't…' her voice faded away.

'Who told you that?' he demanded angrily, stepping away from her.

'Who do you think?'

'You should be old enough to know gossipy old queens believe their own stories a long time before they settle for the boring truth.'

'What's wrong with inheriting!' she said, moving towards him but going right past him to the railings. 'Simply bloody good luck, surely. Look, you can nearly see your place from here if you crick your neck right out.'

'Hey be careful,' he said leaping towards her, 'You might fall.'

'I already have,' she turned and looked up at him. He took hold of her hands.

'I'm still confused. How come we didn't hear you in the UK?' she said, determined not to get it wrong. There was still the possibility that he might be being over-friendly.

'I wouldn't let it.'

'But…'

'This was before the web. My father was a lawyer?'

'Barry told me.'

'He could stop Niagara Falls with his little finger if he felt like it.'

'So we're talking about – when exactly?'

'1986. I was living in Sacramento with my father.'

The way he said Sacramento went right through her. As if in direct response he put one hand on her waist and pulled her closer.

'Until he died. I hated, hated it all. I'm only glad Kylie kept me away from the number one. It would have been even harder to run from.'

'We spent our entire lives chasing the number one spot,' Sally said wistfully. 'And now we're there, my husband is dead and there are no royalties.'

'I'm sorry,' he held her close. 'But Barry only told me last night. He said before your husband was in America.'

'You asked him?' she said, feeling ridiculously flattered, then confused. 'But he knew the truth!'

'But why didn't you tell *me*?'

'The subject never came up. Besides, your interest lay elsewhere, remember.'

He shrugged, 'Only at first.'

'I lied to Barry and Charles originally. A stupid little lie, not even a white lie, a full-on blatant untruth.'

'But why to *Barry*? You thought he was after you?'

'No no no! I came here to get away. To get away from how people see me as much as anything. So that I could begin to see myself. Does that make any sense?'

'Yes. It's your way of being free,' he ran his hand across her back.

'Now you tell me. Why did you let me go on about that track when it was already out there in the world.'

She felt every bone in his body stiffen. 'What I hate, hate is this business talk.'

'Only because you don't have to worry about that side

of things!'

He let go of her. 'Songs come from the centre of your being, Sally,' he began pacing up and down the terrace, waving his arms around in his Greek way. 'Fame is the opposite. A mask to cover your real self. Your being. When it becomes your own face you are lost.'

'It's a lot of pressure I know.'

'When you are alive in normal life it's only a thin mask – we all have it of course, but out there it becomes too much. Strangers, people you don't know, they know who you are. At first it's funny, OK, but they want to possess you, they want more and more until they take control of the mask.'

'I'm sorry.'

'Even your friends,' he laughed sardonically.

Sally was genuinely puzzled for a moment. 'But you don't know my friends?'

'They are the worst!' he continued as if he hadn't heard her. 'Who you think are your friends. You have to figure out which are real. Evil thoughts take your mind and you don't know any more. You don't know. Therapy put me right. Almost.'

'That's what it is about you. You still have that running away feeling.'

'I learnt how to survive. In the moment anyhow.'

'This moment's pretty special,' she said.

'It is.' He stopped pacing and smiled at her. All the tension seemed to drain out of him.

The distance between them felt unnatural but she held her ground.

'You didn't have enough esteem to think I liked you for yourself,' he said softly.

'I knew it!' she laughed.

'It's how I felt when the song took off. A deep feeling of undeserved success. A sense I'd be found out.'

'Paranoia?'

'Paranoia.'

He shrugged. It was such a shrug she parted her lips slightly and knew all she had to do now was wait. He came to her, touched her waist lightly and turned his head sideways and down.

'Oh no!' she leapt up.

'I've – er left the iron on.' She raced to the stairs. 'Don't move! Whatever you do STAY THERE!'

'OK.'

She switched off the iron, darted into the bedroom, pulled on her pants from the travelling pile, ran to the door, stopped, ran back to the bed and undid her suitcase.

She grabbed her toiletries bag. Posh pong or cheap French supermarket cologne? The cologne had always done it for Dom but – no. She sprayed her neck with the smallest hint of the Ormonde Jayne Champaca Ami had given her for Mother's Day. She took three deep breaths and went slowly up the stairs, wafting onto the balcony in a distinct but light cloud of freesia, green tea and musk.

He was seated at the table. She picked up her glass and sat next to him.

There was no mistaking the look in his eyes now. She felt his touch on her skin. They shared a shruggish, wistful smile. He tipped his head sideways and leant down to her. She softened and leant towards him, but he snapped back like he'd been caught nicking the sweets.

'What?'

'Your bell.'

Sally heard a persistent ringing.

'Let it ring!' she said, but the moment had gone.

'Sometimes the Gods still speak here,' he said, shrugging and making to move. Cursing to herself, she followed him down the stairs.

'You'll come back soon, yes?'

'I know I will.'

'We must have some time, some proper time to be together.' He pulled her towards him on the stairs. Their lips touched. A key rattled in the lock. They jumped apart. In the doorway, a tiny but sturdy old woman stood, stock still, gawping up at them.

'Hey you. You're early EARL – E,' Sally yelled, tapping at her watch.

The black widow said something angry in Greek to Loro came inside and slammed the door with a loud thud behind her.

'Get on with it, won't you ask?' Sally said.

'I'll go now.' Loro looked at Sally with a resignation that said don't even begin to try arguing with this woman. The woman turned her mouth down at him with a superior, suburban disgust. She had a sleeping eye, Sally noticed, that made it look like she was permanently winking.

Sally was furious. Furious that the widow's sneering had no foundations. Furious at her helpless foreigner status.

Loro said something to her in Greek. They both waited until she turned her back to them, foraging in the utility cupboard.

He leant forward and kissed her again, just long enough for her to get a hint of exactly what she'd be missing.

'Soon, yes?' he said, stepping out of the door.

'It had better be or you'll be shacked up with a permanent lover and a tribe of black eyed, straggly-haired gypsy children.' She forced a smile before closing the door on him.

'So,' she yelled to the sound of vacuuming up the stairs. 'It's you and me.'

The vacuum roared and doors banged. There was a finality to the sound she couldn't bear now. The Villa Lobos was being prepared for the next visitors. It wasn't hers any more. The sound was hateful and everything was unbearable. She flew upstairs and switched the vacuum off at the mains.

Not realising what had happened at first, the widow clucked and fiddled with the switch before turning round. Seeing Sally, she set her wrinkled old jaw tight and straightened up.

'I have this house until midday!' Sally yelled, 'I have THINGS TO DO, I have IMPORTANT THINGS TO DO. Clean if you want,' Sally mimed cleaning movements. 'Do your scrubbing but no vacuuming. Not until after midday.'

She unplugged the cable. The cord whipped across the rug and vanished with a noisy clunk into its little hole.

The widow looked down then up at Sally, her winking face stiff in amazement for a second before letting off a torrent of Greek at her.

Sally grabbed the bottom of the Hoover before the

woman could retrieve the plug.

With a terrifying, shrieking scream the widow held firmly onto the handle, pulling the vacuum back and dragging Sally with it.

Digging her heels into the terracotta tiles, Sally gave an almighty jerk and tumbled backwards in a puff of dust. She and the widow stared in astonishment at each other before Sally turned and, hugging the vacuum to her chest, raced onto the terrace calling back, 'you clean, you polish, OK! Check for missing teaspoons, do what you want but this time is MINE!' She hid the Hoover under the table.

The front door slammed.

She poured the rest of his brandy into her glass and knocked it back in one.

That was that.

That was fucking fuck fuck that.

What did the world have in store for her now?

For him now it was easy.

Some woman, or girl more likely, was out there, obliviously living her life somewhere, laughing with friends, having 'fun' lots of 'fun' probably. They'd meet, randomly in some bar no doubt, and she'd have his next kiss. And there was another one somewhere else on the planet who'd fall heavily in love, as he would with her, and she'd have his kids one day when.

It was so likely that's what was so sad about it all.

And bloody unfair! Why did life hold such promise for him and not for her when they were the same age?

Yet, as much as she hated the idea of the next woman who'd get him at the same time, for his sakes, she hoped that, whoever she was, she would. For a man like that not to have children would be sad.

She had to accept the facts. His future was filled with unknown opportunities around every corner whilst the rest of hers yawned like a void to be filled with vegetable plots and the Archers Sunday omnibus. That or a series of disastrous internet dates appeared to be her only choice. Men might die sooner but they lived so much longer.

## CHAPTER TWENTY-EIGHT

'I hope you enjoy your stay,' said Spikey hanging the keys on a hook behind the bar. 'Please, take a seat, one last drink from us here for you. Is all right you come back to the Villa Lobos some day, I know it,' he said, not looking at her as he banged the now familiar ramekin of garlicky green olives onto a silver tray.

'And I'll shout and fight and demand heaters,' Sally said, trying not to sound quivery.

'You want heater now?' he chuckled, holding his arm high as he poured a large slosh of Ouzo into a glass.

She sat outside, facing the ferry terminus. The full glare of the sun was tempered by a soft, light breeze coming in off the sea.

She popped an olive in her mouth, clouded the alcohol with a touch of water and sipped. The garlicky taste of the olive mingling with the iced aniseed refreshed and comforted at the same time.

Tourists jostled for their places in the queue for a ship that hadn't arrived yet. Glad of the laid-back attitude she'd picked up from the locals, Sally felt like she belonged. Well, she wouldn't be a Hydra hippie for much longer she thought, admiring the contrast of her turquoise bangles against her brown wrists. That tan would be gone next week, the painted toes would be put away for another year along with the sandals, and soon enough her freefall knots of hair would be moussed into order by Trish of Twickenham Headmasters. Once she'd faded back into the grey of London, she'd be queuing for ships with the best of them.

She tried to keep positive. Like the hours that were ticking seriously down now to that cheese and pickle Mother's Pride sandwich. Ambling in soft, Surrey woodlands. Lakes. Ducks. Swans. Alone. But not. Friends! Family! Life! *Her* life!

'May I?' a voice came behind her.

The old poet in the white panama hat sat down in the chair opposite, crossed his legs, and shook out his newspaper.

'Cheers,' she said loudly.

A pair of watery blue eyes appeared over the top of *The Times.*

'Did you say something?'

'I said,' Sally raised her voice to a shout. 'Cheers!'

'Oh – good. Celebrating something are we?'

'I'm leaving, Graves, hadn't you heard? I'm sorry, why should you? Why should anybody have heard.'

'Ah I see.' He pulled his white earplugs out of his ears, picked up his glass and raised it shakily to his lips like he'd been told his lines in a play.

'I didn't want anybody seeing me off you see. I can't stand goodbyes. But all the same, I thought somebody might turn up anyway, you know like you do.'

'Ah, that's better.' He finished his drink, put his glass down and blinked a couple of times.

'It's like when you say something and you do mean it, but your friends know, down at another level, you don't. So deeply even you don't know yourself kind of thing.'

275

'Any friend in particular?' his old eyes twinkled in a way that told her he knew exactly who she was talking about. This wily old boy twigged so much more than he let on, she realised.

'Do you ever leave the island, Graves? Do you ever get yourself on the Flying Dolphin or the old ferry and give yourself a bit of an airing?'

'Why should I ever want to do that!'

'That's what I'm wondering.'

'All that going and coming back? No no, dear. It all happens when you're not looking you know.' He chuckled, more to himself than to her. 'That's when you've got to be careful. No no, not a good idea at all.'

'Do you look forward to us all going at the end of the summer? Having the place to yourself again?'

'Coming, going, all the same to me really dear, everybody knows everybody goes. In the end.'

'You must have – seen a few go off in your time.'

'Prefer not to have em in the first place now. Easier that way.'

'Do you ever stop missing them?'

'Grief's the price you always have to pay for love my dear.'

Sally took an olive and leant back in her seat.

Loss. Get used to it. This was how it was now. How it would be.

'You know what I do, Graves? I scream. I go to a distant place and scream at the top of my voice to try and get it all out of me. I haven't done that for a week now. Maybe I won't need to do that anymore?'

'It'll always be inside you my dear, but up there, too, with the wind and the sky. As our own Byron of Rock says, there's a crack in everything, that's how the light gets in.' He picked up his paper and shook it out to turn a page.

Behind him she could see the passengers were boarding. She didn't move but sat staring at Graves in admiration. 'And I thought Yeats was more your style!'

'He touches us all in the end.'

'God, or Leonard Cohen?'

'Same breath my dear.'

Spikey rushed out, 'Come come come, you miss your boat you miss your plane you miss everything you can't stay here anymore. Shoo shoo,' he flapped his arms at her in the same way he did at the cats.

So, that was that then. Determined not to cry, Sally said her farewells to Graves and looked around for a familiar face, if not Him, Barry, Charles, Morrissey the dog, anybody would have done, but even the cats had deserted her. She gathered her bags and rushed for the boat. The Harbourmaster threw down his rope as she passed and gave her a gentle farewell pat on her back.

'The island grapevine, does that wither in the sun as well, Pan?'

'Good journey,' he winked.

She took her place on the same sheltered side of the open deck as before, and soon after the ship sounded its horn and rumbled into life. She leant over the railings and watched the island sliding away from her. The jetty was busy with tourists now, making their way to the sunbathing rocks. From the height of the deck they looked different. More purposeful, somehow, like the only people who knew where they were going.

Now she was on her way, she didn't feel so bad.

Nostalgia for what might have been was pointless. The knowledge that there really could have been something with Loro was for keeps at least. Perhaps the fantasy she'd been within a squeak of fulfilling would remain more potent in her memories because it was only that. She was pleased at herself for this mature perspective. There'd been no major peak, but neither had there been any of the nasty troughs that went with the highs of a short love affair either.

The engine picked up its beat. A whiff of diesel floated down from the top deck. They were really on the move now. She focussed on the harbourmaster getting smaller and smaller as he guided a newly-arrived yacht through the maze of boats.

And who better to have stopped it than Dom? She was still Dom's woman as truly and wholly as she would always be Ami and Nick's mum. Wherever she ended up, winter would come and she'd have her telly and chocolate. A log fire in the winter, a flower garden in the summer.

The ferry reached the centre of the harbour and swung round ready to chug out to the open sea. The little horseshoe-shaped town of Hydra spread out before her in all its perfect, symmetrical neatness. Sally caught a final glimpse of her terrace with the lemon tablecloth now draped over the railings by the hag. She looked higher up and over to the right. His windows were wide open, the white muslin curtains billowing like sails.

She imagined him up there, watching her leave. In her mind she told him there was so much else she'd wanted to thank him for. She'd faced rejection square on and survived. Harmonising has its weaknesses, dischord has its place, explosions create the new.

'Adeeo,' she shouted, semaphoring vigorously with both arms, 'Adeeo.'

'*Why are you going somewhere?*'

Sally froze.

What the *fuck* was that!

Now that was not on.

'*What's the matter?*'

No no no. No way. If Dom's voice in her head was always going to be drowned out by Loro's voice in her head… she really, really would not be able to cope.

'*If you're not deaf now, why don't you turn around?*'

Not daring to believe it, she slowly turned and there he was. Leaning listlessly against the doorway with his arms crossed, smiling at her.

Sally's stomach crashed to her knees and shot right back up again.

She gripped the railing behind her and tried to speak. He joined her.

'B, b, but, why? Your apartment, the windows…?'

'I have a cleaner sometimes as well.' He looked down at her with an indulgent, affectionate smile. 'Not the same one as you I'm happy to say.'

'Wh, wh – ere... you…?'

'I have to be in Athens for a day or so, business meeting. I have an apartment there.'

'So. So I…' she said, clearing her throat.

'Barry told you?' he laughed.

'Um yes. He did mention it.'

'Would you like to come there with me?'

'What! Like *now*?'

'I don't mean next year. It's what we wanted wasn't

it?'

'Yes, but, I'm on my way home now. I have a plane to catch…'

'So?'

Could she miss her flight? Could she really? It was only a CheepieGreekie flight, it would be nothing. She'd get back.

He put his arm up and with one finger stroked her cheek. Sally caught her breath.

'One night? One beautiful, special night hm?'

The boat chugged out into the open water. A warm, salty breeze caught her hair and blew it across her eyes. Scared he'd evaporate, she reached out and touched his arm. He lifted her chin towards him and kissed her.

He pulled away and looked down. 'I'll take that as a Yes?'

She couldn't. What would she say to Nick? To Ami? To Val and Tony who had her return date marked in red on their Snoopy calendar and would doubtless be Googling the arrival time of her flight as she stood there now.

'I can't!' her hair blew all over her eyes.

Dom? No, the wind. Simply the wind.

He moved closer. She felt the force of his body against hers, sheltering her from the breeze in a pool of hot white light that felt like it was burning up her insides. And there in that moment, in that puddle of dancing, forgiving warmth, Sally Lightfoot ceased to exist. Becoming as much a part of him as he was a part of her. Now this really was, she thought, melting into his kiss, the best way.

The best way of all to say goodbye.

# CHAPTER TWENTY-NINE

'There were lots of lemon and cinnamon left but I thought we'd try their new pumpkin chocolate chip flavour.' Val slapped the Evening Standard on the kitchen table. 'The girl suggested it said everybody's raving about them so I thought we'd give them a try why not?'

'How many did you get?' Sally took two plates down from the dresser.

Val looked at Sally carefully. 'Three as always.'

'Good.'

In the conservatory, Sally settled in Dom's chair whilst Val, folding the newspaper into four, sat at the table. 'The sevens are the toughies today. If I can get one seven in I've cracked it.'

Remembering Barry and his numbers, Sally smiled to herself. How she wished she could have been there when the news had got back to him.

She looked at Val fondly, glad they'd forgiven her. Tony had been so livid with her for not being on that flight it had been touch and go for a while. She ran the palm of her hand across the worn, frayed tapestry of the chair arm.

Thank God the sale had fallen through. Days before the exchange of contracts she'd discovered that her own solicitor had forgotten to get probate and her buyers had pulled out. Or that was the story. Tony insisted it was the tumbling market. No matter, it gave her the extra time she needed and Nick the base he'd wanted until they'd both sorted themselves out. The sacrifice and duty stage of motherhood was over. She could be there for him and the rent would see her through. For the time being.

Sally swallowed hard. 'I've had a little breakthrough, Val.'

'Oh good.' Val delved into her handbag for her glasses.

'It's early days and it could be false hope but...'

'But?'

Sally faltered, 'You know that job I went for?'

'Which one?'

'The piano bar.'

'The Curzon Street one? Mayfair might be posh, Sally, but it can be dangerous at night you know.'

'I've taken it.'

'Oh well, there you are then,' Val said with a touch of grandness, as if she'd organised it herself.

'I'll be singing four nights a week. There's a car to take me home.'

'Isn't your lovely friend Ramone nearby?'

'She is. She might even join me on stage after her show sometimes.'

'A celebrity! They'll love that.' Val pushed her glasses up her nose and turned back to her puzzle. 'Got it!' she said moments later, scribbling. 'Isn't it funny how you can puzzle over Sudoku forever but as soon as you look away for a moment the answer stares right back at you. Won't be long. On the home run now.'

'No hurry.' Sally tucked her legs under her and sipped

her coffee.

Who'd have thought it, she reflected. Ramone was living her diva dream and a starstruck Val had become her number one fan.

After Ramone replaced Narina Ferina days away from closure, *Montana Mountain* suddenly found its audience. It was so bad it became a cult hit with Ramone inviting the whole audience up onto the stage, Rocky Horror style, for the finale. The Lady Gaga crowd got wind and began turning up in droves dressed as the characters and there hadn't been a spare seat to be had since.

Sally took Val and Tony as a veiled apology for refusing to fill them in on the details of her delay. Whilst a bemused Tony had looked on, Val had had the night of her life, clambering up on stage at the end and belting her heart out with the best of them.

Now Val was booking ahead for every single musical in the West End and Ramone was cultivating a strong interest in gardening. Insisting to Sally that allotments were the coolest things on the planet and did she know Anita Pallenberg had one?

'You don't need to work now though do you, with Nick's rent?'

'No, but I want to.'

'Oh well, that's good then.' Val clicked the end of her biro and filled in a box, humming under her breath.

'There, done!' Val put her glasses away, closing the case with a hollow pop of a snap. 'Now, I must be getting on, lots to do today.'

Would she do something so reckless again? She wasn't sure. Would she ever need to? Unable to suppress the good mood vibe any longer she let the thought surface.

'What I can't work out as I get older, Val,' she said, seeing her out, 'is if sex is a bodily function or an arbitrary add-on? You know? Is it the central heating or the conservatory of life?'

'Well, that depends on the person doesn't it. And who you're with.'

'Who you're with, yes,' she said closing the door and leaning behind it for a moment.

She'd tell her eventually. But for now she was enjoying the tease. Feeding little tidbits here and there. The longer she kept her mystique the stronger she felt.

The right sort of strength was coming through now. The strength that came from being honest with herself and those around her rather than battling to harmonise into everyone else's lives. Nick was working and Ami and Pete were on an even keel. Her family wasn't disintegrating. It was alive and evolving. Her mourning had reached a new stage of acceptance. Dom was a part of her now, an important part, but not her whole being. She'd started remembering all the good years with some joy and serenity, as she was already remembering her island man with a smile.

The uncertainty of that day and that night still gave her goose bumps. She'd been and gone and done it and scored! *There he was!* Ahead of her, carrying her case on his shoulders up those three flights of narrow, twisting marble stairs leading to who knew where. And what?

They'd staggered into his flat, collapsed into the sofa and kissed properly for the first time since the ferry. Her emotions were a jumble of tension mingled with disbelief yet certainty. That she was about to do... it. – ? Really?

His body had been warm, his mouth cool and fresh on hers. How could she have forgotten what kissing was like? She'd thought of how she'd tell Ramone that. Of how she'd tell her everything. How proud she would be of her. But only Ramone, not Ami, Nick and certainly not Val and Tony. Her life was her own again. Love didn't have to mean giving everything away any more than it meant taking everything away.

The moment the pictures of her singing with Loro were up on Facebook, Ramone had been straight onto her with a Like thumbs up and a one-word comment.

'And?'

And how.

They'd taken it slowly. With the rest of the day and all of the night ahead of them it felt like forever. She remembered the strength of him there. The sudden spurt of insane abandon she'd felt as the shadows lengthened and she realised her flight had taken off for Gatwick without her.

An image of the wheels folding themselves inside the plane sprang into her mind. The ping of the seat-belt light going off over her empty seat.

Abandon was followed by panic. She tried to rationalise it. She'd go to the airport tomorrow, where there were lots and lots of planes, and she'd find one to take her home. Simples! It would happen. Somehow.

She'd never forget his flat. The long, narrow windows, muslin curtains, and Flokati rugs. It had all the cool, natural Greek minimalism of his Hydra house. The bachelor slap of the over-sized plasma and the monochrome blow-ups of naked women that looked like landscapes and landscapes that looked like naked women. Like his slip-on shoes and his stage tux, cheesy as hell but she'd even loved that. Precisely, she realised now, because it was so. Because it was part of who he was.

'Greek simplicity, you can't beat it,' she'd said, lounging into his arms.

'You are insulting me?'

'Not you, your flat. White is so obvious but so right,' she gently draped a hand over his thigh. She instantly felt awkward but she couldn't take it away now.

He put his arm over her shoulders.

Staying inside his arm, she leant forward to pick up her glass. 'I think I'll do something with white when I get my new home. If I ever do.'

'You are thinking too ahead.'

'There's a shop in London called the White Company it's very good a one stop shop for everything white though I don't suppose you need that in Greece do you?' she babbled on. He was feeling her now, through her dress. 'Without the photos and the telly, though I can see the attraction of a big screen.'

He tilted her chin towards him and kissed her. 'Stop talking about the decoration!'

'Sorry, I'm a bit nerv... obsessed.'

'So am I. Now shhh.'

There they had made love in the moment with no past, no future, no expectation. Well, maybe a little bit of expectation. But mature Sally had a firm grip of the reins now. She was taking it for what it was. A silly crush followed by a real friendship tinged with lust. They were together now because it was what she wanted, and she'd asked for it.

The next morning, every time she moved to get up he pulled her down and they started making love all over again.

'Why did this take so long to happen,' she'd sighed, stretching her legs lazily under the limp, white sheet and curling them around Loro's thighs.

'You know why,' he stroked her back over and over with one thumb. 'I don't sleep with married women,' his arm tightened around her back.

'By the looks of it, most of them aren't old enough to be married,' she joked, squeezing her damp legs around his thighs in response.

'I don't want you ever to get up,' he said, and then they were kissing again. Short, sharp little kisses.

'I'm not married, I'm a...' he put his hand gently over her mouth.

Their kisses got longer and soon they were slipping down the pillows again.

She thought of the women down at the harbour, '...single woman.'

He ran his palm lightly over her breasts, 'Now I understand.'

'More than me probably. But I do know I'm so glad I found you.'

'I found you. In my bar, remember.' His blows on her neck set the tingles trotting off down her spine again.

'We found each other.'

'Because we were already lost. That is the best way, to lose is to find.'

'I'll have to think about that one.'

He slowly pulled her sheet sarong away.

She pulled it back.

He pulled it off. 'Don't hide yourself. You are perfect.'

'I am so not but thank you for saying that. It means a lot.'

'I mean it.'

'Whatever this is, I'm not expecting anything.'

'Can I come and see you in London?'

'You wouldn't want to do that.'

'Strawberry Hill – it sounds interesting. Like Strawberry Fields – are there strawberries there?'

'No. The only strawberries you'll find are on the shelves of Waitrose. Always on offer for some reason. Like sofas.'

'Sofas?'

'Never mind. There are no hills either, come to think of it. It's as flat as Holland.'

As they talked their bodies began finding each other again. It felt bizarre to be having a normal conversation and making love simultaneously, but, at the same time, the most natural thing in the world.

He suddenly stopped kissing her and pulled away, frowning.

'What?' she said.

'What is Waitrose?'

Sally laughed, 'That's so cute.'

'What!'

'I love it that there are still people in the world who haven't heard of our supermarkets, and I know I know, why should you. It gives me faith in humanity that's all.'

He slapped her bottom lightly. 'I'm glad I am funny to you.'

For a moment she let herself think they really had got something going.

'I tell you what, you can visit me in London if you stop singing those old songs and get a few of your own in. I'll get you some gigs.'

'Nobody will want them.'

'How do you know? If you haven't tried? Will you try it? That one song then? That one song once?'

He didn't answer. They slipped down the pillows and sighed into each other as he found her. Oh! She surrendered to his rhythm.

Afterwards they both lay still. He stayed on top of her, breathing into her neck. She felt like a hermit crab that'd found its shell, protected from everything, for ever.

'That was amazing. The most in the moment moment I can remember,' she murmured.

He kissed her ear.

'I love you,' he growled. 'I want you more and more.'

Sally turned over to face him.

'This is sex, Loro, pure, unadulterated, adulterated adulting, crazy, mad sex. What do the kids call it? Friendship with benefits. Possession doesn't come into it.'

'Do you say that every time you make love with a new man?'

It still made her smile. In the bigger scheme it didn't matter. She put the mugs in the dishwasher and looked out onto what could be the garden when the concrete had been removed and the studio knocked down.

That was a possibility now. The rawness felt more like

a part of her than her very being. Maybe that was the new stage of acceptance the book had been going on about? She still missed him. Desperately sometimes. But a new serenity had crept in. A thankfulness for all the time they'd had together.

And thanks to Loro she'd won the freedom of her intellect over her body. She did alone well now. Instead of being alone with herself she was sure with herself. She didn't define herself by anybody else's need of her.

And this was the only way to be.

No matter what age.

# ACKNOWLEDGEMENTS

In homage to Mr Leonard Cohen, for his beautiful being and songs – the inspiration for several scenes, some obvious, some not so, in this story.

Blackbird Digital Books
The #authorpower publishing company
Discovering outstanding authors
www.blackbird-books.com
@Blackbird_Bks

Blackbird

Printed in Great Britain
by Amazon